Coming To Be
A Novel

Rebecca Thaddeus

Plain View Press   http://plainviewpress.net
1101 W. 34th Street, STE 404, Austin, TX 78705

Coming To Be

A Novel

Rebecca Thaddeus

Plain View Press http://plainviewpress.net
1101 W. 34th Street STE 404,   Austin, TX 78705

ISBN: 978-1-63210-074-0
ebook ISBN: 978-1-63210-075-7
Library of Congress Control Number: 2020934179

Cover Art: three-women-standing: image 3558037 courtesey of pixabay.com
Cover Design by Pam Knight

This is a work of fiction. All characters, places, incidents, and dialogues are a product of the author's imagination or are used fictitiously, and any resemblance to actual persons, living or dead, is entirely coincidental.

To Nancy Kaszyca,

my lifelong best friend,

who helped me understand what

coming to be was really all about

Nothing ever is, but everything is coming to be.
Plato, **Theaetetus,** *369 B.C.*

Chapter One

January, 1983

Interlude

Steppenwolf, "Magic Carpet Ride"

He looks tantalizing, lying on his side upon a white sand beach. His right hand supports his upper body, the angle designed to showcase the musculature of his chest and upper arm. The deep bronze of his nakedness attests to his island heritage, and the sand sticking to his thighs, his taut belly, and his feet and forearms indicates that he recently enjoyed a swim in the ocean, which is visible from behind a small rise of sand, gentle whitecaps kissing the shore. A mass of curly black hair caps his head, and his thin mustache crowns perfect white teeth and an open smile, suggesting that lying naked on a beach in the middle of the day is perfectly natural for him.

Carly can't decide whether his best feature is his deep brown eyes, their seductive gleam inviting her to come play, or his perfectly rounded buttocks barely concealed behind the angle of his right elbow. Everything about his situation, his posture, and his smile, suggests the words "Aloha from Hawaii," which is appropriate, as those are the words printed in yellow approximately a half inch beneath his prone body. Liz will love it, she decides, turning the postcard over to write her message:

How do you like this "souvenir" I sent you—he'll be arriving any day now—don't you wish! Having a great time. Steve took kids to whale wharf at Kanapali while I stayed at resort to work

*on tan. Saw on TV that Michigan got some snow yesterday—
pity. Well, enough gloating. Will call when we get back.*
Love, Carly.

Flipping through the rest of her recently purchased postcard collection, Carly found the one she intended for Beth. Same words at the bottom of the card—"Aloha from Hawaii," this time printed in gold—but there the resemblance ended. This picture was a sunset scene, with silhouettes of palm trees swaying before a background of marigold, ultramarine, and fuchsia against a Dresden sky, the whole card seductive in its invitation to would-be Hawaiian vacationers. She wrote:

*Yes, Hawaii really IS this lovely. You need to come here some
year. Been having a great time. Taking kids biking down
Haleakala volcano tomorrow EARLY a.m.—hope my legs can
stand it! Should do wonders for my pudgy calves. See you at
O'Hare Friday—thanx again for picking us up. Steve would die
if he had to leave his beloved Lexus in that parking lot.*
Love, Carly.

Despite all the changes that had occurred in her life since she first met Beth and Liz sixteen years earlier, Carly's relationship with her two best friends had remained pretty much the same. Beth and Liz always seemed to inhabit two ends of a spectrum, with Carly placed almost dead center between them. From the first day she met them in that hideous apartment on Morgan Street, she recognized herself as the pivot of their see-saw, equally attracted to Liz's life on the edge and to Beth's comfortable conformity.

Carly sorted through the stack of postcards once more, looking for a twin to Beth's card to send to her mother. She thought how much the apartment the three of them had shared differed from the setting where she currently found herself: the word "luxury" must have been created to describe this suite at the Merrit Maui Adventure Resort. Silk drapes. Velvet upholstery. Real gold leaf decorating the dressers. Linens that finally made her understand why Egyptian cotton was so expensive.

She had just found the postcard she was seeking when a knock at the door announced that, as always, she was too late. Sighing, she slipped the unwritten cards into the desk drawer and, stretching to relieve the pressure in her back, walked to the door.

"Beat you again, Slowpoke," taunted nine-year-old Tyler, scabby arms and legs angling out from his Cubs tee shirt and blue shorts. "You're sooooo slow, even for a girl."

"I wasn't racing, Pea Brain," said Celia, with all the disdain a twelve-year-old is capable of articulating. Celia looked pristine as always in designer jeans and a tee shirt advertising a rock group called Nirvana. Carly hoped the group wasn't particularly degenerate.

"What did you see at the whale wharf?" offered Carly. She had long realized that distraction was the best method for heading off arguments between her children.

"Whales," muttered Celia, slipping quickly into her room.

"Mom, you shoulda gone with us. It was really neat. The whale bones were awesome—the skeleton was longer than Uncle Carl's boat." Carly knew she could always count on Tyler to relate to her all the events of his life. "And they had all these little stores that had lots of carved things like boats and whales and little houses, and it was all made out of bones and shells and stuff..."

"Scrimshaw?" offered Carly.

"What?"

"Scrimshaw. Isn't that what they call that kind of carving? Sailors used to carve ivory, bone, shells, whatever they had available, during their long sailing voyages. Usually they carved things they saw—ships and marine life. It's called scrimshaw."

"Whatever," sulked Tyler. Carly made a mental note, for perhaps the thousandth time, to quit interrupting other people's stories with the kind of educational information she found fascinating and was able to call to mind at a moment's notice. Most people seemed to find that trait of hers slightly annoying.

"Can we see some real whales?" asked Tyler, quickly overcoming his momentary pique.

"Sure. We'll probably see some on the boat to Lanai. The brochure says the whales around that area are very active in January."

"And can we go back to the whale place? There's a really neat poster of a whale I want to get." Carly imagined the walls of Tyler's bedroom, speculating that finding space for one more poster would be difficult. "Dad wouldn't buy it for me."

It was only then Carly noticed Steve's absence, although she had to admit that he had seemed absent, distracted and easily irritated throughout most of this trip. She admired her husband's dedication to the business he had founded and built into the successful enterprise it was today. But between his traveling to do computer consultations and his twelve-hour work days when he was home, he had become almost a stranger to his family during the past four years.

Of course, neither of them could have anticipated his future success during those first financially rocky years of their marriage. She had hoped this family vacation would take his mind off business and help him focus on what was most important, their relationship and the relationship he could be sharing with his children. Celia and Tyler were growing up frighteningly fast. If he wasn't careful, he'd miss their childhoods altogether.

"Dad had some stuff to do downstairs," continued Tyler. "Can I go to the pool?"

"You can get ready for the pool, but I want you to wait here with your sister until I come back. I'm just going down to the lobby to mail these postcards and see what your dad wants to do for dinner. Why don't you see if Maui has cartoons on television?"

Carly felt slightly guilty for directing her son *toward* television, but quickly shrugged off her guilt. After all, it *was* vacation. House rules didn't apply. She called to Celia's closed bedroom door, "Honey, keep an eye on your brother. I'll only be gone a few minutes," but she didn't wait to decipher the grumbling she heard from behind that door.

Exiting the elevator to the lobby, Carly was again awestruck by the extravagance, even what one might call decadence, of the Merritt Maui Adventure Resort. She had never seen a room so large; even with dozens of people milling around, she felt lost in its vastness. The lobby, built around an ancient, enormous banyan tree, featured a ceiling half open to the brilliance of the Hawaiian sky. The marble floors and walls added luxury, and island prints and tropical plantings added charm. For Carly, however, the most unbelievable part of this paradise was the free-form pond, where serene white and black swans floated like tiny ships at sea. Five days earlier Carly could never have imagined black swans.

This must be costing us a fortune, she thought for probably the fifteenth time before reminding herself that she and Steve could afford this fortune because of their unrelenting efforts of the past sixteen years. Much of the credit went to Steve, of course, whose devotion to his work had paid off so well. But Carly felt she had contributed to their success as well, what with all those boring jobs she had taken early in their marriage that had just managed to keep food on their table while he had developed his career.

And then later, after he decided to go into business for himself, she had needed to add the demands of raising young children. Finding thrifty ways to manage their household had become a habit to her. But even now, when they were able to afford nice things, Carly felt a nagging guilt at any extravagance. Perhaps that was why she insisted on keeping her job at the music store, although the money she brought in was a pittance compared to her husband's income.

Heading toward the front desk to mail her postcards, Carly almost missed seeing Steve at the last of a long row of telephones along the wall behind the elevator bank. His trim body, honed by hours of racquetball and golf played with clients, and his sandy blonde hair, still full despite his fears of approaching baldness, belied the fact that he was approaching forty. His stance was casual, but it did not hide the hint of pent-up energy and aggressive tension which had always been so much a part of his personality.

As Carly approached him, she was once again aware of how much kinder the years had been to Steve than to her. Her hair, still a brown dark enough to look almost black, was now kept that way through monthly dye jobs. She believed her shoulder-length curls kept her looking young, although not as young as she had looked once she abandoned the much longer style when Tyler was born. Her azure eyes still sparkled, despite the tiny wrinkles beginning to form at their corners. And the twenty-five pounds that had somehow inched their way onto her frame did not help her image of herself: often she felt the same vague sense of inadequacy and gratitude she had felt when she first met Steve in college, when he had first taken her to bed, when he had married her.

Coming closer, Carly noticed in Steve a look that reminded her of the early days of their marriage—his smile open and relaxed, his eyes liquid with emotion. But he seemed startled to see her, and quickly mumbled some closing words into the mouthpiece. He hung the receiver into its cradle as Carly reached him.

"Who was that?" she asked, somewhat taken aback as that air of tension and mild annoyance, customary with him lately, settled back into his features.

"Just someone from work," said Steve, flashing what looked to Carly like a forced smile. "Just another client I have to sweet talk into signing a contract."

"Why didn't you call from the room?"

"Right, with Tyler and Celia bickering in the background. Very professional."

Carly wanted to remind Steve that their offspring were only children, that they were better behaved, she thought, than most, and that they were all on vacation and couldn't be expected to follow proper office protocol. Instead she asked about dinner.

"Carly, I've about had it with the daddy routine for one day," he responded. "Besides, I met a Texan with a cattle ranch who needs some computer advice—I've set up a racquetball game with him for later this evening. He could be a prospective client."

"But you've got to eat," countered Carly, biting back the words she wanted to say that would express her resentment. Why did she have to share Steve with business on one of their rare vacations?

"I snacked all afternoon at the whale wharf. Why don't you take the kids to that Chinese place we saw in town? And then we should all call it a day—we need to get up at 4:00 tomorrow morning for the trip on Haleakala."

Steve was right. Tomorrow was going to be another busy day with the children. Chinese and early-to-bed was probably the best course of action. Carly made a mental note to leave the new midnight blue teddy packed in her suitcase for one more night. She had agonized over her purchase for almost a week before ordering it from the *Victoria's Secret* catalogue. Would Steve appreciate her efforts at seduction, or would he only notice how little her body resembled those of the catalog models? She had expected to find an opportunity to wear it by now, five days into their Hawaiian vacation; this trip had not lived up to expectations in many ways.

"Okay. Don't play racquetball too hard with your new client. Save yourself for tomorrow—you're going to need your strength for the mountain," she answered lightly, turning toward the front desk. Her carefree stride away from Steve belied the dull, anxious ache settling like felted wool overtaking her heart.

"Magnificent," Carly whispered, awed and muted by the grandeur of the first spokes of golden radiance bursting over the horizon. The thirty or so other travelers who stood atop Haleakala seemed similarly transfixed. Within moments, a slender arc of the sun's fiery ball could be seen, impossibly far away, lighting the indigo sky. It shimmered over their island in the sky, which was encompassed by a sea of cloud whose gray mass was turning to ridges of deep blue topped by glints of frothy white.

Moments later the heavy black mountain peak, with its silhouettes of human forms, took on color, the piles of black becoming a reddish mass of treacherous ridges and inclines. The silhouettes became people, young and old, most dressed in bikers' pants of neon yellow, orange or lime green and warm jackets layered over sweat shirts and jerseys, all trying to combat the surprisingly biting cold. Too soon it was over; the sun had risen, the sky was a pale blue, and the surreal sense of being alone in a world swimming above the clouds disappeared as the tourists began to gather in small groups, chatting about the wonder of the experience they had just shared and looking for the guides who would take them down the mountain.

"Wow, Mom, that was the coolest," enthused Tyler.

"Worth getting up at four in the morning?" asked Carly. Tyler nodded ardently, but Celia responded with only the small wry grin that lately had taken the place of the toothy smile which had so graced her face as a young child. *Maybe,* Carly thought, *their quarrel of three hours earlier still rankled.* Celia, whose reactions to any of her mother's suggestions were lately filtered through the barrier of adolescence, had sullenly objected to getting up so early in the morning during her vacation just to see some "stupid sunrise."

"C'mon, troops. Let's find our guide—Chad? Brett? What was his name?" asked Steve, rubbing his eyes. He must be exhausted, thought Carly—getting up so early after tossing and turning the way he had all night—the way he had so many nights in the previous few months.

"It's Brad," offered Carly.

"Right. Brad it is. Let's find Brad the Bikemaster, kids."

Brad was easily found near the dented van which had taken the family up the mountain. Carly had been concerned when she first met him—he had seemed so young and so casual. Learning through his guide chatter that he avidly surfed the high waves every winter and guided bike tours down Haleakala only often enough to support his surfer lifestyle did not help allay her fears. But as he had masterfully negotiated the steep and narrow two-lane road in total blackness, with the only sight of life outside the van being a few lights blinking in the villages far below, Carly was willing to entrust their lives to his expertise for the remainder of the tour. Watching him pass out helmets and elbow and knee guards to the eight tourists under his care—Carly's family, an older couple, and two college-aged men—helped make her feel even more trusting.

"Awesome, right?" asked Brad. "Anyone here not impressed? Y'know, I see that sunrise three or four times a week and it's still like the first time. Now everyone grab your tour bikes—check the brakes—you'll be needing 'em."

The little group chattered excitedly as they mounted the unusual vehicles, which resembled mountain bikes but sported much fatter tires and heavily padded seats. The bike's braking system was more like an automotive system's, with disc brakes attached to their wheel hubs. "I hope I'm up to this," said Carly to Brad. "It's been a while since I've been on a long bike ride—and this is, what, 38 miles?"

"Don't worry, ma'am—you're only gonna be pedaling for about the first 200 yards—the rest is downhill all the way. Stay in single file, everyone—no passing—no hotshot stuff (with a stern glance toward the two college men)—don't get too close to each other. And keep your eyes on the rump of the biker ahead of you in the steeper areas. There's gonna be a few straightaways and plenty of places to stop and take pictures along the way—you'll get a chance to see all the scenery you want. Everyone ready?"

Before she pushed off, ready to tackle the descent, Carly had only moments to be irritated at Brad's "ma'am"—how long had it been since young men and women had started calling her by that term of respect she felt should be reserved for older women? "Celia, Tyler, you need to stay with us," she called out, watching her children pulling up to the head of the small pack.

"That's okay," called Steve over his shoulder as he pedaled ahead. "I'll keep an eye on them."

Carly got into position toward the end of the column as it headed down the rugged trail. Following Brad's advice, she reserved most of her attention for the rather flabbily padded rump of the woman pedaling ahead of her—*some people really shouldn't wear bright, gaudy florals, even in Hawaii*—but she couldn't resist an occasional look over the mountain at the clouds below. She'd seen clouds beneath her while flying at high altitudes, of course, but this was different. These clouds seemed close enough to touch: she could feel their mist caressing her face and smell their ocean tang. She'd never before had the sensation of being enveloped by the wet sweetness of heavy clouds.

But as enchanting as the travel through the clouds had been, nothing could rival the next experience, as the small group of bikers broke through the lowest of the clouds. Suddenly, the cool gray mist atop the mountain gave way to a sky as clear and blue as only a Hawaiian sky can be. And the view below, when Carly chanced a quick peek, was breathtaking. The entire outline of western Maui could be seen, with the Pacific stretching out beyond. Smaller islands appeared, cast out into the ocean like toys flung about by some giant child. Enthralling though it was, Carly was grateful to see the biker ahead of her veer into a clearing where the faster bikers were already dismounting. This was a good time to grab a quick drink, take off her jacket, stretch her tingling leg muscles, and see how Steve and the kids were doing. Mostly, however, she wanted to appreciate in a more leisurely manner the beauty spread below her.

"How's everyone?" she asked, approaching her family.

"Great, Mom. Look at those islands out in the ocean," beamed Tyler.

"This is pretty cool, Mom. A lot better than I thought it would be," admitted Celia, a trace of that old toothy smile appearing on her face. "Thanks."

Carly had only one moment to bask in the glow of her daughter's unexpected gratitude before Brad launched into his tour routine. "Everyone here?" he called. "Everyone okay? Any weak knees yet? Anyone need the rescue helicopter?" The small group laughed, the older couple perhaps not as whole-heartedly as the rest.

"Okay, from here you can see West Maui Mountain—it and Haleakala make up all of Maui. It looks a lot smaller, but that's because it's much more eroded than Haleakala—it's a much older volcano."

"Could it explode right now?" asked Tyler, looking as though that prospect would be a bonus to the tour.

"Nope, both volcanoes have been dormant for millions of years. You'd have to go over to Hawaii Island to see any active volcanoes. There are two there—Mauna Loa and Kilauea."

"Can we go see them, Dad?" pleaded Tyler.

"Maybe next trip, Son. Right now let's listen to Brad."

"Over to the left you can see Lanai—that's where the biggest pineapple plantation in the world is. There's also a great resort there now; maybe some of you will be going there later during your trip.

The smaller island is Kahoolawe. No one lives there, but the U.S. government used to use the island as a bombing target."

"Cool," said Tyler. "Are there sharks in the water?" Carly glanced at Celia, whose eyes rolled upward vigorously enough to seem capable of rolling right into her forehead.

"Yep. All kinds of sharks. Don't ever go swimming too far out or by yourself while you're in Hawaii," suggested Brad. "You folks have got about fifteen minutes to look around and rest. Take in some water; you'd be surprised how quickly you can get dehydrated out here once it gets warmer. Don't go too far off—we don't want to lose you."

The small cluster scattered, most singly or in couples, seeking out the best possible view of the panorama below. Carly walked over to where Steve fussed with his bike. "Don't you want to take in the view? Brad said we only had fifteen minutes."

"Sure—I'm just checking these brakes. How are you doing?"

"Okay. Why?"

"Well, you don't get a lot of exercise at home most of the time. I don't want you to hurt yourself by straining too much."

"Not much I could do about it on top of the mountain, but I'm not really ready for the rescue helicopter yet," said Carly somewhat sharply. His "solicitude" annoyed her. He never seemed to let a chance go by without referring to the extra weight she had put on the past few years. Quickly, however, she forced herself to soften her tone. This bike trip was supposed to be a highlight of their vacation; it was turning into just another opportunity for them to bicker. "This was a great idea, don't you think? The kids are loving it. Honey, we don't do nearly enough of this kind of stuff together—and it's so important for a family."

"Don't you ever get tired of that old song? We couldn't do stuff like this if I didn't work so hard. You always seem to forget that. Without all the overtime I spend at work we'd be lucky to be vacationing at Wisconsin Dells this year."

"Honestly, Steve, I didn't mean...but we had lots of fun at those vacations, didn't we?"

"Yeah, well, next year *you* take in the Tommy Bartlett water show and the campground—the kids and I prefer Haleakala and the Merritt Maui."

"Steve, don't over-react..." But she was talking to Steve's back as he headed over to a distant ridge. *Dammit,* she thought, *we ought to be enjoying the scenery instead of bickering.*

Checking the whereabouts of her children, she observed Celia chatting with Brad (yes, her daughter *was* growing up) and Tyler pointing out some area of interest to the two college students. Her eye caught the elderly couple standing on a ledge beneath her, his arm around her shoulder in what appeared to be the familiarity of many shared years. As they turned toward a different vantage point, the old gentleman took his wife's hand, gently helping her across the rocky ledge. With a small sigh, Carly hurried to catch up with Steve, who was contemplatively peering out at some far point in the Pacific.

"It *is* beautiful. I never could have imagined how beautiful it would be," she said, sliding her arm around his waist in reconciliation. "I just love being here." Together they peered out at the water, taking in the beauty of the expanse of peaceful ocean that became far less peaceful where its waves encountered the rugged shore. Following the flight of a lone seagull, Carly sighted Tyler with his two new friends.

Suddenly she cried "Tyler! Steve, he's too close to the edge."

Jolted out of his reverie, Steve shot a glance at Tyler, then grabbed Carly's arm as she began to start toward their son. "Honey, he's fine. Don't get over-excited—he's just looking at something over the side."

"He'll fall."

"No, he won't. He's not that clumsy. And he's got those two guys standing right next to him—they're not going to let him get too close to the edge."

"Right, Steve, I should trust those two idiots to watch out for my child," Carly huffed.

"Will you stop over-protecting him? For Christ's sake, you treat him like a two-year-old. Let him grow up. Let him take a few lumps. When I was ten..."

"He's only nine."

"Nine, ten, that's not my point."

"You don't even know how old your own son is."

"Dammit, Carly. Don't get hysterical on me. All I'm saying is you've got to let Tyler grow up. You're turning him into a mama's boy, and that's not a good thing. Look, he's far away from the edge now. He's fine."

Even to Carly's eyes, Tyler now looked safe, at least several feet from the edge of the mountain and chatting with the college students. Relieved, she tried to focus her gaze on an island, both to hide and to combat the hot tears stinging her eyes as she tried to think of a good response. She was spared this task by Brad's voice calling his flock back to their bicycles.

"C'mon, folks. Ready to go? We've still got a lot of mountain to get down in the next couple of hours."

Carly spent the next two tour stops with Celia and Tyler in tow, diligently questioning Brad about the native flora and fauna they encountered. They learned quite a lot, as Brad pointed out Hawaiian orchids, hibiscus, and frangipani, and they were suitably impressed by specimens of Haleakala silversword, the exotic plant found only on this mountain, which bursts into hundreds of magenta blooms only once every fifty years. They laughed at the antics of some nene, the awkward, comically striped Hawaiian geese, who skittered up to the tourists, became suddenly shy, and skittered away again. And, of course, the Pacific continued to provide breathtaking views at every stop.

At the last rest stop of the tour, Carly stripped down to her tank top and greedily guzzled the remaining drops of her bottled water. In the relatively short time of their descent, the chill of the mountain peak had given way to Hawaii's normal mid-70s, but the relentlessly beating sun combined with the exertion of cautious bicycling made it seem much hotter, actually stifling. Determined that their latest squabble wasn't going to ruin this excursion, Carly wandered over to the bench where Steve was doing some leg stretches as he gazed at the expanse of Maui and the unending Pacific, now nearly at their eye-level, extending before him. "Beautiful, isn't it?" she asked.

"One of the most beautiful places I've ever seen—probably *the* most beautiful place."

"We really shouldn't waste the time we have together arguing, honey. I'm sorry if you misunderstood me before," Carly purred, linking her arm in his to gaze out at the sea.

"Carly, it's just that...Well, you're not going to like this. We have to...I have to...Well, I...I have to leave...go back."

"What? We have two more days here."

"I know. You and the kids stay. It's...it's that new client, the one I played racquetball with...the Texan. He flew back to Texas this morning. He needs some work done right away."

"He expects you to leave your vacation? Is he out of his mind? Are you?" Carly didn't wait for an answer. The look on Steve's face told her what it would be. "You don't even know him."

"No, but I know a great opportunity when I see one. He needs some consulting work done *now*, and he's not the kind of guy who's used to being put off. He's offering me an unbelievable amount of money. This is too good to turn down."

"But...this trip. We've planned it for so long. We have our reservations for Lanai for tomorrow...can you even get a flight out?"

"Yeah, I can...I already have my ticket. You take the kids to Lanai—I'm not much of a beach person anyway. It's been a great trip, but I've got to get back."

"You know, I'm not even surprised," Carly said icily, turning on her heel. "Go. The kids and I will be fine. It's not like this is the first time you've let us down." Steve would have known about this since last night. He must have known she would be upset; that must have been the cause for his all-day sensitivity. It was so like him to act testily toward her when he knew he'd done something wrong—his best defense was always a good offense.

Fine. Once he got back from Texas, the Chicago freeze wouldn't begin to match the freeze he'd feel in his own bedroom.

On the short ride from the tour station to the Maui Merritt, Tyler and Celia's excited chatter, once commonplace but now exceedingly rare, did much to cover the cool silence of their parents. Once in their room, the children decided to swim off their exuberance in the hotel pool; Carly opted to join them at poolside with her book while Steve, pleading exhaustion and actually looking more tired than Carly ever remembered seeing him, chose an afternoon nap in the room.

But inner peace eluded Carly. The oversized chaise longue was comfortable enough. The Sex on the Beach drink, with its fruity flavors, was well-blended and refreshing, although the thought that this was the only sex she'd experience on this trip had given rise to an unintended grimace as she ordered it. The pool area was spacious and designed to accommodate both active swimmers and passive idlers, and the Anne Perry mystery she brought with her had, up to now, proved quite engrossing.

But Carly was distracted by everything—the colorful flashes of the swimsuits in the water, the quiet hum of activity in the nearby lobby, even the occasional splash from the pool. She tried to follow Steve's lead and take a short nap, impossible with the hubbub of activity around her and the riot within her. She considered taking one of the long walks she had planned for this trip, then, with only slight guilt, figured there really was no reason to begin that healthful regimen right now. Finally, she decided to return to the room to fetch her Walkman; perhaps some soothing James Taylor or her favorite Steve Miller tape would help.

She quickly threw on her beach cover-up, then walked through the lobby to the elevators. Once on their floor, she rustled through her bag for the room key; the last thing she wanted to do was wake Steve—no sense arguing any further this afternoon. On entering the sitting room of their suite, she was pleased to see the Walkman and her tape case on the table near their bedroom door; she would not have to risk waking Steve by entering the bedroom to look for it. Quietly stepping toward the table, she was surprised to hear Steve's voice—probably on the phone talking to his client. Perhaps he had been too agitated by their quarrel to sleep. Good! Why should she be the only one to agonize over their disagreements?

Then she remembered the weariness in his face. He did work awfully hard for his family, and he had needed this vacation at least as much as they did. Deciding to make amends and salvage the rest of the afternoon, she walked back to the bedroom door and quietly turned the knob. The kids were busy downstairs, and the hotel provided plenty of supervision in the lobby. Perhaps the teddy wouldn't be a total waste after all. She could remember quite a few occasions when resolving a quarrel in bed had been a lot of fun.

"No, I didn't tell her. I couldn't. I..." Steve, visibly startled at Carly's sudden appearance, turned from her and quickly ended his conversation. "Look, I have to go. I'll see you tomorrow." Replacing the receiver with a barely controlled force, he turned and glowered at Carly. "For Christ's sake, what are you sneaking up on me for? You almost gave me a heart attack."

"Sneaking up on you? This is *our* bedroom—mine too, remember? Who the hell were you talking to?"

"What the hell business is it of yours?" But the confused look on Carly's face seemed to deflate his anger. "Carly, I'm sorry. It's that damn Texan. I called him back to see if he could wait a couple of days to have our meeting, but he's so unreasonable. Remind me not to act that way once I have millions to spare."

"But...why are you taking it out on me? You're always so touchy lately. I don't understand."

"It's not your fault, sweetie. It's just all the pressure I'm dealing with right now. I don't mean to take it out on you. I'm sorry...come here, let me make it up to you." Steve patted the bed beside him, a penitent smile on his face. "I know I've neglected you this vacation."

She reluctantly sat on the bed, a foot away from him, but he sidled up to her and embraced her, his lips searching out that special place behind her ear. "Don't be upset."

"Steve, don't. You just can't..." But Carly forgot her protests as his kisses, becoming more urgently persistent, began to achieve their familiar effect.

As the Boeing 747 approached O'Hare, Carly contemplated the passage of the last three days. She had enjoyed those days with Celia and Tyler, but the sweet memory of that last afternoon with Steve had made his absence unbearable. They weren't such an old married couple after all—there was still a spark or two left. She couldn't wait to see him again—she'd kindle that spark into the kind of flame that had brought them together in the first place.

Remembering her resolution to call him in Texas just as soon as she arrived home, she suddenly realized that, in the bustle of packing his things the next day, she had forgotten to get the phone number of his new client. "Damn," she thought, "now what'll I do?" She remembered that last phone call he had made before he left. Maybe the client's number was on the bill. She rummaged through her purse—surely she had not lost that bill. Of course, that would not have been surprising in all the confusion of having to check out of the hotel with the kids bickering in the background—checking out was a task Steve always handled.

Ah, there it was, all five pages of it...she found room, tax, room service, then finally phone charges, itemized at the end. There must have been fifteen phone calls, but the one she sought would be the last. Carly was confused; there was nothing with an unfamiliar area code that would be the Texas call. But there were quite a few calls made to one Chicago number and a few, including the last call, the one that he said was made to his client, had been made to their own area code, followed by a phone number that seemed familiar. But whose was it?

It was...

The realization hit Carly in a blinding flash. The world beyond the boundaries of her own body collapsed around her. All she could sense was the beating of her heart—rapid, erratic—and her breathing— shallow and fast, heartbeats and respiration seeming to take up all the space in the cabin. Snatches of bright colors—oranges, rubies, vermilions, magentas—exploded in her swirling mind. Flashes of scenes—Steve abruptly hanging up the phone, the glimpse of him she had caught driving away from their home that day when she thought he was at work, strange looks she had gotten at Steve's last office party—all attempted to establish a foothold but were instantly replaced by other fragments of thought. She burned from within, but in raising her hand to her forehead she felt a clamminess that made her shiver.

"I did not say that, Pea Brain." Celia's voice sounded as if it were reverberating through the walls of a tunnel.

"You did. You promised I could sit by the window during the landing. You did. Ma!"

"Oh, shut up, Doofus. It's too late to change seats—we're about to land. The seat belt sign is coming on any minute. And I did *not* promise."

"Did too!"

"Did not!"

"Ma, she promised!"

Carly finally intervened. "Tyler, baby, just sit still."

"But, Ma, she promised! She said if I let her sit by the window during take-off, she'd change seats for landing."

"Tyler, please, just sit still. Please!" Carly was oblivious to her son's glowering eyes shooting accusations of betrayal toward both his sister and his mother.

The Boeing made a perfect landing into the 12 degree chill at O'Hare and eventually found its way to Terminal G14. As the Brennans emerged from the exit tunnel, they glimpsed Beth waiting for them amidst the bustle of busy airline employees, exhausted business travelers and frenetic vacationers. Beth rushed to help the children with their carry-on luggage, bending to receive a kiss from Tyler and a rather perfunctory hug from Celia. "Welcome home. How was Hawaii?"

"Great," smiled Tyler. "We saw whales jumping at Lanai. And rode bicycles down a mountain. And we brought you back a souvenir."

"I can't wait to see it. How about you, Carly? I thought you were planning to get a tan—you look almost as white as when you left. Where's Steve?"

"He had to leave early—another business trip that couldn't wait."

"What a shame. You both really needed some time together."

"Yeah."

"Are you okay? Now you look flushed. You didn't catch some tropical flu bug in Hawaii, did you?"

"No, I'm just a little tired. You know how much I hate to fly, and it's an awfully long trip. I'm really glad to be home."

"Well, we're glad to have you back all safe and sound. It's been too quiet around here without you guys. Ready for luggage retrieval hell? Carly, are you sure you're okay? Do you need to sit down? You look like you've seen a ghost."

"Really, Beth, I'm fine."

But Beth obviously was not convinced. She asked if Carly was really all right once at the luggage carrel, twice in the car, and finally as they approached the Brennan home. As she helped the Brennans unload their luggage from the back of her Plymouth Voyager, she couldn't hide her concern. "Can I help you get this stuff inside? Let me come in and make you a nice cup of hot tea."

"No, thank you, Beth. I just need to get inside and rest awhile. I...I'll call you later." Carly shouldered a duffel bag and grabbed her suitcase, unsteadily making her way to the house. She unlocked the front door, pausing to let her children battle their way in, each trying to be first, then looked back to see an obviously confused Beth standing in the cold. Beth, her dearest and most loyal friend since their college days, deserved better than this. But her children were resurrecting their earlier squabble and she knew that, in her own confusion and fear, she had no idea what to say to her friend.

She stepped through the doorway and into what she feared might be a very different chapter in her book of life, one she wasn't looking forward to reading.

Chapter Two

August, 1966

Prelude

Led Zeppelin, "Stairway to Heaven"

The address matched the one on the tiny slip of paper that had been posted on a bulletin board in the Student Union. But Carly Novak hoped that this decrepit warehouse did not house the apartment described in the ad: "Roommate wanted. Neat loft apt. near campus. $100 mo. plus utilities. Ask for Elizabeth Romano." Of course, Carly reminded herself, if she wanted the comfortable conventionality of middle-class life she could have stayed in her parents' bungalow in the Chicago suburb of Berwyn.

Her parents would certainly not approve of Carly's whereabouts right now, having warned her repeatedly to stay on campus, away from the surrounding neighborhoods. They'd made it clear that Carly's living at home was the price she had to pay to become the first member of their family to enter college, since they'd always believed decent young girls left home only to get married or to enter the convent. After all, no telling what sort of mischief a pretty girl like their daughter could get herself into away from the settling influence of her family. Finally a bargain had been struck: since Circle was only a thirty minute El ride along the Eisenhower Expressway, Carly could attend classes and still be home before dark, leaving the weekends free to continue waitressing at her parents' family restaurant.

That tiny slip of paper had drawn her away from the stark, futuristic granite and glass buildings that made up the University of Illinois at Chicago Circle. A lot had changed in this neighborhood since Mayor

Daley had fought to build an urban university for the children of the working-class families of Chicago. Set squarely in the conflux of the territory marked out by three of Chicago's groups who were very interested in maintaining their inner-city enclaves— the Italians to the north, the Greeks to the south, and the blacks to the west—the university had begun its existence struggling to establish itself amidst unfriendly neighbors. The Italians had fought the hardest to stop the building of the campus, and Carly could remember *Chicago Tribune* photos of shawled Italian women trying to block the oncoming bulldozers with their bodies. But Mayor Daley had persisted, forcing the often unruly and always unpredictable residents of his city to accept his gift to them.

By the time Carly appeared on campus for Orientation Day the neighborhood had, it seemed to her, accepted the behemoth campus-of-the-future. Italian and Greek restaurants were crowded with professors, staff, visitors and students. Carly was intrigued by Maxwell Street, set right in the middle of the black neighborhood her parents had warned her to avoid. Maxwell Street was famous for its open air markets where anything from fresh vegetables to used shoes to Rolex knock-offs could be found. There was nothing similar in Berwyn, and Carly, as she passed the market on her way to the apartment, was delighted to find the kind of bargains K-mart's blue light specials never offered.

Urban renewal had overtaken many of the neighborhood areas, and it was not unusual to find expensive townhouse projects being built next to ancient tenements. But as she pressed the doorbell marked "Romano/Grainger," Carly mused that urban renewal had not overtaken this particular block of Morgan Street. She determined to overlook the clandestine appearance of this inner-city neighborhood with its graffitti-festooned buildings, littered sidewalks, and dark alleys, and at least check the apartment out.

The normal, everyday din of the busy neighborhood was fractured by the simultaneous sounds of pounding and a female voice shouting "Damn these windows" over the background strains of Mick Jagger hissing "Sh...sh...sh...shattered." *Well,* Carly thought, *at least we like the same kind of music.* Looking up to the source of the noise, she saw a mass of black curls pop out of a third floor window. "You the person who called about the apartment? Come on up—third floor." Before Carly could answer, the apparition disappeared, the window slammed shut, and the door buzzer sounded.

She stepped out of the hazy glare of a torrid August afternoon and entered a dank, musty lobby—no, that was far too generous a word— an entrance about the size of a large closet. As her eyes adjusted to the darkness, she noticed a stairway to her right.

Two flights up, the muffled sound of the Stones directed her to her destination. She knocked only once before the door opened to reveal the owner of those dark curls. Elizabeth Romano, barefoot and attired in a flowing Indian shift, smiled a welcome. She extravagantly gestured Carly into the room with a clattering sweep of an arm glittering with an array of silver and turquoise Navajo bracelets. Carly was immediately taken by the intensity of this young woman, whose dazzling green eyes seemed strangely suited to her olive complexion, and whose large but well-aligned features added, if not beauty, then a certain drama to her face. She also noticed a faint chemical smell lingering over the musky scent of cologne.

"I'm Liz Romano; Beth is asleep in her room."

"Hi, I'm Caroline Novak. But my friends call me Carly."

"Then Carly it is. Come on in and tell me what you think of the place."

What she thought of the place? She hadn't even stepped into it. Carly would learn later that Liz's tendency to make snap judgments made her assume that others did too.

Once inside, dutifully examining the room, Carly noticed a lumpy sofa under an ancient chenille bedspread, a smattering of unmatched chairs, a quite expensive-looking stereo set, posters of Janis and Jimi thumbtacked on the walls, books, papers, a guitar, a worn Smith-Corona portable, sundry clothing items littering the floor and an old lava lamp perched on an orange crate. Sticks of incense, dried-out bunches of flowers in Mason jars, plastic glasses and overflowing ashtrays added to the general clutter.

"It looks nice," Carly lied, "and it's close to campus. Is the neighborhood safe?"

"Is anything safe? Beth and I have been living here for over a year and we haven't had any problems at all. You just have to kind of blend into the neighborhood—become one of the regulars."

"Are you a Circle student?"

"Yeah, trying to be, anyway. Chemistry major, at the moment. Beth is in Elementary Ed. The apartment is just this one big room, a kitchen and three bedrooms," Liz said, beginning a short tour. "The kitchen is over here—sometimes it's cleaner—you just caught us at a bad time. That door to the left used to be a pantry, but I do experiments in there sometimes. You never know what's brewing in there. Better to leave it closed."

Carly now understood the source of Liz's faint chemical scent. "I'm planning on majoring in accounting," she said.

"Great. We'll put you in charge of paying the rent and stuff— maybe things will get paid on time. Your bedroom would be this one," Liz said, moving aside an old drapery panel that provided scant privacy. "When can you move in?"

Carly maneuvered her way toward the doorway and stepped into a small, dark, empty room with faded floral wallpaper. A tiny, unadorned window offered a view of yet another converted factory. The room bore absolutely no resemblance to her bedroom, where French Provincial furniture beautifully complemented the lilac walls, curtains and bedspread and where a zoo of stuffed animals and high school mementoes decorated every flat surface.

"I'd have to talk to my parents first," she answered, smiling at the understatement expressed in the word "talk." "Talking" to her parents did not begin to describe the scene that awaited her at home—perhaps "pleading," "begging," "entreating." "Defying"? Could she defy her parents over this matter? Would she?

"Is someone here?" questioned a voice at least an octave higher than Liz's velvety smoker's tones. Beth Grainger emerged from the next room, yawning, her right hand with its neatly manicured pink fingernails tapping her mouth. Carly was immediately struck by the contrasts between the roommates. Liz was the essence of exotic drama with her gypsy-like coloring and apparel. Beth, on the other hand, looked like a cheerleader gracing the cover of a teen magazine. Pretty and petite, with short-cropped honey blonde hair and an upturned nose sprinkled delicately with freckles, Beth was clad in a short, fuzzy pink bathrobe with neatly manicured pink toenails peeking out from fuzzy pink open-toed slippers. Another yawn was followed by a broad smile that revealed small, perfectly aligned, perfectly white teeth.

Carly reflected that, physically, she occupied the middle road between the roommates. She was dark-haired, but without the exoticism of raven-tressed Liz. Short-statured, but not petite like Beth. Her complexion was the exact balance between Liz's dramatic olive coloring and Beth's peaches-and-cream, and she would have gladly traded the color of her deep brown eyes, although they were certainly her best feature, for Liz's emerald shade or Beth's jay's-wing blue.

Perhaps living here would be a good fit.

"Are you the person who called about the apartment?" asked the vision in pink. Carly nodded in answer.

"It's usually much nicer than it looks right now—Liz has a tendency to just kind of let things drop when she's working on an experiment. She's probably already pressuring you for an answer on whether you'll take the place or not. Did she at least have the decency to offer you a cup of coffee?"

"No, not yet," Carly laughed.

"Then come on." Beth led Carly into the kitchen where she cleared a space on the small white table, removed books from three chairs, and picked three mugs from a shelf displaying a motley assortment of kitchenware, pouring strong black coffee in each. "Sit," she offered, "We'll get acquainted. Are you just starting at Circle this semester?"

"Yes. I was really planning on commuting here from Berwyn— that's pretty much what my parents are expecting me to do. But after orientation and signing up for classes, I think I'm going to be on campus a lot more than I expected. When I saw your ad, I thought I'd look at housing options available near campus."

"Well, part of going to Circle is the atmosphere," responded Beth. "You'll really need to be near the campus to take advantage of outside lectures and different extracurricular activities, plus all the plays and stuff you can get to downtown. And you'll probably be spending a lot of late hours in the library."

"Yeah...that's what you can tell your parents, anyway," offered Liz, flopping into a chair and reaching for the cup of coffee Beth had poured for her. "Tell them the El is unsafe after rush hour, and that's the only time you can get into the library or any of the science labs. Parents always fall for that kind of shit."

"My parents are really counting on my waitressing at our family's restaurant. That's part of the reason they want me to stay at home."

"So what's the problem? Tell them you'll be home weekends to work at the restaurant, but that you'll really need the time here during the week to keep up with your school work," Beth suggested. "You can even go home one or two weekends before you tell them you have all kinds of group projects and stuff that you can only do here—you're really sorry, you really wanted to help, college is just so important to you—you'll figure out what to say. It's not like they'd never be able to find another waitress. Trust me, a couple of weeks here and you'll never want to go back to your folks' place."

"Beth is right. You have to kind of take the initiative in pushing away—at least I did. Eventually they'll come around. And the truth is, once you're out of the house for a couple of weeks, they'll find out that they can do just fine without you."

Carly doubted her parents would ever react in quite that manner.

The next several hours flew by in easy discussion, first over coffee and later over pizza and Cokes. Carly learned quite a bit about the women who would become first her roommates and then her best friends, and found that she could talk with Beth and Liz more easily than with the girls she had known in elementary and high school.

Liz, at twenty-one the older of the two, had been born and brought up in Boston. Her parents, first-generation Italian-Americans, had made a great success of their back room beauty parlor that had grown into a chain of high-priced salons. They indulged their only child outrageously: the University of Illinois was her third college, and chemistry her third major. Liz had enjoyed the advantages of designer clothing and sporty cars throughout high school and later at various colleges, but she had been an indifferent student at best, very bright, but bored with most of her classes and restless in whatever situation she found herself. Carefree and generous, extravagant and unpredictable, she had grown up to be as indulgent with herself and her friends as she herself had been indulged. Her current interest in chemistry, however, seemed to have the potential to last, although Liz hardly fit Carly's image of a scientist. When Carly asked what drew her to that field, her answer was swift and sure:

"The order."

"Order?" asked Carly, surreptitiously eying the mess surrounding her.

"Yeah," responded Beth, "it might not look like anyone here is a neat freak. But you should see Liz's lab. It's pristine." Still, Beth expressed doubts about whether chemistry would be Liz's final career choice, mentioning a closet containing the litter of paints and easels, guitars and songbooks, fabrics, design books, sculpting clay and other paraphernalia that evidenced the many interests Liz had eagerly adopted and then suddenly abandoned. "Chemistry is Liz's *passion du jour*," asserted Beth, despite Liz's protests that she had actually, finally, found her true calling.

Beth, on the other hand, was in every way a product of suburban Chicago. Born to well-to-do parents in the affluent suburb of

Northbrook, her childhood was full of activities: Brownies, Girl Scouts, piano lessons, ballet classes, swimming lessons, soccer, recitals, and later in high school, drama club, chorus, French club, the school paper and cheerleading. Her father was an executive for an electronics firm, and her mother, a housewife involved in many volunteer activities. Beth's good nature and loving spirit, her ability to achieve good grades and to avoid serious trouble, made her the ideal suburban daughter throughout the nineteen years of her life.

When Carly asked her why she had chosen Elementary Ed as her major, Beth just smiled sweetly and shrugged her shoulders. Further questioning made Carly realize that teaching second or third graders was intended to keep Beth respectably occupied while she had time to pursue her true calling—finding a suitable husband who earned a substantial income, purchasing a suburban house even nicer than the one she had grown up in, and raising happy, healthy children. Carly mused that Beth's thoughts were much like her own father's the first time she had mentioned going to college: he had suggested she find a job waitressing near the DePaul or Loyola campuses. He told her that she would be sure to find a nice, Catholic, college-educated husband there.

When it became Carly's turn to disclose her major, she found herself repeating almost verbatim what her father had advised her once he realized she was determined to actually *attend* college: that accounting would be her most practical choice, what with her strong math grades and good memory. It was also a profession that met his own needs in running their family business. Owning a small business was hard, constant work, and a small restaurant succeeded on very little margin. A daughter who could keep accounts and prepare financial statements and the necessary tax documents would be extremely helpful and cost-saving.

"What kind of restaurant do your parents own?" asked Beth.

"A Polish restaurant—the *Little Warsaw*—on Roosevelt Road. Maybe you've heard of it? It's pretty popular."

"Well, I don't get into the western suburbs very much. Do you serve only Polish food there?"

"Pretty much. *Pierogi, kielbasa* with *kapusta, golumbka.*"

"That's all Greek to me," laughed Liz, reaching for another slice of pepperoni pizza.

"Stuffed dumplings, sausage with sauerkraut, and pigs in a blanket," Carly translated. "You'll have to come out to the restaurant some time. But watch out—my mom would see 'fattening you up' as a pretty worthy cause."

"My diet!" groaned Beth.

"It can't be helped. Mom lives by the motto of the Polish housewife."

"Which is?"

"If it moves, feed it. If it doesn't move, clean it."

Once their drinks switched from Cokes to Budweisers, the subject turned to names. Carly learned that both Liz and Beth had been christened "Elizabeth," and Liz was certain that their different nicknames had developed from their personalities. "Beths are quieter and more studious," she had said, "and Lizzes are girls who like to have a good time. Look at Liz Taylor—a 'Beth Taylor' would never have made it in Hollywood."

"What do you think, Beth?" Carly asked. "Are you quiet and studious?"

"Well, yeah, but Liz is forgetting that still waters run deep," Beth answered, a devious smile wrinkling her perfect nose.

"How about other nicknames for Elizabeth? Do they come out of personalities, too?"

"Yeah—there's Betty," offered Liz. "Betties are the sensible, hardworking type. They're always somebody's secretary or best friend."

"Like Veronica's friend Betty in the *Archie* comics," offered Beth. "Veronica is the heartbreaker who gets all the guys; poor Betty is always just the best friend."

"Or Betty Rubble," added Liz, "always second fiddle to Wilma Flintstone."

"How about Betsies?" asked Carly.

"They're little girls, not women—they're the type that never grows up. Like Betsy Wetsy!" offered Liz.

"And then there are the Elizabeths of the world—the ones who never use nicknames at all, like Queen Elizabeth," added Beth. "Could you even imagine a Queen Betsy? Elizabeths take themselves pretty seriously—or sometimes they're artsy types. How about your nickname? Or were you christened Carly?"

"No, Caroline. Well, actually Carolina," responded Carly, softening the vowels and rolling the "r" in her name's Polish pronunciation.

"Caroline? Didn't you say your brother's name is Carl?" asked Liz.

"Yeah, we were both named after my father—his name is Karol."

"Carol?" asked Liz. "Isn't that a girl's name?"

"Karol with a K. It's Polish for Carl. My mom's name is Zosia. Sophia in English."

"Wow—is your dad some kind of control freak or something? He named both of you after himself? What was your mom—just the delivery system?" asked Liz.

A little hurt, Carly defended her family. "No, both of my parents liked that name. And in a Polish family the husband is sort of expected to make a lot of the decisions. Maybe a little more so in my family, with both my parents working in our restaurant, and Dad being the manager—Dad's pretty much Mom's husband and boss, too. But my mom's no pushover. She has her way of getting what she wants a lot of the time."

"How does she do that?" asked Beth.

"Well, you know—you have to be a little devious with men. Make them come around to your way of thinking without letting them see what you're doing. At least that's what my mom says."

Beth nodded her agreement, but Liz protested. "I don't see why men and women can't just be more honest with each other—why it all has to be such a game. I never wait for a guy to ask me out. If I want him, I just let him know—it works out fine for me."

"That's because you're such a slut," suggested Beth. Carly was surprised Liz did not seem to be bothered at all by being called such a name. "Some of us aren't into sleeping with a different guy every two weeks," Beth added.

"Right. And what I do is worse than your serial monogamy? You act like you're still in high school, 'going steady' with a different guy every six months and playing games with all of them. I'm just being honest and natural, and there's nothing wrong with that."

"Well, maybe you are 'honest and natural,'" retorted Beth, "or maybe you're just a nympho!" Liz's response, a deep belly laugh, astounded Carly. How could neither of the girls be offended by what the other was saying?

"What's wrong with being a nympho?" countered Liz once her laughter subsided. "It beats jogging or eating a pound of chocolate at one sitting. Sex is good exercise. And you know what else I believe? All the moralists—the priests and nuns and television preachers—all the people that tell us we should wait until we're married or that we all need to practice self-control? I'll bet they're all people with low sex drives. That's why they just don't get it—why they can't understand the rest of us. I bet a lot of those moralists are the way they are because they're nothing but fucking virgins."

Carly was taken aback by Liz's casual use of a word that she had never herself uttered —one that was never heard bouncing around the halls of St. Stanislaus Girls' High School. She wondered if she should mention that "fucking virgins" was an oxymoron—would they think that was funny? Or would she sound too pretentious? Her brother Carl was always telling her that her mind was a storehouse for useless knowledge.

But the subject matter turned suddenly to her. "How about you?" asked Liz. "We haven't gotten any true confessions from you yet. What about your sex life?"

"Well, I dated a lot in high school."

"And?" persisted Liz.

"I guess I never got real serious about anyone." Of course, she thought, any kind of sex life would have been awfully difficult to pull off with her parents insisting on knowing her whereabouts at all times. And they had the cooperation of her whole community! Her mind flashed back to a vision of *Pani* Soberska, the elderly widow who rented the second floor of the bungalow adjacent to Carly's home, peering through the lace curtains of her kitchen window every time one of Carly's dates escorted her to the front door for a modest good-night kiss. One hot summer night she had rebelliously given her date a far more passionate kiss than her norm, and had then sung sweetly up to her neighbor, "You can go to sleep, *Pani* Soberska, I'm going in now." *That* had seemed incredibly bold behavior at the time.

"You mean," persisted Liz, her cocked head and raised eyebrows reflecting her amazement. "You haven't done it *yet*? Not with anyone?"

"Well, I guess not. Not really."

"You guess not? I should think you'd know if you had. You do *like* guys, don't you? It's not that you like...I mean, you're not a daughter of Lesbos or anything, are you? Not that it would matter."

"Honestly, Liz, aren't you a little bit out of line here?" said Beth. "You're about the last person who should be commenting on anyone else's sex life. And everyone who isn't sleeping with a different guy every weekend isn't necessarily gay. Maybe Carly's saving herself for her husband."

"A virgin? Hell, that would be worse than liking girls instead of guys."

"Liz!" Beth's arched eyebrows signified her disapproval.

It was time for Carly to intercede. "I like guys—I really do. I guess I just haven't found the right one yet."

"Stop embarrassing Carly. I think saving yourself for your husband would be kind of sweet." Carly recognized Beth's gentle smile for what it was: an attempt to smooth over what was becoming a difficult situation.

"Sweet? That's a fine thing for you to say," laughed Liz. "Virginity's one bridge *you're* never gonna be able to cross back over! But I'm not picking on you, Carly. It's just that it seems like you're missing out on a lot. You're only young once. But, hey, it takes all kinds to make a world. Different strokes and all..."

"Right. As long as it's *your* decision," added Beth.

"Hell, it's *your* body."

In the early evening the topic changed to music. Beth was the owner of the somewhat battered but still quite usable guitar Carly had noticed when she first came into the apartment. Beth could play pretty good renditions of several popular songs. Carly had always wanted to learn to play guitar but just never had the time. She asked where Beth had taken lessons.

"Lessons? For guitar?" questioned Beth. "I just learned from my brother Jason—he's awesome at guitar, and he taught himself. Sit down. I can show you how to play C, F, and G in about twenty minutes. You'll be able to play about a hundred songs once you learn those. Of course, it takes years of practice after that to actually get any good." Carly was delighted when, after the promised twenty minutes, she was able to painstakingly strum her way through "Michael Row the Boat Ashore," with Liz and Beth singing along, both fighting giggles as they held the notes long enough to allow Carly time to find the chords. Liz promised to take Carly to a local pawn shop where she could pick up a second-hand guitar cheap.

Later, Beth expertly rolled a joint and passed it to Liz, who inhaled deeply. "Care for some?" she offered Carly, who did not know quite how to respond. Was this some kind of test? Would she be rejected if she didn't join in? Of course, she knew about pot—some of the girls she knew in high school had tried it. But she had not. Well, she thought, this was an evening for firsts. She accepted the joint from Liz.

Liz laughed hysterically at Carly's awkward attempts to smoke the marijuana, holding the joint much like one would hold a cigarette and, being a non-smoker, coughing violently when she tried to inhale. But Beth intervened. "Here. Hold it like this—two fingers on top and your thumb on the bottom. Then inhale slowly, like this," she instructed, demonstrating with the *elan* of the veteran toker. "Don't let Liz get to you—you would have laughed yourself silly if you saw me my first time."

"It's that obvious?" Carly wailed.

"Well, yeah. But like I said, I was pretty funny my first time. Jason almost wet his pants laughing at me."

"Your brother taught you how to smoke marijuana?" Carly couldn't even begin to imagine her own brother smoking pot, much less teaching her how to do it.

"Yep, and a mighty fine teacher he was. You'll have to meet Jason some time. He's kind of an atypical suburbanite."

"Actually, I think Beth's parents see him as the anti-Christ," added Liz, laughing much harder than her comment deserved.

"Is he that awful?" asked Carly.

"No," defended Beth, who seemed proud of her brother the rebel. "He's just kind of irreverent—he always sort of stood out in our neighborhood of preppies whose biggest concerns were whether or not the football team would win and wearing shirts with alligators on them. And Mom and Dad were really upset when he didn't go to college, especially since he's the family brain. But he's a good guy at heart."

"And he's got a fine ass!" added Liz.

"Hey, watch it—you're talking about my brother." But Beth's objection initiated three-way hysterics. For the past hour, the girls had found themselves laughing hysterically at just about everything.

Much later, as Carly got on the El heading west, she considered, somewhat disjointedly, the arguments she would use to convince her parents that she needed to live in that decrepit apartment on Morgan Street. It wasn't the pot or the impromptu guitar lessons. It certainly wasn't the ambience of the physical surroundings. And she had never been one to jump to conclusions, to make decisions without first thoughtfully considering all options and possible liabilities. But something made her want to move in with Liz and Beth more than she had ever wanted anything in her life.

Coming to some agreement with her parents on her hoped-for living arrangements had been tricky. "*Matka boska,*" Zosia had wailed, lifting her floured hands out of the enormous pile of *pierogi* dough she had been kneading. "You know you papa never gonna say yes. He don' want you live away from home. And you got it so nice here—you got beautiful room and everything. We never have nothing like that when I was old as you. Why you wanna move?" She tucked a wayward curl back behind her ear, leaving a dusting of flour on her brow. The years of hard work in the restaurant left little physical impression on her, Carly thought, looking carefully at her mother, whose dark eyes flashed in a round, open face free of any signs that would betray her almost fifty years, and whose short dark curls were just beginning to show signs of gray. She looked much as she had when Carly was just a child. "What you got there you don' got here?"

"Mama, college is different—I feel different already. It's a lot more work than high school, and if I'm going to be successful there, I have to be around for all the evening activities."

"Parties? You gonna drink? Smoke? Run around? We expect maybe you brother gonna do things like that, but not you! Is that what you papa and me work so hard for?"

"No, Mama, lectures. The library. Science labs." Carly found herself desperately ticking off Liz's list of arguments.

"Never! Never! You papa never gonna say yes."

"It's mostly the El ride, Mama," added Carly, feeling guilty for using her mother's over-protectiveness and fear of the city to her own advantage. "I don't feel safe coming home alone so late. And, Mama, I know you and Papa can't afford a car for me," she added, disappointed with herself at sounding like a spoiled ingrate.

Miraculously Zosia, finally won over by her daughter's lies, was once again able to work her wifely magic. A compromise was reached. Her parents would consider allowing Carly to stay in Chicago during the school week, but would expect her to come home most weekends and all holidays and breaks. "Don't tink you gonna go to Florida for wat dey call...wat dey call it..."

"Spring Break, Papa? It's not real likely I'd be going anywhere for Spring Break," Carly said, trying to remove even the slightest hint of sarcasm from her voice.

"Watever dey call it," he thundered back, his normally ruddy coloring turning absolutely livid. "You not gonna become one of dem crazy college kids." But by that time in the negotiations her father was speaking more for effect than to make any actual point. And although Carly was able to forestall her parents' desire to actually see the apartment, pleading her own lack of time and their busy schedules, she had to capitulate in agreeing to bring her new roommates to the restaurant to meet them before actually signing a lease.

That experience was more of an encounter of contrasting cultures than anything Carly had ever read about in *The National Geographic*. Beth and Liz were on their best behavior, which was quite a stretch for Liz, whose normal conversational patterns needed a great deal of restraint for this situation. But Liz managed to deftly steer clear of the expletives that normally added so much spice to her speech. The most difficult time for Beth, on the other hand, was when she discovered, to her horror, that the *czarnina* which, as the restaurant's specialty, was made in the traditional manner, featured duck's blood as its main ingredient. Beth handled the situation with aplomb, swallowing quickly the mouthful she had just taken and managing to push the remainder of the soup aside, covering it with a napkin, while Liz hid her laughter behind her own napkin. She make a point to eat the *czarnina,* and even requested another bowl.

"Nice girls," Karol commented once Beth and Liz had left the restaurant. "Dat little blondie one, she maybe a little bit Polish?"

Carly beamed, realizing that her objective was gained. "Well, Papa, her name is Grainger, but you never know. She might be."

"Yes, very nice girls," added Zosia. "But so skinny. They must not have very good food at that university."

"Probably not," responded Carly diplomatically. "But then, I'd be eating a lot of my meals here, so that wouldn't be a problem."

And so the deal was sealed.

Living with Beth and Liz was not quite the serendipitous experience Carly had hoped for. From the start, her roommates had begun taking advantage of both her dependability and her desire to get along. She had gladly taken over paying the bills for the apartment, a task she was certainly more qualified to do than Beth, whose checks seemed to bounce monthly, or Liz, who simply never got around to writing the checks in the first place. And the cleaning...well, she had to admit Liz was right. If living in a pigsty didn't bother Beth or herself, and it only bothered Carly, then Carly was the person to do something about it. Carly didn't want to be reminded that the girls got along very well in the apartment without her for over a year.

Of course, there were advantages to living on Morgan Street. The freedom of living away from home was intoxicating. She had become pretty fair at the guitar. She had made many more friends, and very different kinds of friends, than she would have made as a commuter. And she had found college to actually be much more demanding than she had expected, and that the excuses she had made to her parents about long nights in the library and the science labs had turned out to be dishearteningly true.

Carly realized that, despite her frequent periods of annoyance with her roommates, she had inexplicably found herself liking them more each day. During the long gab sessions which had become a bonding staple of their existence together, she had learned how different their experiences growing up had been from hers.

She was mystified by her roommates' relationships with their families. True, Liz's family was in Boston—she couldn't very well visit them every weekend—but Beth's family lived only a few miles away. Carly could not imagine living so close to one's parents and not being expected to attend dinners and parties with assorted extended family members and friends, or summoned to help out with various household tasks and projects.

Yet both Beth and Liz shared a complacent expectation of consummate support from their parents; Carly could scarcely believe such parents existed. Carly was amazed one day when Beth discussed her first car, a Toyota her parents had given her on her sixteenth birthday. Beth had totalled the car in a rollover accident six months later.

"My Lord, Beth, what did your parents do?" Carly had asked.

"They were both pretty mad, especially Dad. But all in all they were happy that I wasn't really hurt. And insurance pretty much covered the cost of the new car they got me."

"What? They got you a new car! I'm surprised they didn't ban you from driving forever."

Liz interjected, "Compared to Jason, her parents think Beth is a saint. They're just happy they never had to bail *her* out of jail!"

"Jail? Your brother?"

"Well, not for anything serious," Beth defended her brother. "Some minor drug use—just pot—ignoring a lot of tickets, stuff like that."

"And your parents accept that kind of behavior?"

"Really Carly," said Liz, "there's not much parents can do by the time you're a teenager." Carly had a hard time imagining her parents taking such a cavalier attitude toward adolescent indiscretions, although she realized neither she nor her brother had the temperament to test their parents to the limit.

"It's not like they haven't tried with Jason," added Beth. "They took him to the most expensive child psychologists and psychiatrists on the north side. They tried everything—my mom has every damn creative parenting book that was ever published and she's been in support groups forever. Jason was even on Ritalin for a while. It was supposed to control his mood swings."

"Did it work?"

"Well, actually, I guess we're not quite sure. He moved out a couple of years ago—about the time he and Dad were really into it about his not going to college. He lives in the city somewhere—I don't think any of us has his address. But he keeps in touch with them for holidays and stuff and I see him once in a while. He's stopped over here a few times. Maybe you'll meet him one day. And it's not like he's a bad person. He's sweet and caring—really pretty good for a big brother. He never cared about sports or dating very much, and as far as school was concerned, he could never be bothered with it. But he's real smart in his own way. He reads more and knows more about all different kinds of stuff than anyone I know."

"You sound pretty close to Jason."

"She oughta be," said Liz. "He really took the heat off her while she was growing up. Jason never gave them the time to figure out what Beth was up to!"

"And just what *were* you up to?"

"Oh, nothing, just the usual stuff—some beer, some pot, a little bit of shoplifting—all the usual teenage rites of passage." Carly reflected that none of these had been part of any rites of passage she had experienced. Had her mother noticed any hint of indiscretion, she would have pounced on her daughter like a calico on a hapless mouse. And shown about as much compassion.

Damn, it's almost 6:00, thought Carly, pushing the door of the Morgan Street apartment open with a quick thrust of her right hip (the only way the warped door would yield) as she clutched two bags of groceries in her left arm and tried to keep her overloaded bookbag from tipping her over. *The guys'll be here in an hour. I wonder if Beth cleaned up.*

"Hello...anybody home? Oh, shit," she moaned as she observed that the apartment, impossible as it seemed, was messier than it was when she had left it ten hours earlier. Hopscotching over Beth's guitar, Liz's new jeans, and a pile of tapes scattered haphazardly on the floor, she dashed into the kitchen where the faucet dripped methodically over piles of dirty dishes and two bags of garbage stood sentinal against the back door. "Damn!" Deciding that the living room looked the worst, she grabbed an empty plastic bag and the kitchen sponge and began frantically emptying ashtrays, dumping pizza boxes, and wiping off surfaces gray with ash.

As Carly began to see some improvement in the living room, she advanced toward the kitchen to unpack the groceries she had picked up on her way home from classes. Dumping the contents of yet another overflowing ashtray into her rapidly filling garbage bag, Carly realized the apartment was actually beginning to shape up. Almost as if on cue, she heard Liz and Beth chattering in the hallway, followed by the expected thump of a hip dislodging the door.

"Oh, Carly...you should have waited. I was going to do that," sighed Beth, expressing what, had Carly not known better, would have sounded like true penitence. "Let me help you finish up."

"Thanks. We only have a half hour before the guys get here, and I was planning on fixing some snacks." Carly tried to keep any hint of scolding out of her voice.

"That's awfully sweet of you. Those vultures are always ready to eat us out of house and home," cooed Beth.

"As if they'll really be here before 10:00," added Liz, heading for the bathroom. "Don't turn on the kitchen faucet," she called from the bathroom as she turned on the shower.

"But the dishes...they still need to be done."

"Carly, the guys are bound to be late. I'll do the dishes once Liz is out of the shower. I can help you with the food, too."

Carly was dubious that Beth would be much help, but chose to keep that thought to herself. "Okay. So who's coming?"

"Well, Jason maybe. I invited him when he stopped over last week. And Marty and Tony—I think Tony's bringing a date. And Liz asked a couple of the guys she knows from the club—Dirk and Eric—they're the ones who are trying to put together a band, and they're bringing some guy named Steve that I haven't met yet. Suzanne said she'd drop by later—her roommate might be with her."

"I should have bought more food."

"Don't worry. We can always order pizza later on, and maybe Suzanne will bring something. As long as we have enough beer we ought to be okay." Sighing, Carly decided she might as well stop worrying about the apartment and just plan to have a really good time. It had been a particularly long and stressful week at school, and she deserved it.

"Hey, Liz," she called, all annoyance with her roommates suddenly vanishing, "can I borrow that black embroidered blouse you bought at Carson's last week?"

Chapter Three

February, 1967

Prelude

The Doors, "Light My Fire"

"Today we are going to cover accruals. The purpose of accruals is to match income to expense in the period that the expense or income is incurred. We are looking to both the income accounts and the expense accounts as our source for the accruals, and I will cover both today."

"Accruals," wrote Carly on her full-sized yellow legal pad, "purpose—match income to expense—period when incurred. Income & expense are sources." It looked like another interminable lecture from Professor Fishman. How could he stand up there for fifty minutes three times a week, droning on in his mind-numbing monotone, referring constantly to a stack of notes withered and yellowed with age, without ever taking a question or using the blackboard?

"Generally, income is approached first. The type of business that the corporation is in is an important note for your accruals. If a distributorship, segregate the shipping papers at the time of the inventory. Obviously, anything that was shipped prior to inventory should be looked at for accrual purposes."

Obviously? Who thinks this is so obvious? thought Carly. *The other 250 kids in the room?* Carly imagined that "anything that was shipped prior to inventory should be looked at for accrual purposes" was obvious to only the thirty or so students who sat in the front rows, turning their intent looks away from Professor Fishman only long enough to scribble notes, nodding sagaciously every so often, even occasionally cracking a smile. They had actually laughed out loud when he had told his inventory joke last Monday, something about inventory being FIFO, LIFO or FISH—First In-First Out, Last In-First Out, First In-Still Here. What was so funny about that? Was Fishman actually a raconteur, and was she just too dense to understand?

Carly had started the semester in those first rows, when she still had time to read the assigned chapters of her beginning accounting book at least twice before Fishman's lectures. But gradually, as the semester plodded on (*can it actually be only the middle of February?*) she had drifted back to join the majority of students, those who tended to fill the back half of the auditorium. She glanced quickly at her new comrades-at-arms, some of whom tried to look attentive as they took meaningless notes, while others chatted companionably at the back of the room and still others were already slumped in half-doze. "Income—distributorship—shipped prior to inventory—look at for accrual purposes—-<u>OBVIOUSLY</u>," she wrote, frantically trying to catch up to the professor's unrelenting monotone.

"If manufacturing, the same holds true but you must also include work-in-process accrual, which should be addressed at the time of inventory. Service organizations are less difficult, as only work billed to date will be included, and construction accounting includes percent of completion of work in process accruals."

"Manufacturing—same holds true—also work in process addressed—address—*get Steve's new address— Don't forget!!!*—service easier, only work billed to date—construction—% of completion of work." Carly tried to jot down the information as Professor Fishman droned inexorably on, words beginning to blend into a distant buzz.

"Address expenses that pertain to your sales accrual, like freight, taxes, carrying costs, etc. Shipping date is the criterion for picking up a sale for accrual purposes, not date received by your customer, so all shipping documents must be addressed."

"Expense—office-type—accrue—percent—vendors—both periods. *Hope I don't get my period tonight.* Shipping date—*date—date with Steve. What to wear? New jeans? Too tight—nope, Steve likes them tight—just won't breathe.*" Fishman's voice drifted away to a far-off, barely perceptible hum, as Carly's notes took a decided turn toward a far more interesting topic. "Steve—Steve Brennan—Steven Brennan—or Stephen Brennan—which one? Have to ask him. Funny that never came up. Mrs. Steve Brennan—Mrs. Stephen Brennan—Ms. Carly Brennan—Carly Brennan—Mrs. Carly Brennan—Mr. and Mrs. Stephen Brennan...and family."

Damn, thought Carly ruefully, *what am I? Twelve years old? What happened to that efficient, responsible college student I'm supposed to be?*

As Fishman droned on, she realized what happened. Steve happened. Carly had to admit she was not prepared for the overpowering attraction she felt for Steve from the moment she had first seen him at that party in October. He came in late, after midnight, having missed his ride with Dirk and Eric, the rock star wanna-bes.

The party reached its mellow stage: pizzas were ordered and eaten, along with every tray and bowl of snacks Carly had prepared; Liz, Eric and Dirk were companionably sharing a joint, while Carly and the others contentedly sipped the Coors Suzanne had been extravagant enough to bring. Quiet conversation was occasionally disrupted by peals of laughter.

Carly knew Jason Grainger was Beth's brother the minute he walked into the room. Same jay's-wing-blue eyes. Same freckles. Same honey blonde hair, but with a bit of strawberry tossed in. Same confident, personable manner. He was taller than his sister by over a foot, but other than that, Carly almost felt that she was in the presence of another Beth.

On meeting her, Jason asked how her guitar-playing was progressing—Beth must have spoken to him about her. When she admitted she'd been too busy to practice much, he offered to show her a thing or two. He was in the process of showing Carly a new chord—B minor, which was certainly a lot trickier than B flat—his arm casually draped around her shoulder feeling warm and friendly as they shared the old loveseat Carly had found on one of her forays onto Maxwell Street. And then Steve walked in.

Some people purposely arrive late at parties to effect an entrance, but Carly was to learn that this wasn't the case with Steve, who managed to become a commanding presence in any group. He was tall, a couple of inches over six feet, lean but muscular. His clothing was simple, practical, and somewhat conservative for this group: Levis and a dark green knit shirt. The first impression Carly had of Steve was one that she would retain for years: *My God*, she thought, *he's a golden man.*

It might have been the effect of the entrance light shining down on him that first moment she saw him, but Steve seemed to emanate a tawny sheen. His hair, which others might uncharitably describe as dishwater blonde, caught the light with glints of gold and copper as he walked in. As Steve removed his jacket, Carly noticed that the short, fine hairs on his arms flashed gold against the aureate tan of his skin. Later she would notice his hazel eyes, always steady and direct, glittering with golden flecks. Carly found him enormously compelling; his golden sheen and the lithe but powerful smoothness of his movement, intense but controlled, reminded her of the lions she had seen pacing in their cages in Lincoln Park Zoo just a week earlier.

"What was that?" Jason asked, in response to the hideously flat chord Carly had just produced. "Carly, are you still with me? Pay attention if you want to learn this." Carly obediently tried to focus her thought on the new chord Jason was showing her, but she definitely was no longer "with" him. She was too preoccupied sneaking peeks at the leonine young man who was now following Beth into their kitchen to seek out a Coors. Now sipping his beer casually as he chatted with his friends. Now thumbing through the cassettes stacked in a precarious pile next to a loudspeaker. At last Jason, seeming impatient with her sudden disinterest in the whole range of B chords, got up and headed to the kitchen for a beer. Carly, softly strumming chords, tried not to appear so intent on her task as to suggest that she did not desire company.

"Have you been playing long?" asked the golden man, suddenly appearing at her side. His voice, deep, sure and sonorous, fit him perfectly.

"No, I've just started. I'm really just a beginner."

"Is your boyfriend coming back?"

"He's not my boyfriend...I just met him tonight. He's Beth's brother."

"Well, in that case..." he drawled, settling himself next to Carly on the battered loveseat in one lithe, fluid movement. "I'm Steve Brennan. I don't think we've met."

"Carly Novak. Are you a musician too?"

"Me? No. What gave you that impression?'

"I thought you were a friend of Dirk's and Eric's."

"Yes, but I only know them from the club. What else do you know about me?"

"Well, nothing...I mean," Carly stammered, feeling curiously thrown off-guard. "It's just that Liz mentioned that a friend of Dirk's and Eric's was coming over tonight. I figured you must be the one."

"Well, then, in the event that I am *The One*, what would you like to know about me?"

That had been how the most compelling, most distracting component of Carly's current life had begun. She was convinced Steve had been as strongly attracted to her in those first few moments as she had been to him. How else could she explain the time he spent with her in the past four months, time he could barely spare from the rigors of completing the coursework and final project for his graduation in the spring from Circle's data processing program (and graduating with honors as well) and his almost full-time job at a local warehouse?

But he found time for her: time for long walks on the miles of public beach abutting Lake Michigan, its beauty now frozen and still; time for visits to the Field Museum and the Art Institute and to coffee houses and the artsy movie theaters she had discovered on the near north side. Steve had no money to spare for the more expensive amusements Chicago had to offer. Every penny he had went to tuition and other school expenses. But he didn't let that stop him from showing Carly a good time.

One of their favorite haunts was Lincoln Park Zoo. Situated right on Lake Michigan, just a few El stops north of the campus, the zoo was free and open to the public every day. Carly had gone there with her parents once or twice when she was a child, but recent renovations designed to bring the animals out of cages and into more life-like surroundings made the zoo seem like a much friendlier place.

Steve had dropped by unexpectedly one Saturday afternoon when the thermometer was frozen at five degrees. "Wrap up warm, sweetie, I'm taking you out," he announced as she opened the door.

"But, Steve, I wasn't expecting you. I thought you had to work."

"Got the day off. It's just too beautiful an afternoon to waste."

"Beautiful? It's freezing!"

"Yeah, cold, sure, but crisp. The whole city's sparkling. And it's almost warm in the sun."

"But I have a test to study for—accounting. I need to..."

"When's your test?"

"Monday."

"Come on. You've got two days to study for the test. Besides, a couple of hours outside will clear out the cobwebs and make it even easier for you to study later."

"Outside? We're spending the time outside? Are you crazy?"

She had determined that he was, indeed, crazy, when they got off the El and she realized where they were headed. "The zoo, Steve? In this weather?"

"This is the perfect time to visit the zoo."

"But there's nobody here."

"That's the point, exactly. Nobody's here. We have the park almost all to ourselves."

"There's a reason the park is empty!"

"Oh, come on. Think about the animals—they're still here. Don't you think they get bored during these long winter months when nobody comes?"

"Bored? Animals get bored?"

"I bet they do. And besides, this is the best time to see seals and polar bears. This is their kind of weather." Carly thought that if it were their kind of weather, they were welcome to it.

"Did you come to the zoo often when you were a child?" she asked.

"No—well, maybe. I don't remember. Come on. Let's head over to the Arctic enclosure."

They spent a good half hour there, and Carly found that Steve was right—the polar bears seemed determined to put on a show for their solitary couple of visitors. Two chased each other, splashing magnificently into the frigid water, then suddenly mounted the rocks, sleek and slim from their icy bath. A smaller bear did a little two-step into and out of his cave, shaking his immense head every time he emerged.

"They're so cute!" raved Carly. "Especially the little one. It's hard to believe that they're the most fierce of all the bears—even fiercer than the grizzly bears."

"Is that so?"

"Yeah, they're a real danger to people. They'll attack with no notice. Even their keepers have to be very careful around them."

"Well, I guess it's all a matter of perspective. I imagine, all in all, a lot more bears have been the victims of people than vice versa. And I'd probably be pretty pissed if someone put me behind the bars of a cage."

"But they've got a beautiful area here—rocks and a pond. And their food is always there for them—they don't have to hunt or forage. They're probably luckier than polar bears in the wild."

"Luckier? How can you say that? Would you be happy in a cage—even a beautiful cage, full of everything you'd ever want? Away from the way of life that's natural for you?"

"Not if you put it that way. But then why do you even want to come to the zoo?"

"Because, Carly, zoos aren't something I'm likely to be able to change—I just have to accept them. And if I have to accept them, I might as well enjoy them. But I can't help feeling, when I look at that polar bear, that I know pretty much what he feels like right now. And if I was him, and got out somehow...well, I wouldn't want to be you right now!" With that Steve grabbed her, squeezing her, pawing her, snarling as he nuzzled and mouthed gentle bites into the bare area between her woolen cap and her coat collar. Carly laughed until her tears carved hot, slick streams on her frigid cheeks.

"Now I've got you," Steve growled, lifting her into his arms. "Off to my cave! You're going to be a tasty morsel!" He carried her, lumbering in a believable impression of a bear, all the way across the park, to a massive glass building trimmed in white, where he released her. "Let's get you into the conservatory, baby, so you can warm up. You're almost blue with cold."

They stepped out of arctic freeze into tropical splendor. Carly smelled the warmth—dense, loamy, heavy with moisture—before she began to feel it. Leaving the conservatory lobby to enter the main greenhouse, she was overwhelmed by the voluptuousness of unfamiliar fragrances—jasmine, hibiscus and oleander—and by the vibrancy of the green surrounding her. Towering banyan, date and coconut palms, lush ferns and bamboo abounded, and a separate room, across a bridge from the main greenhouse, contained a variety of orchids: blue speckled vandas, phalanopsis pouring from pots attached to the ceiling, dense stalks of cymbidian, showy, frilled cattleyas. Carly felt as if she were melting, even after she removed her heavy winter coat.

"Good," said Steve, placing his arm around her and holding her close. "I knew this place would warm you up."

"I feel a lot warmer now," she answered, although she wondered whether it was the orchid room itself or the closeness of the man himself that was warming her so thoroughly. "Steve, I could stay here forever. It's paradise."

"I knew you'd love it. This place is heaven—especially when it feels like winter is never going to end."

Carly had hoped this day would never end, but all too soon Steve was depositing her at the apartment, kissing her gently and admonishing her to get back to her homework. She couldn't concentrate on accounting with sweet memories of their day drifting through her mind. Yes, Steve was handsome and intelligent. But it was more than that. Carly was struck by his sensitivity—imagine worrying about animals getting bored! His take on life was so different from hers, and so fascinating. He made her think about things she'd never considered before.

Sunday morning she awoke with a raw, ragged throat, an aching body and a fever of 101 degrees. Rest, a salt water gargle, and plenty of hot tea with honey and half a shot of whiskey—her father's prescribed remedy for all manner of aches and pains—did not help. When Monday's 6:00 a.m. alarm rang, Carly was already awake and in the middle of yet another coughing spell. She knew she could not make it to class, even if she had been prepared for her test.

But Chicago weather, for once, was her salvation. When Carly was able to pry open her sticky eyelids and glance out the window, she saw nothing but white—swirling, wind-blown white—a genuine, city-halting blizzard. There would be no school today, or for the next two days, while the city dug itself out of over thirty inches of snow. A blizzard of this magnitude was difficult enough to deal with anywhere, but in the central city, with its dense population packed into so little space, there was simply no place to put the snow. While streets and sanitation workers concentrated on plowing major thoroughfares, it was up to the populace to dig out their own cars and to forge inroads through the clogged side streets. No wonder residents placed old chairs and other pieces of furniture in the spaces they had shoveled out, jealously guarding their parking spaces. More than one brawl started when some outsider dared to move an old chair and try to park in a place he had not himself shoveled.

Carly resigned herself to a break from seeing Steve; after all, his apartment was on the South Side, almost three miles from Carly's, and none of the bus lines were running. So she was surprised when Beth knocked on her door later that afternoon and told her she had a visitor: Steve, bearing containers of mushroom barley soup, cans of butterscotch pudding, and a small bunch of yellow tea roses. "Barley soup and pudding. That's what Ma always made for me when I was sick. How did you know?" she asked.

"Oh, I have my ways of finding things out."

"And how did you even get here? Are the buses running?"

"Nope. Just the snowplows. That's how I got here. Walked part of the way, hopped onto snowplows the rest. Besides, it's the least I could do. I should never have taken you to the zoo in such cold weather."

"Steve, it's not your fault. I've probably been coming down with this for a while."

"Okay, be forgiving. But let me take care of you anyway. I'll just heat this soup in the kitchen, and then after you eat I'm going to read you to sleep—I brought this old copy of *David Copperfield*—that ought to do it. I bet you didn't sleep a wink last night."

How could she help but fall in love with him?

But then there were other times, disturbing periods of up to a week when she did not see him or hear from him at all and when he did not return her calls. Once when she had confronted him about his neglect he had reacted with surprise.

"But honey, I didn't mean to hurt your feelings. I was able to pick up some extra time at work. And with classes and everything, I just couldn't get away. You forgive me, don't you? Don't be mad. I can't stand it when you're mad at me." He put his arm around her and, holding her very close, softly kissed her. How could she remain angry?

She chose to ignore signs that could have warned her if not to back off, at least to slow down. But he was such an enigma, and she was enjoying her attempt at solving the puzzle he presented. He often caught her off guard and made her wonder about things she had taken for granted. Once he had stopped to give two dollars to a homeless man aggressively importuning passers-by on Morgan Street. "Honestly, Steve," she had said, "you only encourage them when you do that. He's probably going to take the money and just get more to drink, which is the worst thing he could do for himself. You didn't do him any favors."

"Boy, that's a pretty sharp judgment," Steve had countered. "I guess you don't know a lot about life in the city."

"I do so," she responded. "I've lived near Chicago all my life. And I know that if we give people like that money, it'll only encourage them to keep on begging instead of going to work, which is what they should be doing." As she said these words, she heard echoes of her father having said the same thing.

"People like that?" he had responded. "Are we being a bit Lady of the Manor, Miss Silver Spoon?"

"I beg your pardon. My parents have worked hard all their lives, and they taught me to work hard too. Nobody ever gave us anything."

"You haven't got a clue, have you?" he had responded. "You think that bum could never be you or your parents, right? Because you work hard? Because you're special people? You have no idea how easily that could be you or me living on the streets. It wouldn't take much."

"But, Steve, you work harder than anyone I know. You could never be like that bum—you're the exact opposite of him. You of all people should know that he's that way because he wants to be."

"Sorry, baby, he's just another side of me—and of you, too. You just don't see it. You've grown up as one of the haves of this world, and you can't see how your having what you want is built up on the backs of all the have-nots."

"Is that how you see yourself, as one of the have-nots? Is that how you grew up?"

But Carly already knew any mention of Steve's family and of his life as a boy tred onto difficult terrain. Although she knew he was the oldest of a big family that still lived in Chicago, he seldom mentioned his parents or siblings and evaded all her attempts to find out more about them. Usually he did this with a diverting laugh or smile, but sometimes she could see tension stiffening his shoulders and anger clouding his eyes. This confused Carly, for whom discussion of family, even when she was complaining about them, was completely natural and expected.

Steve was confounding: sometimes attentive and loving, other times distant; sometimes sensitive and open to her moods and ideas, other times almost despotic in asserting the superiority of his own. Yet she found him irresistible. Any time she did not spend with him physically she spent mentally and emotionally attached to him, contemplating his actions, thinking of their time together, trying to make sense of her attraction to him.

She had tried to discuss her feelings with Liz one cold December day as they companionably folded clean laundry together. "So," Liz questioned, her cocked head and sly smile revealing her interest. "Have you two done the Wild Thing yet?"

"You mean sex? Well, no, not yet," Carly responded in mid-fold of a large Turkish towel.

"That explains it all, then. You've got the hots for him. What, by the way, are you waiting for? Isn't he interested?"

"Yeah, he's interested. I've practically had to fight him off a couple of times."

"Well, then? You do plan on having sex at some time in your life, don't you? Isn't it time to seize the day? After all, 'The grave's a fine and private place, But none, I think, do there embrace.'"

"It's nice to know you learned *something* from that English Lit class we took last semester—leave it to you to memorize only those two lines from Marvell!" Carly laughed.

"It was kind of nice to find *something* relevant to my life in that awful course," Liz answered. "But you're changing the subject. Back to you and Steve. You like him, don't you?"

"Of course."

"Do you love him?"

Carly paused for a moment before answering, "I think maybe I do."

"Then what are you waiting for? Are you afraid? Of getting pregnant? There are lots of ways to make sure that doesn't happen, you know. I can help you there. Or are you afraid it's the wrong thing to do? That you'd go to hell or something?"

"To hell...well, it's not quite that simple," laughed Carly. "You don't know the complete Catholic school scenario. Yes, of course I'll get pregnant...the first time. Then my dad will throw me out, and Steve, finding out that he's about to become a father, will have nothing further to do with me, and I'll wind up having the baby by myself in an alley somewhere in the middle of a blizzard, and I'll die in childbirth. Then and only then will I get to go to hell."

"Sounds pretty grim." Liz laughed. "But you don't really believe that."

"Well, no, but, you know that line about Catholic girls starting too late."

"Yeah, but the next line of the song says it comes down to fate. Don't you think Steve would be an appropriate fate? Damn, I wouldn't think twice."

"I don't even understand the attraction I feel for him. I want to be with him all the time, even if sometimes I just want to kill him. I've never felt this way about anybody before."

"If you ask me, you think too damn much. You always have to figure out every angle about everything before you make a step—that's not the way to live your whole life. For some things you just have to follow your heart, and if not that, at least your yearning, sex-starved body."

"Our time is just about up. During Friday's class we'll discuss payroll accruals, and I'll delve more deeply into the mechanics of the accrual process. Quiz on chapters 8 and 9 for our next session."

Damn, thought Carly, looking somberly at the pathetic scratchings that served for her class notes for the day's session. *Fishman's done for the day. I wonder who I can get notes from?* Most of the students who had been sitting near Carly were already streaming toward the doors, and the few remaining front-sitters were clustered around the teacher, asking questions. It would not be wise to ask any favors from that group. She packed her materials into her backpack, vowing to find some kind soul to lend her notes before the next session, but already losing that good intention in thinking ahead to seeing Steve that evening.

"Flowers? Steve, what a wonderful surprise."

"Well, it's almost Valentine's Day," he countered as she gently unwrapped the dark jade florist's paper to find long-stemmed American Beauties, their lush, velvety petals just short of bursting into perfect full bloom.

"These must have cost a fortune!" she exclaimed, hoping that he could not hear her heart, suddenly beating a crescendo. She wondered what such an extravagant gift, a Valentine's Day gift, might signify in terms of his feelings for her.

"Ah, now, let's not worry about that tonight. Find some water for them and let's head out before we're late for the movie."

Finding a vase in the poorly stocked kitchen was out of the question, but after a bit of searching Carly found a tall, only slightly chipped German stein, probably the relic of some long-forgotten Oktoberfest party, hidden behind battered aluminum pots on a bottom shelf. The cobalt of its background coloring would showcase the richness of the roses' crimson.

"I love them, Steve," Carly said, placing the roses on the old bureau, noticing how their classic beauty made the room look even more shabby than it did before. "Thank you. What's this movie we're seeing?"

"Paradise, Hawaiian Style," he answered, taking her good wool coat from the counter and helping her into it in his best gentlemanly fashion. "It's an Elvis movie."

Hours later, she was comfortably snuggled in the corner of an old but still serviceable sofa in the tiny living room of Steve's apartment. His building was at least as old as the girls' warren on Morgan Street, and the shabbiness of the apartment's walls and woodwork reminded her of theirs, but there the similarity ended. Steve's apartment was meticulously tidy, well-scrubbed and polished, without so much as a book or sock out of place. And his walls were surprisingly bare—no posters or pictures intruded upon their stark white. No family photos or knickknacks cluttered the set of maple end tables, chipped and scuffed, but obviously recently polished.

"Does the fireplace actually work?" she asked, looking at the last vestige of the room's old grandeur.

"Yes, it does. Would you like a fire?"

"No, that's okay. Don't go to any trouble," she responded. But he was already kneeling before the grate and in no time was lighting a match to the small stack of logs he had expertly assembled. The fire caught suddenly, and the blaze illuminated Steve, washing his hair, face, and arms with a soft, golden glow.

"Would you like a beer? I've also got some white wine in the fridge, if you'd prefer," he offered.

"The wine sounds good." He brought it to her on a rosewood tray, which held not only two crystal stems and the bottle, but a single rose, obviously a match to the dozen he had brought her, in a glass bud vase. Had he been *that* certain she would be coming to his apartment this evening?

His left arm was draped with a white tea towel. "Does Madame desire anything further?" he asked, offering her the wine with a flourish and a slight bow.

"Well, perhaps Monsieur sitting right here beside me," Carly laughed as she patted the deep blue velvet of the sofa. He was so sensitive and charming, she thought. How could she ever have doubted him?

"Ah, but of course," he smiled, easing to her side and casually slipping his arm around her. As Carly sipped the wine, gazing intently at the fire, Steve softly kissed her eyebrow, then her cheek, then that dangerous, sensitive area just behind her ear.

"What did you think of the movie?" she asked suddenly.

"Oh, I thought it was great."

"I love Elvis, but don't you think it was a little far out?"

"No, not really."

"I liked Blue Hawaii better. But I've never really been crazy about movies where people start singing all the time."

"So you're a realist, not a dreamer."

"I don't know. Maybe a little of both."

"But you must have liked the Hawaiian scenery."

"I did, I'd love to go there sometime."

"Well...maybe one day we will."

"Uhh...maybe...but..." She found she could not complete her sentence as he placed his arm around her, pulling her close, as he gently brushed her cheek with his lips. "I do know that," Carly said. But her words seemed negated by a sudden subtle stiffness in her body and a pulling away from his embrace.

"Carly, I've never felt this way about anyone before in my life. This close. But maybe you don't feel for me what I feel for you."

"Steve, I do feel...I..."

"I want to show you how much you mean to me...make you want me the way I want you. Carly, you are so beautiful, so special. And you don't even know it." His fingers gently stroked her cheek and neck and rested there just a moment before deftly slipping down to the top button of her silk blouse.

"Steve, I don't think..."

"Darling, for once, don't think. Let your feelings take over. Don't you feel that what we have is special? Don't you want to be with me in every possible way, the way I want to be with you?"

"Yes, very much," she sighed, as his fingers rested gently on her breast. "But..."

"Trust me," he pleaded, easing her body down and gently lifting her legs up onto the sofa. He knelt beside her and began to undo her blouse with one hand, lingering over every pearl button, and very slowly, very gently, very delicately kissing every inch of the flesh he exposed. "Just tell me to stop and I will. I swear it. But, baby, please, I'm hoping to God you don't tell me to stop."

As Carly lay there, glancing at her fingers running languidly through his hair, which danced with glints of reddish gold reflected from the fire, she felt her body flame, then melt, then flame again wherever his fingers or his lips made contact. Every inch of her exposed skin became a well of desire—her body throbbed in ways she had never felt before. Peeking at Steve through her own slitted eyes, she saw such hunger in his, such delight—hunger for her, delight with her. She felt a power she had never felt before, a power born of surrender.

Carly's early training told her it was time to stop him, time to ask him to take her home. But how could she talk, how could she walk out of the room, with this new body, weak almost to liquidity, she found herself inhabiting? How could she tear away from the sight of him, his shirt tossed to the floor, his tight chest muscles and shoulders glowing gold in the flickering light of the fire? And how to ask him to stop, before the hollow hunger she felt deep within her was satisfied? As passion, urgently powerful in its first true inception, washed over Carly, stopping Steve became unlikely, then improbable, then completely inconceivable.

Chapter Four

May 1967

Prelude

Heart, "Magic Man"

*C*ome on, Carly coached herself, *time to face the music. Putting this off isn't going to make it any easier.* Still, she remained at the kitchen table, her head propped heavily on one hand, listlessly lighting yet another cigarette from the previous one, sickened by the acrid pungency of her own breath. *One more cigarette and another cup of coffee couldn't hurt,* she concluded.

She dreaded the upcoming visit to her parents' home. She had made up her mind two weeks earlier; certainly she was old enough to make her own decisions and to take steps toward pursuing her own happiness. Perhaps she should have accepted Steve's offer to accompany her on this visit home. But no, this was something she needed to do by herself. She owed her parents that.

And afterward she would be free—free to continue along the path she'd stepped onto that evening in Steve's room. What a big step that had seemed at the time; she'd imagined virginity looming before her like a castle wall, dense, high, unassailable. Steve knocked the fortress down...with sweet words, wine, roses.

Walls offered protection, but they could also incarcerate, keeping her away from experiences that could set her free. Her experiences of these past few months were an education in themselves. That first night with Steve—she felt such a fool, fumbling, frightened and confused. But he had been gentle and loving, both that night and the many glorious nights that followed. And, as always, she had been an apt pupil. Before long she felt more comfortable and more herself with Steve than she did with her family or with Liz and Beth.

She had so many delicious firsts to reflect upon: waking before him that first morning, which gave her the opportunity to examine his sleeping body, completely relaxed from his usual highly strung tenseness, his face as vulnerable as a child's; making his breakfast that morning, tenderly feeding each other orange slices and cinnamon toast; their first joint forays into the local supermarket and the laundromat, where the sight of their clothing jumbling together in the suds paralleled the intimacy they were beginning to share; that first time he had stepped into the shower with her...well, better stop thinking of that or her knees would become too weak to carry her to the El station.

Of course, there had been difficult times as well. She didn't enjoy the visit to the sterile environment of the University Clinic, where she received her first prescription for birth control pills: the alternative, a visit to her family GP, her father's good friend Dr. Kowalski, was clearly out of the question. She was also disappointed with the way her grades suffered that semester, just pitiful C's replacing her accustomed A- average. That only made her decision seem more appropriate: she clearly wasn't college material after all, a sad realization.

And then there was the Como Inn. She should have suspected something momentous was about to occur when Steve invited her to a romantic dinner at the legendary Italian restaurant where the booths, arranged in a grotto-like setting, assured maximum privacy. Many serious contracts, decisions and pacts had been negotiated over a decanter of the Inn's chianti. Steve was so mysterious that evening, telling her to wear her best dress because they had something to celebrate. He kept her waiting through the antipasto, the minestrone, the fettucini Alfredo, even the cannoli and coffee, before he shared his news. "Sweetie, you know I've been job-hunting."

"I don't know how you find the time with work and finishing your degree. Any luck?"

"Definitely. I've gotten a couple of offers, but one is just what I'm looking for, and I've decided to take it. I'd be starting out in junior management with Southwest Systems—they do a lot of implementation work with Kirtland Air Force Base. The salary's almost twice what I had hoped to begin at."

"Southwest Systems? Is that over by Aurora? I don't think I ever heard of it."

"Not southwest Chicago, you ninny," Steve laughed. "Southwest United States. Albuquerque, in fact."

"Albuquerque? In New Mexico?"

"That's the only Albuquerque I know of. I hear it's a great town—very up-and-coming, and the computer business is just booming what with the base and the atomic energy site."

"But, Steve...I thought...I thought we were..."

"Oh, honey, that's the best part. I'll be making a lot of money, more than I ever expected." He gently took her hand across the table and looked deeply into her eyes. "I want you to come with me."

Carly's heart leapt. Steve was asking her to marry him! In the merry-go-round spinning in her head she completely missed two or three of his next sentences, but re-entered real time and space to hear him say "...decent furnished apartments are pretty hard to come by, but the company will help find us a place for the time being. I graduate early next month—we could leave right after that. My old Buick ought to get us there."

Next month? Carly thought. She could never arrange a wedding in, what, two weeks. What was he thinking?

Wait...what was *she* thinking? This wasn't a marriage proposal. Trying to recover from her disappointment, she stammered out, "But, Steve, what about school?"

"You're not listening. This is *after* I graduate next month."

"I meant **my** school."

"Oh yeah. I've already checked it out. There are two universities in Albuquerque—the University of New Mexico and the University of Albuquerque. You can transfer your credits there. Circle isn't the only school in the country, you know."

"My folks, though, Steve. My mother..."

"Of course your folks aren't going to approve. That's a given. They've got that Old World morality, and besides, they'll always see you as their little girl. But you're an adult now, ready to make your own decisions. Please...just think about it. Do what *you* want to do. But think about *us*. I love you. You know that, don't you?"

"Steve, I..."

"It's not someone else, is it? Not Beth's brother, or..." he stopped as he saw the surprised look on her face. "I'm sorry. I guess I'm just a little disappointed. I thought you wanted to be with me as much as I want to be with you."

Before the evening ended she had agreed to move.

Albuquerque!

Her storehouse of useless information failed her—she didn't know one thing about that town. Well, she'd have to learn. And after all, the whole prospect was very exciting. Other than a family vacation to Niagara Falls and her senior high school trip to Springfield, Illinois, she hadn't been out of the Chicago area. It was time for her to spread her wings. And she would be with Steve—even if it was not as his wife. She'd been flaunting conventionality a lot lately. Wasn't this just one more hurdle she needed to get over to become the person she truly wanted to be?

She promised Steve to keep their plans a secret, at least for a few days, but found that impossible once she got back to the apartment— Liz and Beth had an uncanny way of sensing when something was up. But after her excited, almost delirious explanation, she was dumfounded at her roommates' reaction. "Albuquerque?" questioned Beth. "Carly, are you sure? "

Beth's query was drowned out by Liz's outburst, "Have you lost your mind?"

"What do you mean?" Carly was astounded. "Aren't you the one who's always telling me to seize the day? *Carpe diem* and all?"

"Christ, Carly, yes. But this is all brand new for you. You know that thing he's got between his legs that's got you so mesmerized? They all have one of them—all men! He's not the only one! I thought you'd be smarter than to fall apart like this. You ought to at least wait and see what else, or even *who* else, is out there."

Carly was furious. Who was Liz to berate Steve in this way? What did she know about real love—so different from the sleeping around she seemed to have confused for the real thing. "Steve's right," she cried angrily. "You don't like him. He could tell from the start you never did!"

"Carly," soothed Beth, "it's not that we don't like him. We don't even know him, really. And that's the whole point—neither do you. Why can't you give it some time?"

"Because we don't have the time. This is a great opportunity for him—for us."

"No, you were right the first time—it's good for him!" countered Liz. "Dammit, Carly, you have to think about yourself because obviously he's not thinking about you at all. What about school? Or is moving toward a career suddenly a non-issue for you?"

Liz's statement gave Carly pause. Was she abandoning all her future plans? Not that she found accounting exhilarating, but still...

"I'm not quitting," she finally responded. "Circle isn't the only college in the world. There are schools in Albuquerque." The thought that she sounded just like Steve flitted through her mind. "Anyway, it's not like I'm doing so great at Circle. And besides, I can't explain it, but there's something, oh, I don't know, magical between Steve and me, something really special."

"Ah," harrumphed Liz. "A Magic Man. Honey, they're all Magic Men when you've got the hots for them. Give it time, and your Merlin will turn into a mere mortal again soon enough."

"This doesn't even sound like you," Beth said, reaching a hand out to Carly. But the evening ended with harsh words and slammed doors.

After a couple of tense days during which Carly refused to utter any but those phrases absolutely necessary for co-habitation in close quarters, her roommates finally capitulated, letting her know they supported her in whatever decision she made.

For once the El ride seemed too short; before Carly knew it, she was standing at the wide front porch of her childhood home, her parents' Berwyn bungalow. Strange that she was already thinking of it as her parents' home and not her own.

It was so like all the surrounding houses. Long, squat buildings, perfectly designed for the narrow city lots on which they were situated, predominated in this middle-class neighborhood west of Chicago. Mostly built from yellow or reddish-brown brick, they generally featured large bay windows flanked by massive cement staircases leading to large porches; often, the only distinguishing feature of adjacent houses was the relative placement of their windows. The houses reminded Carly of the picture of Noah's ark she had seen in one of her childhood Bible stories picture books—low, flat, built to last.

Carly noticed the straggly remains of spring tulips and daffodils lining the sidewalk leading to the front door and dandelions and crab grass taking over the area under the yews; this was a good sign. Obviously, her mom had not had time to oversee her spring gardening projects, which usually meant business in the restaurant was good. Strange that she had no idea how the restaurant was doing—her parents had stressed the importance of the restaurant's success since she was born.

As she climbed the steps, fumbling through her purse for her front door key, the porch light flashed on as the door cracked opened. "Sis," greeted Carl, opening the door widely,"come on in. I was just about ready to walk back over to work. Long time no see."

As Carly arched on tiptoes to plant a kiss on Carl's cheek, she could see why her once shy and bumbling brother had become the neighborhood Lothario. Tall and athletically slim, with a swatch of dark blonde hair tumbling over his blue eyes, Carl had developed over the past two years into a young man who combined a powerful physical presence with social poise. Their parents were disappointed three years earlier when he notified them that college was not for him, but their disappointment turned to delight when they learned his dream was to learn everything about the restaurant business; after all, who could teach him more about that than they could?

Carl started working full time for them immediately after graduation, walking every day to the restaurant just two city blocks from home, doing everything from bussing tables to cooking short order to taking on the least desired responsibility: arriving at the Fulton Fish Market at 4:30 every morning to select the evening's seafood special. When he turned 21 he found his true niche, as the restaurant's head bartender.

"Got a few minutes?" she asked.

"Always for you. I try to catch a few minutes' rest at home on Saturday nights between the dinner stragglers and the late-night partiers. Wally can hold the fort until I get back." Carly knew the restaurant's Saturday-night clientele had changed greatly since Carl had taken over at the bar. The old group, mostly contemporaries of her dad's who would hang around all night nursing their bottles of Schlitz beer and discussing old times in the Old Country, were now in the minority. First came some of the young single women in the neighborhood, followed, quite naturally, by the young men. Now Harvey Wallbangers and Tequila Sunrises outsold Schlitz every Saturday night.

"Is Mom still at the restaurant?"

"Yeah. She had a big party come in late—family graduation group. Hey, you must be pretty near the end of classes, too, right? How's it goin', college girl?" he asked, affectionately chucking her under the chin.

Sitting down at the dining room table, Carly examined the surroundings almost as if they were new to her: the gold shag carpeting about ten years out-of-date, the heavy walnut table and chairs, the matching buffet displaying her mom's best lace doilies and lead crystal. Carly's eyes stopped at the serving table, where her mother kept her shrine: framed pictures of the Black Madonna of Czestochowa, President John Kennedy, and the current pope, each with a votive candle placed before it. A crystal vase of yarn roses had been placed reverently in the triangle formed by the pictures. Carly sighed, deeply: what had she been thinking? Her parents would never understand.

"Sis, what's wrong? You're cryin'. You sick?"

"No, it's...it's school. I'm not going back in the fall."

"Ma and Pa aren't gonna like that too much, what with all the fuss you made about wanting to go." Carl sounded upset, but a look at Carly's desperate face softened his voice. "But, hey, they'll get over it. You can take some of those accounting classes over at the junior college—can't you? And the folks can always use you at the restaurant. Don't worry—it'll all blow over. Ma never really liked you being in that neighborhood anyway."

Carly wished it were all that simple. "It's more than school. Steve got a great job offer—I'm moving out of state with him."

"Steve? The tall, good-lookin' guy you brought to the restaurant a couple times? Hey, congratulations, Sis! You guys gonna have a traditional Polish wedding? 'Course, he's not Polish—Brennan. Irish, right? Does Pa have to learn how to make corned beef and cabbage now?"

Carl paused. His sister's expression must have told him something was wrong. "You kids are gonna have the reception at the Warsaw, right?"

Carly took a deep breath before answering. "Carl, Steve and I aren't getting married. At least not yet."

"What, are you crazy? You know what Ma always says—'nobody's gonna buy a cow if he can get the milk free.' Take it from a man—she's right." The look on Carl's face suddenly shifted from incredulity to pure wrath. "Hey, he didn't knock you up, did he?"

"No, nothing like that," Carly replied, genuinely alarmed. "It's just that Steve has to leave in two weeks. His new job's in Albuquerque. I'm going with him. It's already settled. Carl, I love him," she pleaded, hoping to make her brother understand, to convince him to support her decision.

His eyes only grew darker. "Albuquerque? New Mexico? Without a ring? Jesus, what has that bastard done to you? Did he brainwash you or somethin'? I thought you were a smart cookie, that you had some sense. Pa's gonna kill him. Christ, I oughta kill the lousy..."

"Carl, you gotta stand by me in this. It's not what you think. Steve... he loves me. He's good to me."

"So if he's so good to you, why isn't he marryin' you?"

"He will, someday. He just thinks differently than our family. A lot of people do. You'd be surprised. Steve and I aren't really doing anything wrong. Carl, it's not 1950—the Sexual Revolution's been going on for a long time."

"Right, like I'm not aware of that. But Carly, a lot hasn't changed, not even now, and probably never will."

"Yeah. You're the one to talk—a different girl every week."

"It's different, Carly. I'm a guy. It's different for girls. Yeah, I see a lotta girls, and I screw a lotta them too. But they're not the kind of girl I'd ever ask to marry, or even bring home to meet the folks."

"Boy, do you ever sound like Dad. The times are changing. Things are the same for girls and guys. Girls can have freedom now too."

"Not in Berwyn!"

"What's not in Berwyn?" Carly looked up to see her mother coming in from the kitchen. She must have entered the house through the back door.

"We got everything in Berwyn. Oh, my darling," she just then noticed Carly, and the smile that rolled over her features almost replaced the exhaustion Carly had seen around her eyes and the tenseness in her jaw. "When did you get here? Come, give Mama a kiss. You hungry? I got some *golumbki* in the fridge."

"No, Ma, I'm not hungry. I just got here a few minutes ago."

"And I gotta get back to work," said Carl.

"Can't you stay a little while longer?" pressed Carly, still hoping to make an ally.

"No, you gotta talk to Ma by yourself. I'm outta here." His weak smile told Carly that, although he sympathized with her to some extent, he was not going to help her deal with this. As Zosia turned her cheek to receive his good-bye kiss, Carly could see tension coming back into her face. No one was better at ascertaining nuances of emotion than her mother.

"Something wrong?" she asked. Carly forged directly ahead with her story, not whitewashing any information, never once stopping to give her mother a chance to respond. Zosia's eyes widened with astonishment, then flashed with fury, and, most disheartening to Carly, dulled with utter disappointment and resignation. As Carly stopped to catch her breath, the sight of her mother crying softly into her hands, her shoulders shuddering with muffled sobs, was almost more than she could stand. Finally, Zosia looked up. "Carolina, you are so young, and this place, this Albuquerque, is so far away, no?"

"Ma, I'm older than you were when you came here from Poland, and that's a lot farther from here than Albuquerque."

"But this is not like you. To act like this."

"I don't think I'm the person you think I am...or even the person I thought I was."

"But this man, this Steve. You hardly know him."

"Oh, Mama, I do know him. Not for a long time, I know. But it's just—I know this is right. He's a good man, you'll see, a lot like Papa, and he loves me. And I love him."

"What you know about love? This is not love you talk about. Love is what keeps people together, makes them work hard together to make a life, to make a family. Is that what you feel for this man?"

"No, not yet. But I will. You think I'm a child, but I know this is right."

"You are a child. You are acting like a child. And this will kill you papa."

"No, Ma, it won't. Pa will come around. You can talk to him for me, can't you? You can make him understand." Zosia slowly shook her head from side to side, but the look of defeat in her mother's eyes told Carly that she had already capitulated, relying on practicality and overcome by love for her daughter in the face of the inevitable.

As she watched Steve load the last of her collected paraphernalia into the massive but already over-packed trunk of his Buick, she realized that her father's reaction had saved a tearful family parting scene. She hoped that, in a few weeks or perhaps months, her father would accept her decision. But this turned out to be one of Carly's biggest misconceptions. Zosia was not able to work her magic on her husband this time. Karol did not come around, and certainly did not understand before she and Steve left for Albuquerque. He absolutely forbade his wife and son to have anything to do with Carly, and other than a few surreptitious phone calls to her mother, Carly had no contact with her family in the weeks before she and Steve left.

Parting with Beth and Liz was difficult enough. Steve, with the long trip in mind, had insisted on a ridiculously early departure time, 5:30 a.m., but this had not stopped Beth and Liz from dragging themselves out of bed to bid their tearful farewells. Carly once again wondered at the closeness they had developed in so short a time. After one last hug and kiss from Beth and a devout promise to write and phone regularly, Carly settled into her seat for the long ride ahead.

They made their getaway from the city going west on the Eisenhower Expressway, surprisingly crowded at that early hour but not nearly as jammed as it soon would be. Before too long the view changed from city high-rises and residential areas to flat green fields that stretched before them interminably. Carly dozed on and off during the first few hours of the trip: every time she awakened she felt as though she were in exactly the same place. Wasn't that the same white farmhouse, the same red barn, that she had gazed upon just before her eyes had shut? Weren't those the same black and white cows, the same manicured fields? Were she and Steve somehow stuck in time?

But no, they passed through occasional small towns, Buckley, Rantoul, Arcola, Neoga, each one a reassuring half inch farther from Chicago on the map Carly occasionally referenced. The small towns were a wonder to Carly. How did people live out here? What did they do for a living? What did they do for fun? She hoped Albuquerque was a lot bigger and livelier than these towns, then remembered with alarm that she knew next to nothing about where they were headed. *This is an adventure*, she forced herself to think. *Everything's going to be all right.*

Later that morning they crossed the Mississippi into St. Louis, much more a river town, economically, historically and culturally, than Chicago had ever been. After St. Louis the scenery changed. Missouri was different, with rolling green hills and forests. It too had a Springfield. *Two Springfields in one day, and the towns so close to each other!* Carly thought. She was beginning to think that she had really lived a limited life—but now things were going to be different.

By the time they approached Tulsa, billboards advertising motels began to be the only thing that attracted Carly's attention."There's a

Holiday Inn coming up in Tulsa," she suggested. "How about stopping there for the night?"

"Are you tired?"

"No, how could I be? I've just been sitting here. You're the one driving for such a long time. Would you like me to drive for a while?"

"I'm okay. I can go on for a while yet. I really don't feel like stopping, unless you need to rest."

And on they went. Carly had thought Illinois was flat, but Oklahoma made her home state look ruggedly mountainous by comparison. Or at least that's the impression Carly got as she stared out into a night only partially illuminated by a full moon. As they approached Oklahoma City, she tried again. "Honey, according to this map, there's not a lot between here and Amarillo. Maybe we'd better stay the night in Oklahoma City."

"I can make it to Amarillo," Steve answered, sipping on perhaps his twentieth coffee of that day. "Unless you're tired."

Carly's eyes felt suspended in sockets filled with sandy saltwater, and her throat was raw from supplying most of the chatter during the trip. She became painfully aware of every muscle in her body, but none so much as her tail bone, which felt permanently welded to the Buick's passenger seat. "No, that's okay. But I can't believe you're not tired."

Amazingly enough, Steve did not look tired. Determined, perhaps, and concentrating even more seriously on the road. But he looked as fresh as he had when they had begun this trip—*was it three days ago?* she wondered. Of course not, only that morning. "No, I'm fine," he said. "Why don't you look for a different radio station? I'm getting tired of this country music."

By the time they got to Amarillo, stopping for the night was out of the question. For one thing, it wasn't even night anymore; dawn had come as they passed an exit sign for Twitty and Lutie (such strange town names!) just over the Texas border. Besides, considering the amount of country they had already traveled, another 284 miles seemed inconsequential. Although Carly slept sporadically much of the night, waking several times to the guilt of the errant shotgun rider who has fallen asleep on the job, Steve, remarkably, seemed unaffected. He chatted amiably with Carly, was always aware of where they were, and seemed most concerned for her welfare, asking whether she needed coffee, something to eat or a rest stop. "How can you do this?" she finally asked as they passed the last few straggling establishments west of Amarillo.

"What?"

"Drive like this."

"It's fun."

"But don't you ever get tired? This is almost inhuman endurance."

"Nope. I never get tired when I'm driving. Especially when I'm going where I really want to go with the one person I really want to go with."

After Amarillo they had miles of serious desert to traverse—the kind of scenery Carly had seen only in old westerns. Stark yellows, reds and oranges replaced the cool grays and greens of the city landscape Carly had known all her life. Even the interstate signs spelled out the romance of the Old West—Tucumcari, Portales, Santa Fe, Las Cruces, Los Alamos.

In just over twenty-four hours, Carly had been pulled into what seemed a different world. She saw her first big cities that weren't Chicago, her first mountains, her first cactus, her first desert. Granted, she saw these things a little more fleetingly than she would have wished. One more set of mountains to cross and they would be at their destination, which Carly had to admit had a name that sounded as romantic and exotic as any they had passed.

They checked into the first decent-looking motel they saw on the outskirts of Albuquerque, although by that time Carly would have happily crawled into a cave if that were the only habitation available, and promptly passed out, fully dressed, on the lumpy motel bed. Carly first woke at about 3:00 the next morning and, stepping outside, got her first deep breaths of the nighttime's cool desert air and her first glimpse of a black, black sky sporting an infinity of silvery stars. These were the same stars that shone over Berwyn, she knew, but Chicago's haze, smog and constant light had made them invisible to her until now.

Steve slept until about 2:00 that afternoon, and woke ravenous for her and for breakfast, in that order. Later, perusing menus as they lounged in one of the three booths in the motel's Buckaroo Diner, Carly gazed at a landscape more empty than any she had ever imagined. Still, she recognized a certain beauty in the starkness of endless miles of sand, with occasional cacti reaching their arms skyward, but not a single tree or building in sight.

Soon a pert blonde, blue-eyed apparition, wearing a snug pink uniform with white fringed cowboy boots and a name tag with "Bonnie Sue" spelled out in what was meant to represent a lasso, sidled over to their booth. "What kin ah do ya for, honey?" she drawled to Steve, ignoring Carly altogether.

"What do you suggest?" Steve asked, a lazy smile overtaking first his lips, then his eyes.

"The cook does a great job on them *huevos rancheros*," she suggested, leaning over the menu in a way sure to display maximum cleavage. Steve was no longer looking at the menu.

"Ahem," interrupted Carly. "I'll have the blueberry pancakes."

"Sure," Bonnie Sue answered offhandedly.

"And I'll go with your suggestion," Steve grinned, handing her the menu. She gave him one more electric smile before she sidled back toward the kitchen, leaving an overpowering scent of hibiscus behind her.

"What the hell was *that* all about?" The tone of Carly's voice wrenched Steve's eyes away from the departing waitress.

"What?"

"You and *Bonnie Sue*."

"Oh, for Christ's sake, Carly. You're going to be jealous of a waitress? She was just being friendly. We're in the South, you know. They're all known for that. You better get used to it."

"How about you? You're not from the South. You looked like you wanted *her* for breakfast."

"Dammit, Carly. I'm a man. Don't think you can stop me from looking. That didn't mean a damned thing."

Carly, clumsily getting out of the booth, made a beeline for the door marked "Cowgirls." After a few shed tears and a quick couple of splashes of cold water to her face, she was able to convince herself that Steve was right, she was tired and cranky from the long drive and had probably overreacted. She returned to the booth with a weak smile on her face, but her pancakes tasted like sawdust.

Over the next few days, the multitude of tasks that accompanied their move—locating Southwest Systems and meeting Steve's new employers, moving into the furnished apartment the company had found for them, finding a grocery store, drug store, post office, department store, calling the phone company, the electric company, adding the touches to the apartment that would make it their own—occupied their time and their thoughts.

Carly was surprised one morning to realize they had been in Albuquerque for almost two weeks. Steve was already working late every night and coming home exhilarated with his new job, but too exhausted to do much more than halfheartedly eat the meals Carly had carefully prepared and then stumble into bed, usually to fall immediately asleep. She decided, in honor of their new home, to experiment that evening with preparing Mexican food for the first time—enchiladas, after all, were just kind of a very spicy *pierogi*, and they would taste wonderful washed down with Corona and lime. She saw this evening as the true beginning of their New Mexico adventure.

"What do you think about this plan for the weekend?" Carly asked, dishing out lime sherbet to counteract the spicy heat of the enchiladas. "I was talking to some people at the grocery store yesterday. There are a lot of neat things to do close to town—some ruins of Indian pueblos in the mountains and a park—Petroglyph State Park—where you can see old Indian carvings on lava. Maybe we could take a picnic out there. And everyone said the Old Town district is really fun—kind of touristy, but with lots of nice restaurants. There's also one restaurant in the mountains that you have to take a trolley up to. I bet that's pretty cool."

"Honey, I thought I told you, I'm working this Saturday."

"Working? You didn't tell me—I would have remembered. Well... then Sunday. How about Sunday?"

"Okay, maybe. But I've got a lot to do this weekend—papers and manuals I have to go through. I'm the new kid on the block—I got a lot of catching up to do."

"But, honey, it's the weekend." While Carly despised the whine she heard in her own voice, she persisted. "I thought we'd have some time together."

"We do have time together—right now. Let's not spoil it by arguing."

"But I feel trapped here all day—you have the car every day and there's no real public transportation—not like in Chicago—and there's not much for me to do in the apartment—it's so small. And I don't know anybody here."

Steve grimaced his frustration. "You're right. You do need to get out more." But his expression suddenly brightened. "Have you thought about getting a job?" Carly wondered whether this idea had come suddenly to him, or whether his sudden, friendly smile was caused by seeing an opportunity to suggest something he'd been thinking about for a while.

"School starts in six weeks. I didn't really think it made a lot of sense getting a job and then quitting so soon."

"Yeah, but six weeks is a long time. You'll be bored silly before that time is up. And we could really use the money. I think I can make a lot eventually at Southwest, but I have to work up to it. We're gonna start feeling the pinch pretty soon if we don't get some more money coming in. And maybe we could get a second car. That way you wouldn't feel so trapped."

"I guess I could get a job waitressing—but damn it, Steve, I could have just as well stayed in Berwyn if that's what I'm going to do."

"Are you threatening me?"

"What?"

"Are you threatening to leave? 'Cause if that's what you want to do, go running back to your mama and papa at home, you just go right ahead. Don't let me stand in your way."

"I'm not...I didn't...why did you think that was a threat?" But Carly was talking to Steve's back. The only response she received was the crash of the door he slammed behind him, and the screech of the Buick's tires as it careened down the driveway.

That evening seemed eternal to Carly, who alternately was terrified at the prospect that Steve would not come home, and terrified at the prospect that he would. As the earliest of the sun's rays broke through the slats of the blinds in their sparsely furnished bedroom, Carly tried to devise a plan. She considered calling Southwest just as soon as they opened for business but then worried that Steve would be furious at her sharing their problems with his colleagues. A call might even hurt his reputation at work. She considered calling the police, but knew nothing would be done about a grown man who had been missing for only several hours. In desperation, she considered calling home, but realized that any unkind response from her parents that smacked of "I told you so" would be devastating right then.

Ultimately she did nothing useful in the interminable day that followed. That evening, about a half hour after Steve's usual arrival time from work, she heard the back door open. Hurriedly wiping her eyes, she rushed to the door to find it slightly ajar, a very familiar hand waving a white handkerchief and a dozen American Beauty roses through the crack. She didn't quite know how to react, but Steve took the initiative, popping his head through the door with a pitiful sounding, "Is it safe to come in?" Soon he was inside, his arms around her, his eyes glistening with tears.

"Honey, I'm so sorry. Forgive me, please. I was terrified at the idea of you leaving me."

Carly felt relieved, but also confused. "But, Steve, I never said I was leaving," she said, wondering how he'd come to that startling conclusion.

"I know it's hard for you, living away from your family and your home, but I need you so much it scares me. I swear sometimes I feel like you're the only thing that anchors me to the ground, that I'd just fly off into nothing if you weren't with me."

"Oh, Steve, I..."

"Do whatever you want. Work or don't. Go to school or not. Whatever you want, baby. Just promise me you'll stay with me."

"I promise. I'll stay. I'll never leave you." Steve's renewed passion that night allayed all Carly's fears. She was Steve's. He was hers. That was the way it would always be.

Finding a job in Albuquerque wasn't difficult for Carly. By Tuesday morning she was working full time in a Mexican restaurant just a few blocks from the apartment. But when September came, they'd both become accustomed to the extra income she was bringing home, and they both felt they really did need that second car and probably a bigger apartment. And to be honest with herself, Carly had to admit she did not feel ready to return to the rigors of college.

Halloween passed, and then Thanksgiving. Carly's parents had never adjusted to these all-American holidays, so her family's celebration of them had always been somewhat lackluster. But Carly knew that Christmas, with its wealth of Polish tradition culminating in the Christmas Eve celebration of Wigilia, would be a trial. In keeping with her new surroundings, she sent home presents that represented the Southwest—hand tooled leather wallets for her father and brother and a lovely turquoise and silver pendant for her mother—but she waited in vain for a call from home, or even a card. By contrast, the day Beth and Liz received the kachina dolls she had sent them, all wrapped in a funny Christmas paper that featured Santas surrounded by cacti, they called immediately, and Carly spent a glorious fifteen minutes catching up on things back at Circle and sharing only some of the elements of her new life with them.

Carly prepared for Christmas by dragging Steve out to get a small but traditional tree, which they decorated with strings of popcorn and cranberries and the cheapest ornaments she could find. But her first Christmas without snow...strange how the one thing she had hated most about Chicago was the catalyst that brought into focus all the other things she missed.

Still, Albuquerque displayed its own brand of Christmas charm, and Steve, who must have sensed Carly's loneliness for her family, attempted to replace her old family traditions with new experiences. They took the tram up Sandia Peak to dine at the Summit House, a restaurant she had wanted to visit for months. From there they toasted their first Christmas Eve together, enthralled by the vision of twinkling lights.

The Mexican church where Steve and Carly attended midnight mass later that night had an altar decorated even more ornately than St. Casimir's, with hundreds of pointsettia plants looking more beautiful, here in their natural habitat, than in Chicago. The nativity figures, so much darker than the blonde, blue-eyed Jesuses and Marys and Josephs of Carly's childhood, seemed so much more appropriate. Luminaria twinkled in a friendly, companionable way along every sidewalk they passed on their walk back to the apartment. Carly, at last, began to believe she could grow to love this place, with its warmth and intense spirituality, if only she weren't so far from her family. If only her father would quit being so unreasonable. If only Steve had more time to spend with her. If only she could find some valid purpose in what she was doing here.

The next morning, after she and Steve exchanged presents and sipped egg nog under their first shared Christmas tree, he slyly grinned and said, "Santa left one more present for you—you must have been a very good girl this year. Check under the bed."

Carly ran to the bedroom and bent down gracelessly. Pushing aside shoes already covered with dust bunnies, she found a triangular patch of Christmas paper. Pulling it out, she discovered a long, slim package—she did not have to unwrap it to know it was a pair of skis. "Oh, Steve, I've never skied before, but I always wanted to try it. Is there skiing in Albuquerque—up in the mountains?"

"Probably. But you'll be using them somewhere else, and very soon."

"On a vacation?" Carly could hardly contain her delight. "Where are we going? Can we afford it? You sneak, what are you up to?"

"Well, not really a vacation, although it'll probably feel like one. We're moving to Colorado."

"Colorado?"

"Boulder, to be exact. You'll love it. Everyone I talk to says it's beautiful—in the mountains."

Boulder? Boulder, Colorado? Carly realized she knew even less about Boulder, Colorado, than she had known about Albuquerque before their sudden move.

"Does Southwest have a branch there? Are you being transferred?"

"No, Southwest just isn't what I expected it to be. My manager's a real jerk. I've been really frustrated there the past few weeks. And when I heard about this new job..."

"But why didn't you tell me you weren't happy at work? Why didn't we talk about this first?"

"I didn't want to worry you. I know how hard this has been for you—leaving home, coming to a new place, working at the restaurant. I didn't want to add something else to all the stuff you've been concerned about. And this is a better opportunity for me—for us—Keller Technologies, an older firm, much more established. We have to be there in two weeks."

"Two weeks! I'll never be ready to move in two weeks."

But of course, she was. And a few months later they moved to Denton, Texas, and then to Bakersfield, California, and to Overland Park, Kansas, where they stayed for over a year, long enough for Carly to begin to feel actually at home, and then to Twin Falls, Idaho. And for such a short time in Minneapolis that Carly could never remember whether Minneapolis was before or after Overland Park. Every new place started off as the latest opportunity of a lifetime for Steve—the place where he was sure to settle down and eventually call home, the place they would start a family. And every job did offer him exciting new responsibilities and more money, even though they never seemed to get ahead financially. But within just a few short months, the opportunity of a lifetime would become just another stale and oppressive sinkhole to him, and he was ready to move on. And, of course, there was always another restaurant for Carly to waitress in, or occasionally an office that needed a receptionist with no real experience required.

Steve did finally propose to Carly, on a long weekend trip they took to Las Vegas at about the time when both of them were thoroughly disgusted with the nightlife available in Twin Falls. But it was certainly not the proposal Carly had dreamed about as she had lain surrounded by her stuffed menagerie in that Berwyn bedroom a million miles away and a million years ago. Carly wasn't impressed by Vegas' glamor and glitter, and was alarmed at Steve's obvious enchantment with the city. And the gambling! She didn't even want to imagine how much Steve had lost at the blackjack tables. As they got back to their hotel room very late Saturday night, she confronted him, enflamed by the resentment and tension that had simmered through her all evening.

"So how much did you lose tonight?"

"Christ, Carly, I don't know. Maybe a couple hundred. I was just having fun."

"Fun? It's going to be a lot of fun coming up with the rent and the car payment this month."

"Don't you ever let up? It's Vegas—people come here to have a good time. Do you even know what a good time is? Damn, I feel like I'm dragging a ball and chain sometimes with you."

"Ball and chain? That's sweet. You can unchain yourself any damn time you want to, Steve Brennan."

"Threatening me with leaving again?" Carly was too angry to notice that she had threatened nothing. "Christ, Carly, can you find another threat—this one is getting old. Besides, it's *my* money—I'm the one who works my ass off sixty or more hours a week for it."

"And I don't? Or maybe you think I just love my job at the diner—that it's what I wanted to do with my life. Dammit, what have I done! Ma was right. I'm getting out of here. Right now." Carly had wanted to say this many times before, particularly when his thoughtlessness about her feelings and his frequent outbursts had aggravated her beyond belief. But this time she had actually said it, making the possibility of her leaving seem more real. With blinding determination, she wrenched open the closet door and grabbed her travel bag. Slamming it on the floor in front of the dresser, she began dumping drawer contents into the open bag.

"What the hell do you think you're doing? It's the middle of the night, dammit. You're not going anywhere." Steve grabbed her arm and pulled her toward him.

"Let me go—you're hurting me!" Carly was stunned by his reaction. Steve had never before laid a hand on her in anger. She believed he never would.

"Hurting you?" But with these words Steve's anger seemed to vaporize. "Hurting you?" Dropping her arm, he shook his head slowly. Carly could see his shoulders sink in what looked like abject defeat. "Don't you think you're hurting me? Do you really want to leave me? After all we've been to each other?"

"No," Carly cried. She certainly did not want to leave Steve. "But it's not working out. Maybe we just need a little time away from each other—a little time to think."

"I don't need any time to think. I know what I want, and it's you. I don't want anything else in the world. I love you. Can't you see that?"

"I love you too. But, Steve, we're fighting all the time. Neither of us is happy."

"You're right. You've been right all the time. I know what's bugging you—it's been bugging you since we got together. We should get married."

"Married?"

"Yes, now. Right here. In Vegas. This is the place, baby, and now is the time. We can find one of those little chapels. We can be married before we leave."

"But, honey, without our families? Our friends?" She doubted that her family would even come to a wedding with Steve, but surely Liz and Beth would. And what about Steve's family? Steve had told her she'd get to meet them on some future trip back to Chicago—their hasty move had negated any opportunity of getting acquainted. But to her knowledge, he hadn't communicated with them during their time together.

"Yes, here and now. Just us. Just the two of us. I don't need anyone else, Carly. Only you. Only you forever."

"But it's just that...well, it's not the way I thought I'd be married. I thought there'd be a church, a reception, a white dress..."

"Kinda late for that white dress, don't you think? I didn't know that crap was all that important to you. I thought you felt like I felt—you needed me like I needed you."

They married that weekend, in one of the strip's indistinguishable wedding chapels, their witnesses being the elderly man and woman who ran the chapel, and they laughed uproariously about the tackiness of it all and their youthful impulsiveness all the way back to their hotel room to "consumate" the marriage.

And a year later, when Carly inexplicably forgot to take her birth control pills for a few weeks and surprised Steve with her unexpected pregnancy, she was able to talk him into heading back to suburban Chicago, with the promise of continuing work after the baby was born so he could pursue his dream of starting his own consulting company. They had been gone for over three years, but there, she was sure, back home, really home, they could actually become the couple—and soon the family—they were meant to be.

Chapter Five

July 1982

Prelude

The Rolling Stones, "19th Nervous Breakdown"

"Daddy! Daddy!"

"Celia, wait! Your shoes! You can't go outside..."

Hearing the screen door open, Carly realized she was already too late. "Celia! Don't let that door slam." The sudden bang of the door annoyed her: Steve had promised to fix it weeks earlier.

Glancing quickly toward the kitchen island she saw a dozing Tyler squirm in his infant seat, then settle with a sweet baby sigh. She sighed as well: she had spent a long afternoon, made much longer by the addition of two cranky children while shopping for a new living room sofa. This had led to no nap for Tyler, whose normally sunny disposition turned stormy whenever his nap was delayed. In a few minutes, she hoped to take him up to his crib without waking him. A late nap was better than no nap at all.

She grabbed another potato to peel. Through the kitchen window she could see Celia running to greet her father. *One thing she and Steve did exceptionally well together,* she thought, smiling, *was produce beautiful children.* Celia was tall and willowy, all long legs and fingers designed for the piano. Her shoulder-length, cinnamon-colored hair and eyes of darkest amber spelled future heartbreaker, especially when she smiled in her irresistibly winsome way. Tyler was a blonde, Dresden blue-eyed giant, whose sturdy three-month-old body was already becoming too big for his infant seat. Carly felt inordinately blessed every time she looked at him.

She could now see Steve, Celia perched triumphantly on his shoulders, walking up the driveway. "Duck, baby," she heard him say as the screen door opened once again. Depositing both daughter and briefcase on the island, Steve gave her a perfunctory kiss, then stepped toward his son.

"No, Steve, let him sleep. I was just about to take him up..."

"Aw, he can sleep later. Right, Big Boy?" he said, lifting the still-dozing Tyler to his shoulder. "What are you making?"

"Potato salad," Carly answered drily as Tyler's eyes popped open. She'd be the one soothing Tyler once his exhaustion overcame the excitement of seeing his daddy.

"Barbecuing tonight?" Steve reached into the bowl to pluck out a plump piece of potato.

"No, this is for Beth's party tomorrow, so keep your hands off," she responded, tapping his offending hand sharply with her wooden spoon.

"Ouch! Tyler, see what a meanie Mommy is," Steve said, gently pinching his son's cheek. "Is Beth's party tomorrow? I thought it was on Sunday."

"No, I told you at least twice..."

"You know I'm golfing tomorrow."

"Not again." She knew Steve didn't particularly enjoy Beth and Marty's company—he said he didn't have a lot in common with them. But she'd spent plenty of time in trendy downtown restaurants when they'd first moved back to Chicago trying to make sense of what he and his computer friends were discussing. Bits. Bytes. RAMs. All English words, but completely incomprehensible to her in this context, making her feel stupid and out of place. He owed her at least a bit of graciousness to compensate for the time she had to spend with his friends.

"It's Marc's first birthday," she continued. "Even Liz is coming in for it." She immediately wished she didn't add that last sentence. While Steve wasn't particularly fond of Beth and Marty, his relationship with Liz ranged from difficult to hostile. They'd never gotten along.

"Don't worry," Steve said in his most conciliatory tone. "The party's in the afternoon, right? My game's in the morning. I'll get there, maybe a little late."

"But how will I get to Beth's?"

"You can have the car. I'll get a ride, okay?" Carly gave Steve the kind of look that signaled it was not okay. "Here," he said, handing her a now wide-awake Tyler. "I'm going to get changed."

Tyler, already starting to fuss, squirmed in her hands as she watched her husband leave the kitchen and head toward the stairs. "Steve..." she said, hating the whine she heard in her voice. "I'm kind of busy here..." But he'd already reached the staircase, Celia trotting behind him, plaintively asking, "Wanna see the picher I colored for you today, Daddy?"

"You think this will be enough?" Carly asked. She placed a huge, gaily-striped bowl of potato salad on Beth's kitchen table while juggling Tyler on her hip.

"Looks like you made enough for an army. Here, let me take Tyler. Okay if I put him on the floor in the family room?"

"Of course." Beth's lush family room carpeting was almost clean enough to eat on. Carly watched over the half-wall that separated the two rooms as Beth effortlessly placed Tyler on a waiting blanket while simultaneously reaching for a book to keep Celia entertained. Beth's actions were always so graceful, so purposeful.

Beth's home reflected her sense of grace and purpose as well. Compared to Carly's modest suburban home, Beth's was palatial, sporting fireplaces, granite and marble surfaces, several spare bedrooms, and a lawn that looked like it was trimmed daily with manicure scissors. Banks of blooming hydrangeas and beds of roses in reds, pinks and yellows showcased Beth's green thumb.

Not that Carly was at all ashamed of her own place. The three bedrooms and two baths, the separate dining and family rooms, were a great improvement over the two-room apartment she and Steve had shared when they'd first moved back to Chicago. Their apartment had become even more crowded when Celia came—babies seemed to require a great deal of paraphernalia, most of which Carly had acquired at the lavish baby shower Beth and Liz had thrown for her.

Once Tyler was on the way she was able to convince Steve they needed a home in the suburbs, where the streets weren't so busy and the kids could have a yard to play in. Fortunately, Steve's prospects were looking up; the business he and his business partner had set up to implement computer systems for medical clinics was starting to make a profit, so Steve's concerns about being able to buy a house held less weight in their frequent, occasionally heated, discussions.

But she knew from the start he wasn't completely on board. To Carly, they were leaving a third-floor, crowded walk-up with leaky plumbing and squeaky floors, while to Steve, they were leaving dazzling nightlife, Wrigley Field, and an easy commute downtown. To her, they were going to good schools, more space and easy parking, while to him, they were going to a thirty-year mortgage, a lawn to mow, and a long train ride into the city every morning. True compromise was impossible.

"Where's Steve?" Beth asked.

"He's coming later. He couldn't get away from a meeting." Carly looked for signs of disbelief in Beth's face, then seeing none, asked when Liz was expected to arrive.

"Pretty soon. She left Michigan early this morning."

"How long is she staying with you?"

"Until the middle of next week. She took a couple of days off from work."

"Boy, that's unusual," Carly answered. Liz had left college passionate about chemistry and acquired a plum position at the Dow Chemical plant in western Michigan, where she threw herself into her work. Now she was involved in major research in their plastics division. She didn't often spend this much time away from work.

"Even more unusual," Beth continued, "Jason is coming. Marty is picking him up at O'Hare as we speak."

"Wow! I haven't seen Jason in, what, three years now? How is that good-looking brother of yours?"

"Doing pretty well. His band had a couple of decent gigs in California, and there's talk that they might be an opening act for part of the next Guns 'N Roses tour."

"Quite the celebrity! Will he even deign to talk to us today?"

"Well, you know Jason. He never changes."

Carly wondered if that was possible. When Jason had moved to LA several years earlier Carly worried that he had entered the world of drugs and rock and roll—a legendary path to destruction. She wondered if Beth's sweet-natured brother could resist their appeal.

"Is he still seeing Amy?"

"As far as I know."

"What do you think of her?"

"Actually, I haven't met her yet. She was on some kind of business trip when we went to see him in California last month." Carly thought it a bit strange that Beth had not yet met her brother's fiancée. Jason and Amy had been seeing each other for over four years. But then, it took Steve three years to introduce her to his mother and some of his siblings; once she met them, it wasn't too difficult to figure out why he waited so long. Steve's father had left his mother when Steve was only five years old, and he and his step-father, a hopeless, often violent alcoholic, never got along.

"Anyone else coming?"

"Just some of the neighbors, but not for another hour or so. I thought the three of us could use some time to catch up. I don't know what's keeping..." Beth was interrupted by the sound of the front door opening and wheels rolling on hardwood.

"Anyone home?"

"Liz! You made it!" Beth and Carly rushed into the foyer to welcome her.

"Just barely! Traffic was a bitch on 94—a damn semi almost took me out near Gary. Oops! Sorry!" Celia's face could be seen peeking into the hallway at the sound of Liz's voice. "How are you, sweetie? Come give your Auntie Liz a big hug!"

Hugs were shared, children were admired, and special attention was given to Tyler, whom Liz was meeting for the first time. Carly could not stop looking at the vision that was Liz. Her tight designer jeans were topped by a black spandex camisole trimmed in lace, and that was topped by a sleek fuchsia gabardine jacket that featured the wide shoulder pads all the fashion magazines were showing. She could not imagine how Liz negotiated those three-inch heeled sandals, knowing she herself would be flat on her face after just a few steps. Liz's wrists jangled with numerous Navajo bracelets and her ear lobes were adorned with silver chain earrings that spilled almost to her shoulders.

Carly looked down at her own baggy walking shorts and loose tee shirt. But what could anyone expect? She'd had a baby just three months earlier and was still a nursing mom. At least she dieted and exercised herself out of her maternity clothes. That was something. Fashion could come later, once she lost the rest of the baby weight. Besides, she consoled herself, Liz always had a tendency to over-dress.

"What's that heavenly smell?" Beth asked once they had settled in.

"Patchouli. Everyone's wearing it. I brought a bottle for each of you."

"It smells so exotic. I can't wait to try it," said Beth.

"Me too." But Carly wondered where she would wear a scent like that. To the grocery store? The pediatrician's office? She quickly chastised herself for being so negative. "I love your hair," she said, trying to shake herself out of her sudden sour mood. "What's that color called?"

"I can't remember what the stylist said, but I call it burgundy. So what have you two been up to?"

Beth recited a list of activities: church committee meetings, scheduled play dates for Marc, ideas for redecorating her already perfectly stylish home. Carly's list was shorter, but then, she was a new mom again, which ate up most of her time.

"Are you still working for your mom and dad?" Liz asked her.

"Sure. But I only have to go to the restaurant once a week." Once Celia had been born, Karol consented to see his first grandchild, and when Carly held the baby's christening party, he had, somewhat grudgingly, attended. This was the beginning of the development of a somewhat normal relationship. After Tyler's arrival—who, from the moment of his birth, was treated by his grandfather as the Second Coming—the relationship became even less strained. But Carly had to resign herself to the clear knowledge that her husband and her father were not destined to ever become friends. They might briefly discuss home repairs, the economy, the Cubs, but most of the time Karol Novak and Steve Brennan spent together was largely devoted to silent staring at some sports event on television.

Carly hated having to work when Celia was a baby—hated to leave her in day care to spend eight hours waiting on customers in the housewares department of a local store. But they did need the money, as little as it was. Once she became pregnant with Tyler, she convinced Steve that the money she made at work wasn't worth the cost of keeping two children in day care. And if she was home all day, the savings from such economies as cooking at home instead of eating out and selling their second car would make up the difference. Some weeks it actually did.

Fortunately, in the middle of her second pregnancy, her father asked her to do the bookkeeping for the restaurant, complaining that their current bookkeeper wasn't doing a good job. Carly could come in on Tuesdays, their slowest day, and bring the kids—no need for a babysitter when Grandma was delighted to watch them—and she'd be doing him a favor. When he paid her for her first day's work, she was sure he had made a mistake. Her check was almost equal to what she would have made in a week at the department store.

"Dad, this is too much," she had stated.

"No, no, is just right," he had assured her.

"I can't take this. Steve would think it was charity."

"So, you gotta tell you husband everyting? You tink he tell you everyting? What if he never ask?" Carly had handled all the minor household finances from the beginning of their marriage, and Steve never did ask about them. Soon the bills started getting paid on time.

She turned her attention back to Liz. "How about your job? What are you doing these days?"

"Glad you asked. I'm working on improvements in silicone breast implants."

"No!" Beth and Carly replied in unison.

"Sure. Dow-Corning was the first to make breast implants in the early sixties. Betcha didn't know that."

"Well, no," said Beth, "but aren't those dangerous? Leaking gel and stuff?"

"Yep, and that's where I come in. I'm helping design elastomer-coated shells to prevent that from happening. They're a great break-through."

Some good-natured questioning about possible discounts on boob jobs and remembrances of the old rolled-up-sock-in-the-bra method of breast enhancement so popular in junior high school followed. But Carly was impressed, and she imagined Beth was too. Liz was doing important work. Who would ever have expected that?

"Wow! Look at my brother the Rock Star!"

Carly had been gently placing a sleeping Tyler in the play pen Beth had set up for him in an upstairs bedroom. She peeked out the open window that overlooked the patio, where Beth and Liz were sitting on the deck with some of Beth's neighbors, just in time to see Marty and Jason stepping through the sliding glass doors. Jason was dressed in black: tight black jeans and motorcycle boots, black mesh tee, and a jacket that had to be designer. She'd never before thought of him as a fashion maven: maybe LA had finally changed him after all.

"Aviator shades, too," Beth observed as Jason, joining her at the table where she sat with several of her neighbors, bent to give her a brotherly kiss on the cheek.

"You don't expect me to appear at LA International looking like a Midwesterner, do you?" he teased. "Wouldn't be good for my image."

"Got a kiss for me?" Liz demanded, sidling up beside Jason, who complied with a smile. "Ooh, you're bristly," she complained. "But the beard looks great on you."

"Yep. It's today's mandatory amount of stubble. I work very hard to keep it looking this scruffy."

Beth took the next few minutes introducing her brother to her neighbors, none of whom had ever met him. She offered him a beer, but he said he wanted to change into something more comfortable first. "Well, you know where the bedrooms are," she said. "Put your stuff in the first one to the left of the staircase."

"Is Carly here?" he asked.

"Yeah. She's putting the baby down for a nap."

Upstairs, hearing a rustling sound from the playpen, Carly bent to gently rub Tyler's back. Convinced he was sleeping soundly, she tiptoed out the door and closed it softly behind her, almost bumping into the man in black who'd just stepped into the hallway. Jason's smiling face took her back to the apartment on Morgan Street. Despite the rock star gear, that smile convinced her Jason was the same sweet, friendly guy she'd always known him to be.

"Carly? You haven't changed a bit."

She didn't believe that for a moment, but then she remembered the gentle kindness that had always been a part of Jason's personality. She chalked his compliment up to that. "And look at you! Rock stardom must be good to you."

"Don't get too impressed. It's mostly façade." Jason smiled, that smile Carly remembered from their time in Chicago—slow, beginning with a slight parting of lips that crinkled his cheeks, culminating with a sparkle in his eyes. "Is the baby asleep?"

"Yes. Do you want to see him?"

"No, I wouldn't want to wake him. But Beth pointed out your daughter playing in the yard. Such a beautiful girl. She sure takes after her mother."

Another compliment: or just more kindness? Carly didn't know what to say.

"Do you still play guitar?" he asked.

"Sometimes." She wondered why she lied. She hadn't touched the guitar in years. Well, she did strum a chord or two when she moved it from her bedroom closet to the attic storage area a couple of months earlier—maybe that counted as "sometimes." She decided to change the topic. "How are things with you and Amy?"

"Oh, pretty good. Actually, our relationship is pretty casual. Beth makes more out of it than really exists. I guess she wants to see her little brother all settled down." Carly had to wonder why Amy, or some other girl, hadn't nabbed Jason in all this time. He was good-looking, even with that new obligatory facial hair. But more than that, he was a wonderful listener, someone she could talk to for hours on end. There was a certain sense of comfort she felt with Jason, something she'd never experienced with any other man. *Not even Steve,* she realized, *especially not with Steve.* That was certainly a disturbing thought.

"Well, I'm dropping this off," he said, pointing to his backpack, "and getting changed. See you downstairs?"

"Sure," Carly said, almost tripping on her way down the stairs.

"Another Harvey Wallbanger, anyone?" Beth asked.

"I'm good," responded Carly. "I need to drive home pretty soon." Carly wasn't looking forward to going home. She'd already mentally rehearsed several renditions of the argument she and Steve were going to have when she got there. The problem was, none of the argument scripts she formulated ever worked with Steve; it was impossible to foresee how he would respond in any situation. Carly would have thought that by now, years and two kids into their marriage, she would have figured him out. But she was still unable to fathom what went on in that powerful brain of his.

Like the day she'd come home and found him emptying most of the contents of their refrigerator into a black plastic garbage bag. "What are you doing?" she cried, wresting an almost full bottle of catsup from his hand.

"It's got sugar in it," he responded. "Sugar is a killer. It'll kill us all."

She tried to stop him with every argument she could think of—"all things are okay in moderation," "scientists don't agree," "we grew up with sugar and look how well we turned out"—but he was adamant, a man on a mission.

Two days later he brought home three giant Hershey bars to share with the family.

Or the Friday afternoon one January when he had called from work, telling her to pack for an overnight trip. Surprised and delighted, she had arranged baby-sitting with her parents and packed her prettiest negligee in an overnight bag. As they left in ten degree weather, she relished the fact that he was being so mysterious, refusing to tell her where they were going.

After five or six hours on the road, she became restless. Memories of their trip to Albuquerque plagued her. Was he ready to spring another surprise move on her? That hadn't happened in years, but still, with Steve one never knew. She questioned him about where they were going, her questions becoming more and more insistent as the trip progressed. He only nodded and smiled at her.

Nine hours later, with only short stops for fast food and gas, they arrived at Virginia Beach. A full moon lit their way to the shore, where the two of them, eerily alone on the beach, spent fifteen minutes silently gazing at the dark ocean, its waves splashing listlessly on the shore.

"Isn't it beautiful?" Steve finally asked.

"Yes, Steve, but...?" Carly didn't begin to know how to ask the questions that tumbled through her mind. Why were they here? Did this trip mean something special? Did he have some kind of hidden agenda? Was he going to spring some new challenge on her?

"Okay, babe, I know this whole thing might seem a little strange. But I just needed to see the ocean. I can't explain it—don't even ask me to try. But I know it's what I needed to do."

They spent a few more minutes gazing out at a peaceful sea. Then, "Okay, time to go back home," he'd said, placing an arm around her shoulder. "But it was an adventure, wasn't it?" he added, smiling as he hugged her tightly.

She tried to console herself by considering that at least their "adventure" had lifted him out of the dark mood he'd been in for several days.

"Earth to Carly." Beth's voice jolted her out of her remembrance. "Did you want something else to drink? Another iced tea?" Carly accepted.

"Anyone else?"

"I'll stick with beer," said Jason, with Marty nodding his accordance.

"How about iced tea instead?" Beth asked her husband. Carly wondered at the look that passed between them as Marty reached for a beer. The years had not been kind to Marty; he'd put on a lot of weight, especially in the belly. Carly thought Beth might be concerned about his health.

The five of them had been sitting on Beth's deck for more than an hour after all the other guests had left, snacking on leftover hors d'oeuvres or birthday cake, depending on their proclivity toward tangy or sweet, enjoying the earthy, early-evening fragrance of recently cut grass and overflowing flower boxes, talking about old times. The children, exhausted from the day's excitement, napped in the family room. All that was missing was Steve, thought Carly, although she knew the entire ambience of the evening would be replaced by a strange tension with him there.

"Do you want to call Steve again?" asked Beth.

"No. I left a message."

"Are you worried?"

"Not really," she answered, ignoring the quizzical looks her response garnered.

"So, Liz," said Jason, breaking what could have soon become an uncomfortable silence, "you're not my image of an organic chemist."

"Really? What does an organic chemist look like?"

"A man," responded Marty.

Following Beth's and Carly's cries of "Sexist pig!" and Jason and Marty's high five, Liz responded. "I don't look like this at work. There it's a blue lab coat and nurse's shoes, no make-up, not even nail polish. Oh, and a very attractive hair net—the kind all of our grandmothers used to wear."

"That must be very painful for you," teased Jason. "To dress like a professional every day at work. You must be very dedicated."

"Actually I am, you dork. But I can dress any way I want away from work. Look at you. You don't look much like a rock star either right now." Jason, now attired in khakis and a Cubs tee shirt, looked more like the man they remembered.

"Well, you gotta look the part in my business."

"How's your business going?" asked Marty. "Did I hear something about a Guns 'N Roses tour?"

"That's up in the air, like everything in LA. That place thrives on rumor. But actually, I'm thinking of leaving the band."

"No." "Really?" "You gotta be kidding," the group responded in unison. Finally Beth's voice stood out: "You've put your heart and soul into Hött Lïxx! Why would you want to quit just when the band's starting to make it big?"

"Yeah, I know it sounds stupid. But the life's not what I expected. All anyone ever sees is what happens on stage. They don't see the all-night rehearsals that end up with arguments—sometimes even fights. Or the long bus trips. The people who drop out of your life—most of them from overdoses. Or the fact that as soon as you manage the tiniest bit of success, the vultures and leeches are all over you."

"Have you discussed this with the other guys?" asked Liz.

"Not yet. But LA's crawling with good guitar players. Lïxx! wouldn't have a hard time replacing me."

"What would you do? Would you come back here?" Beth asked. Carly detected a hopeful tone in Beth's voice, making her wonder why she and her own brother Carl, although they lived just a few miles apart, didn't have the close relationship Beth had with Jason, who lived over a thousand miles away.

"No—I'd stay in LA. And I'd probably stay in the music business, just not as a performer."

"Then as what?" asked Marty.

"Oh, I don't know. I think I'd like to manage a band—maybe even Hött Lïxx!. I couldn't do worse than the last two managers we've had."

As the conversation continued in the ambience of the sultry evening, Carly found her mind drifting back—way back—to her time on Morgan Street. Who would have thought her old friends' lives would have taken the turns they did? Beth's life was no big surprise: she had seemed destined to become a happy suburban housewife from the moment Carly first met her. But Liz? That scattered, exotic flamingo of a roommate had spread eagle's wings. And Jason, already a success, was reaching for another, better dream.

And what of her? She'd produced two beautiful children. That was an accomplishment. She never really wanted a career. And her marriage? Was that a success? She wondered why she'd never before asked herself that question, and why she was asking it now.

The last of the day's light faded as Carly pulled into her driveway. After struggling to get the kids into the house, into their pajamas, and into bed, she was in no mood to find Steve dozing in the family room recliner.

94

"Dammit, Steve!"

"Oh, babe, you're home," he yawned, stretching to wake up. "How was the party?"

"Don't go acting like everything's all right. Where the hell were you?"

"Oh, well, it couldn't be helped," he began. "Tony got here late and we missed our tee time—we had to wait a couple hours at the club before we got another time. And then the lightning held us up..."

"Lightning?"

"Yeah, about 2:30. Didn't you see any at Beth's?"

"No—it was a perfect summer day. A beautiful day for a party. Blue sky all afternoon." Carly's voice dripped acid.

"Well, you know how localized summer storms can be: stormy in one area, quiet just a few miles away. And you wouldn't want me out on a golf course in lightning, would you?"

"You don't want an answer to that right now..."

"Oh, come on. Give me a break. By the time we finished eighteen holes, it was already too late to..." But Carly, abandoning her rehearsed argument, had already turned her back on Steve and was stomping up the stairs. What was the point? She could argue with Steve from now through eternity—it wouldn't change him at all.

She'd been tossing in bed for nearly an hour when he joined her, gently placing his arm around her and brushing her cheek with a light kiss. Pushing his arm away, she turned from him again, pulling most of the light comforter with her. She felt the mattress lift as he got out of bed, heard the soft thumps of his bare feet walking down the hall. She began to regret her actions, to long to have him by her side, whispering apologies in her ear, assuring her of his love.

No, she realized with a start, that may have been what her mind wanted, but it was not at all what her body needed. She wanted him back, insisting, taking no denial, pressing her to do what he wanted, what she really wanted. Making her scream in anger, then in passion. Losing themselves in each other. It could happen. She could go to him now.

But she didn't. She couldn't. Not tonight. Her passion finally washed itself out with the tears on her pillow.

Chapter Six

February 1983

Interlude

Roy Orbison, "It's Over"

Carly wasn't a die-hard Roy Orbison fan, but tonight, listening to his dulcet, plaintive tones both depressed and soothed her, a combination that somehow felt right. She realized she needed to wash all the clothes from their Hawaii trip and to do some serious grocery shopping, But instead, she rewound the tape for perhaps the twentieth time, and listened from the beginning about golden days. Golden. Like Steve. Her Golden Man. Yes, it broke my heart. We're so through...*But Roy was wrong on that one—it's the men who find someone new,* thought Carly. *It's men who are untrue, and women who are left behind to pick up the pieces.*

"It's o-o-ver, it's over, it's over, it's over. It's ooo-ver." *Well, Roy got that one right,* she thought bitterly. *When it's over, it's over. Even after fourteen years, two kids. Just like that. It's over.*

Carly took another deep swallow of scotch. Scotch was not her drink—she was more the occasional glass of white wine type—but this night was different. The first sips had seemed so bitter—why did Steve love this stuff? Because it was old and rare? Because it was expensive...very expensive? But subsequent swallows had tasted better and better. Now she almost liked it—at least her nose no longer twitched and her body no longer shivered with each sip.

Thank God Beth had been able to take Tyler for the evening and Celia had wanted to spend the night with her friend Ashley. Carly just couldn't hold things together any more. Just attempting to sound normal on the phone to Beth had squandered every bit of control she still maintained.

She feared she was entering the same vortex of the storm her two best friends had occupied the last few years. Of course, Liz had always been drawn to chaos in her personal life, so her lightning-fast marriage to Antonio, a young Italian chemist who was interning for the summer at Dow, was not a complete surprise. But then, neither was her divorce only five months later.

But Beth and Marty's break-up had been a shock. Carly listened for years to Beth's complaints about Marty and had shared many of her own about Steve—but she assumed this was just the "men from Mars, women from Venus" syndrome that was all the interpersonal rage these days. When Marty left Beth for a neighbor—someone Beth considered a friend—she was devastated, but had survived.

What if Steve left—for good? Could she survive? She found herself wanting to cry, scream, throw things, especially after yesterday's awful fight. Not that they hadn't been fighting a great deal in the past few months—she had hoped the week in Hawaii would have helped get them over this latest rough spot. Maybe she was wrong in insisting they go with the kids—maybe they could have rediscovered each other if they were alone, which was his suggestion. Maybe it was her fault...

But wait! What was she thinking! The bastard had just waltzed in, kissed her, talked about his new Texas client as if everything was fine. Texas client, his ass! Thank God the kids had already been in school.

When she asked him about all the phone calls to Meredith's house, her voice quavered with the foolishly unfounded hope that he would have some plausible explanation for the calls.

"Meredith's house?" he asked, attempting a look of injured innocence. "Phone calls from the hotel? Why would I call Meredith at home? Where's that phone bill?"

"Steven!" How could he deny it? Meredith Tillman was his secretary—she'd worked for him for only a couple of months. Carly had noticed Meredith's home phone number on Caller ID a few weeks before they left for Hawaii—Steve had said she needed to contact him about some emergency concerning a contract. If it weren't for Meredith's unusual phone number—one that ended in 0001—Carly would never have made the connection.

"Look, give me the bill and I'll call the hotel and clear this up. I'll call from the office. I have to go in anyway," Steve stammered, looking flustered.

"For Christ's sake, Steve, how stupid do you think I am?" Carly shouted into his flushed, sweating face, seeking out his averted eyes. She was reminded suddenly of the way Tyler looked when caught in a lie. "Are you trying to destroy the evidence? Look at me, Steve. Look at me and tell me there's nothing going on between you and Meredith."

Steve seemed incapable of looking directly at her. Finally, staring solidly at his hands clutching the back of a kitchen chair, he responded. "All right. But I kind of thought you knew."

"What? You thought I knew?"

Steve straightened, suddenly becoming defensive. "For Christ's sake, Carly, if you didn't know, you should have. Grow up: married people have affairs. It doesn't mean anything."

"You bastard!"

"Look, just because you're Little Miss Perfect, it doesn't mean the rest of the world has to be saints."

"You sure as hell are no saint. How can you do this to me? To our family?" Carly spat out her rage. "You never loved me, did you?"

"I do love you. Even now. But you can't be so blind that you've seen nothing wrong with our marriage the last few years. You must have noticed how bad things got."

"Noticed? Noticed what? That my lousy husband was having an affair with his secretary? Damn!" she cried. "Isn't that the oldest cliché in the book?"

"The affair is just a symptom. The problem is our marriage. The affair doesn't mean anything." Steve tried to embrace Carly, but she pushed him away, so hard he almost tripped.

"Sure, it doesn't mean anything to you! But what about to me? And why Meredith?" Meredith, of the blonde hair and sky-blue eyes. Meredith, of the perfect make-up and designer outfits. Meredith, of the massive boobs and slim, tight hips. Meredith, who had sweetly introduced herself to Carly at the last Christmas party, asking about Celia and Tyler, about her job. What a bitch! And wasn't Meredith a married woman?

"Yeah, with Meredith. With Meredith, who knows how to make me feel like a man. Carly, I have tried so hard the last couple of years. Even the vacation to Hawaii—I tried to commit myself to our marriage—to the way I used to feel. But I couldn't do it. I couldn't live that lie any more. Every minute I tried I felt more and more like a hypocrite. I couldn't stand it. Not even for one more day. That's why I had to leave early."

"You couldn't stand it? Couldn't stand being with your wife and kids? No, you had to run home to your slut."

"Yeah—right—it's all me. It's all my fault, like always. You have nothing to do with the way our marriage has fallen apart, right? Christ, Carly, have you looked at yourself lately? You're about one and a half times the woman I married. I can hardly get it up in bed with you any more. Not that you'd ever notice. How many times have you turned me down the last few months?"

"Turned you down? Well, maybe when you get in at three in the morning...What the hell do you expect?"

"Three in the morning, two in the afternoon. It's always the same. You're tired. You're not in the mood."

"That's not true. And why shouldn't I be tired?"

"Right. You're just so busy. With the kids, the house, even your pathetic job at the music store and your volunteer work. Everything but me. You put me last...like you always have."

Last, Carly thought! *Last!* How could Steve even think such a thing? She felt her whole life, since they had met, had been nothing but a struggle to subordinate her wants and needs to his. "This is *our* house," she screamed into his face. "*Our* children, yours as well as mine!"

"No, Carly, it's all yours. It's always been. This is *your* life, the life you always wanted. Not the life I wanted. And I'm tired of living someone else's dream. I'm getting out."

"Good! Leave. Leave me and the kids. Don't ever come back, you bastard!" Steve just missed being hit by the television remote she threw in his direction.

But she didn't mean it—despite everything, she didn't wanted him to leave. She knew that the moment she heard the door slam. Her mind reeled thinking of what her best approach would be when he came home.

But he didn't come home. Where was he? When would he come back? Why should she care? Time to rewind Roy.

And time for more scotch. Oops, she spilled some getting it into her glass. Oh well, the carpet needed cleaning anyway. And why was she drinking this crap? Didn't Steve have some good brandy, too? She'd like that better. Swaying her way into the family room's adjacent half-bath, she poured the small amount of scotch that had made it into her glass into the toilet. Then, with a bemused smile on her lips, she followed this with all the scotch remaining in the bottle, watching the toilet water turn a lovely pale caramel color.

She foraged the liquor cabinet for the brandy, then attempted to find the beginning of the song on the tape. After a few minutes, she succeeded and began listening once again to *her* song, now. Hers and Steve's. Shit, how did she let things just fall apart?

For she did. She knew that. She let things fall apart. It was her fault, of course. She was no longer young...no longer pretty. What did her mom always say—if the man gives 25% and the woman gives 75%, that's a good marriage. Maybe that was it: she just hadn't given enough.

She swayed with Roy's voice—how she had loved to dance. She and Steve had danced together so well. When was the last time they had danced? The last time they had done anything together—really together? If he only came back, she'd make it right. She knew she could. He still loved her—not that bitch Meredith. He said so, didn't he? She could get him back, out of the grips of that whore. That slut. It wasn't like Carly Brennan to give up without a fight.

But then what? What if he did come back? Could she forgive him? Could she ever trust him again? She hadn't suspected anything. How had she been so stupid? She should have known something, should have *sensed* something. Her Steve—*her* Steve—with another woman. Holding her, whispering to her, making love to her. How could she make love to Steve ever again, knowing that? How could she bear that pain?

Would she even *want* him back? Where was her pride? And if he came back—would he give up cheating? Or would she just have to settle for the crumbs of affection he threw her way. Dammit, she'd been settling for years. The bastard! He wouldn't give up his cheating ways—they never did. Either a man was a cheat or he wasn't. That's all Steve was—a cheat, a liar, a total bastard.

The light seemed suddenly too bright. She turned it off, enjoying the dimness in the room, peacefully enshrouded in darkness, not able to see anything clearly. Time to rewind the tape. Time for that brandy.

Ah, Roy Orbison. Steve had always said he was one of those... embryos? No. That wasn't the word. What was it? Palominos? No, she giggled, those were horses. Oh, yes, albinos, that was it. Steve said Roy Orbison was an albino because of the glasses he wore, to hide his eyes. Steve was stupid. What did he know? Steve was stupid about a lot of things.

But not about everything. Steve was smart, too. She relied on his advice so often. And he was so beautiful. Were men beautiful? Yes, of course. Steve was beautiful. His eyes, bright and cat-like, hazel with brilliant gold flecks, were beautiful. And his body...those little gold hairs on his arms. And on his chest. How she loved to tease her fingers down his chest, down to his flat belly, down lower, lower, to where she could drive him wild with passion. What happened to that passion? Carly clumsily tore the wrapping from the new bottle, then looked for the tumbler she had been using, but could not find it in the dimness. She sipped from the bottle, grateful for the warmth pouring down her throat, washing away the hollowness deep within.

She thought of how Steve had made so much of himself. She had every right to be proud of him, especially considering how difficult his early life had been. Why, his father deserted the family when Steve was only six years old. His mother had to work two jobs, just to keep their family alive, which by this time included his three sisters. When she became ill, Steve and the other children were placed into foster care. By the time the family was reunited, his mother had remarried; the then nine-year-old Steve hoped to have a father once again. But his step-father was an alcoholic who often took his frustrations out on Steve and his sisters. Carly felt it was amazing that Steve survived that upbringing.

No wonder he delayed her first meeting with his family. By the time he introduced her to his mother and sisters, he was already a financial success. She and Steve helped his mom, had found her a new place and paid her rent—he was a good man that way, although he tended to avoid his own family get-togethers. Carly often wondered if this was because his mother and sisters were too much of a reminder of the hard times he endured.

Despite the poverty and neglect of his early years, here he was—a great success. A self-made man. A great provider. Provider? Carly felt panic pushing its way through her sorrow. What would happen if they got a divorce? Would she lose the house? How could she ever tell the kids? She and Celia were going through such a difficult time already—her daughter was sure to blame her. And Tyler adored his father. Hadn't she read articles about the problems boys suffered when their fathers weren't around?

And how about her folks? The shame—no one in her family ever got divorced. How would they respond? Her parents certainly experienced hard times together, but their marriage survived. She would be the first—certainly not a stellar achievement.

How about Liz and Beth? Suddenly, even through her alcohol-induced haze, she realized she felt a modicum of self-satisfaction at her friends' divorces. She never completely forgave them for rejecting Steve early in their relationship. She now fervently hoped that Liz and Beth never suspected her true feelings. Although she had sympathized with their pain, she believed her marriage with Steve was impervious to such a collapse, that she and Steve shared some special quality that would not allow their relationship to fall into disarray.

They had all warned her, her family, her friends. They had advised her to wait to marry him. That mad dash to Albuquerque—what was she thinking? Would her family and friends remind her? Certainly her dad would. Oh Lord, how was she going to tell her father?

But, really, none of this mattered, she thought, sadness predominating once again. Only Steve mattered. How could he think that she put him last, that he wasn't the most important thing in the world to her? How had she not made that clear? Oh, damn. She had screwed up royally. She rewound Roy, chugged more brandy. But inside she was empty...hollow...barren. And so tired. If only the world could just go away. If only she could disappear. If only tomorrow morning wouldn't come.

But it would come. It always did. How could she stand being alone? How could she survive even the first week? That's how she would have to do it, one week at a time. Or one day at a time. Or maybe even one minute. Right now she knew what she needed: one more swallow of brandy. The tape had stopped, but it didn't matter. She didn't need Roy Orbison to tell her it was over.

What was that faint sound...the knocking, the ringing? Where was she? What was she doing on the family room floor? She had always been one to go to bed "right," had always insisted her kids do the same. Teeth brushed, face washed, clean jammies. Only uncivilized people just plopped down to sleep wherever they were—in front of the TV set, or lying on a couch reading a book. Going to bed involved a routine, almost a ritual.

There was that ringing again. The doorbell. Was it morning? Maybe Steve...oh, the thought made her head ache—ache more, anyway, than it already did. But Steve had a key. He wouldn't ring the bell. He would just walk in.

More knocking. Oh, of course—she knew who it was, finally remembering through her uncharacteristically hazy thought process. Beth was bringing Tyler home early this morning because he had some scouting activity this afternoon. The one with the little cars...Soap Box Derby? No, that was the big cars. Pine-something...Pinewood Derby. Damn, Steve was supposed to take him to that. All the other boys would have their dads there. Well, maybe it was time for the Boy Scouts to come into the 20th Century. Dads weren't always around anymore.

She must look a fright. And it sounded like they'd been knocking and ringing for a while. Did she have time to run upstairs and run a comb through her hair? No—but she did rush into the bath to splash cold water on her face and gargle a mouthful of tepid water. What an awful taste—how could water taste so sour? But she felt at least marginally better than she had with that stale, cotton-mouthed feeling she had awakened to.

She ran upstairs and breathlessly opened the kitchen door. "Sorry, guys. I was...just putting in some laundry." In tumbled Tyler and Marc, chattering excitedly, followed by Beth, who was already eyeing her strangely.

"I was beginning to wonder if you were home. But we saw the car..."

"Yeah, well, just doing laundry, like I said. I guess I didn't hear the doorbell."

"Oh...boys, why don't you go up to Tyler's room? Tyler, Marc wanted to see your Derby car."

"Okay, Aunt Beth. Race you, Marc!"

As the boys clattered up the stairs, Carly felt a strange uneasiness at being alone with Beth. What would she say to her dearest friend? How could she keep her secret? Maybe she should tell Beth. But would this be the right time? Would there ever be a right time to tell anyone this news? "Can I make you some coffee? Or are you off on a million errands this morning?" she asked, wishing for Beth's answer to her second question to be in the affirmative, anything to give her more time to think of what to do.

"No, nothing really important to do this morning. Here, let me make the coffee." Beth took the pot out of Carly's trembling hands and reached in the cabinet for coffee and filters with the assurance of a woman who was as comfortable in her friend's kitchen as she was in her own. "You sit down. Did you call Dr. Wright?"

"Oh, no. I forgot. I've just been busy."

"You promised me you were going to call the doctor. You look even more out of it than when I picked you up at O'Hare. Your eyes look so tired. Have you been sleeping? You must be coming down with something."

"No, like I said, I'm fine." What could she tell Beth, that she was coming down with divorce, with abandonment, with betrayal? But why tell Beth now? Maybe she and Steve could fix this problem. Maybe no one would ever have to know. What was she thinking? Nothing was going to fix this problem—not ever.

"Please tell me what's wrong. Maybe I can help." Beth sat at the table across from Carly and took both her hands, giving them a reassuring squeeze.

"Oh, Beth, it's...it's..." Carly looked into Beth's eyes, as clear and blue as the Hawaiian sky, and knew she could tell her anything. "Beth, I..."

"Ma, do we got any juice?" Carly hadn't even seen Tyler dash into the kitchen, Marc close behind.

"*Have*, Tyler," Carly answered wearily.

"What?"

"*Have*...do we *have* any juice? Yes...orange and cranberry. The cranberry is in the yellow pitcher. Get a glass for Marc, too."

"Boys, take your juice and go on upstairs with it," suggested Beth tentatively.

"No—not on that beige carpet on the staircase," countered Carly. "Boys, you drink your juice in the kitchen. Then I guess we have to get ready for Scouts. Thanks for taking Tyler last night, Beth. I know how much he loves to play with Marc's video games."

"Yeah, Marc gots...*has*...a new Nintendo game. And I won three times!"

"Great, honey. Finish up and get your uniform together. Thanks again, Beth."

Beth looked uneasy as she got up and herded Marc toward the kitchen door. "Carly, call me later, okay? Are you sure...?"

"Beth, everything's fine. Couldn't be better. Sorry to rush you out so fast, but we have to get ready for the Derby. I'll talk to you later in the week."

Carly watched as Beth slowly, hesitantly walked out to the Voyager with Marc.

Chapter Seven

February 1983

Intermezzo

The Rolling Stones,
"You Can't Always Get What You Want"

*S*unday
    "Ma, do we really have to go?" whined Celia. "Dad wouldn't make us go if he was here."

"Well, guess what? He's not. Going to mass isn't going to kill you, Celia." Celia looked surprised at the unaccustomed steel in Carly's tone. But Celia was right; if Steve were here, the family probably wouldn't go to church. He'd most likely talk Carly into a leisurely brunch at the local Big Boy and an afternoon lazing before the televised football game. She'd always known it was wrong to give in to him—if their kids' religious education wasn't their responsibility, whose was it? But he was so seldom home. And when he was, she really didn't want to spend all their time arguing.

"Where *is* Daddy?" moaned Tyler. "I thought he was s'posed to be home a coupla days ago."

"Well, honey, his trip got extended a little bit. He'll be home soon." Carly wondered how long this lie would sound convincing.

"At least we get to go to Grampa's. Did you find my souvenir for him? The little lamp with the shark on it? You think he's gonna put it on his desk?"

"It's on your dresser. I'm sure Grandpa will put it on his desk. Run upstairs and get it before we leave."

Today's visit would be a trial—how would she ever get past her mother's sharp instincts for trouble? Still, it was better than staying home with the kids, waiting for the phone to ring, jumping every time it did.

"Ma, do you think Grandma is going to serve Klingon food again?"

"Oh, Celia, stop that. If Grandma serves *kiszka*, just don't eat it."

"Ma, it's made from duck's blood. Yuck. Can't I just go to the mall with Ashley and Maria instead?"

"Honey, you haven't seen Grandma and Grandpa in weeks. And they'll want to know all about our vacation. Did you finish unpacking? Don't you have a souvenir for Grandma? Run on upstairs and get it."

"Still in Texas? You husband is never home, Carolina," Karol commented as he plopped another spoonful of *kapusta* onto Tyler's plate. "Eat dis," he responded to Tyler's wrinkled nose, "is good for you."

"Steve works hard, Dad. You can hardly hold that against him. You worked hard when we were kids—you still do. You'd be complaining if he didn't work so hard."

"But we was always together, in the restaurant or at home. Like a family."

"Well, Dad, not everyone can own a restaurant." Carly considered how little choice she and her brother had growing up and how much they would have preferred spending more time with their friends. "Steve's work isn't like that."

"Still, is not so good for man and woman to be so long apart. You know, a man is a man." Carly fought an angry response to her father's self-satisfied, knowing look, then glanced quickly, almost guiltily, to see whether her children had noticed anything. Celia was engaged in a quiet conversation with her grandmother and Tyler was disconsolately heaping the unwanted sauerkraut into a tiny mountain with his spoon.

After dinner, washing dishes in her mother's old-fashioned kitchen, Carly almost lost her battle for self-control. "Carolina," Zosia said, handing her a large platter to dry, "you look so tired. And you hardly ate nothing. You no longer like my cooking?"

"Ma, it's almost a miracle how wonderful your meals are, coming out of this kitchen. When is Dad going to remodel it for you? You need a new stove, a bigger fridge, a dishwasher. For heaven's sake, everyone has a dishwasher today."

Zosia scrutinized Carly carefully before answering. "Don't be mad at you Papa. He's only worried about you, about how tired you look. After vacation you should come back rested, not so tired. Are you sick?"

"No, I'm okay, really." Carly turned away from her mother, seemingly intent on rubbing the rose pattern off the platter she was drying. She then attacked the already-spotless counter.

"You not..." Zosia hesitated so long that the gentle click of the old electric wall clock began to pound in Carly's ears. "Maybe, maybe you got another bun in the oven? You been always tired the first coupla months."

"No, nothing like that. I'd tell you if I was pregnant." Near tears, she thought that would be just about the very last complication she would need right now. Weeks ago, she would have loved the thought of having another child. But now...

"Steve is all right? I thought he was gonna come home with you an' the kids."

"I told you, Ma, he found a client. Someone from Texas." She hated the sound of impatience in her voice. Her mother was just concerned, like any good mother would be.

"Maybe you and Steve need some time for just you two. A vacation with the kids—this is very nice. But you two maybe need some time for just you."

"You and Dad never took any time for yourselves. You were always working or taking care of Carl and me. I don't remember you two ever taking any time away for yourselves."

"You papa and me was different. Was different times then. You and Steve, you are modern couple. Modern *American* couple. What if Papa and me take the kids next weekend? You two could go away for coupla days."

"Oh, Ma, I..." Carly bit her lower lip, hard, and turned away from Zosia, ostensibly to set the platter in its accustomed place high in the cupboard. "Maybe...I...I'll let you know. I don't...I don't know when Steve is coming back from Texas."

"You think about it, okay? To be strong family you gotta be strong man and wife first."

Monday

"Vacation" finally over, Carly struggled out of bed when the alarm shrilled at 6:00. Another interminable night—she had last peeked at the clock at 3 a.m.—and the thought of getting the kids up for school and herself ready for work was almost more than she could bear. She looked at the bedclothes, once again tumbled about, pillows on the floor, the sheet more than halfway off, and thought her mind must be just as disheveled.

At least she had survived the weekend. And the distraction of being at the record shop, being away from the house and the kids, might help.

But it was hard, maintaining a work face with colleagues and regular customers who asked about her vacation, about Hawaii, about Steve and the kids. After lunch, she asked the store manager, Roger, who at 24 was very difficult to see as a boss, if she could spend the afternoon catching up on back orders. He looked surprised and pleased; after all, none of the employees at Sound Decisions liked to do paper work. Carly was thus able to snatch a twenty minute nap in the back room.

And then home. And back to her normal routine of dinner for the kids, homework, an hour or two in front of the TV. But how much longer could she go on like this, her body inhabiting one world and her mind another? And when would she hear from Steve again?

Tuesday

On her day off, she realized she could no longer postpone a trip to the supermarket unless her kids would settle for a dinner of graham crackers, creamed corn, and Coco Puffs.

Standing in a long line at the local Stop and Shop, Carly had time to reflect on the roller coaster that had become her life. What made this day different from the others was the new path of worry her mind had chosen—that perhaps something terrible had happened to Steve. Surely he felt as torn as she did—was he capable of doing something terrible? Of hurting himself?

He, too, was probably distracted, not sleeping. He might be just as upset as she was—maybe even thinking about changing his mind. Maybe in his distraction he'd had a car accident. Terrible things happened in Illinois during the winter. Sometimes cars went off the road into snow drifts or under partially frozen ponds and weren't found for days. Maybe she should call the police. Then what? Her call might cause a search that would be covered in the "Police Blotter" column of the local suburban weekly—that awful rag that detailed all her neighbors' indiscretions from DUIs to kids' shoplifting. And what if, after all that, he was just fine?

Of course he was fine. What was she thinking? He was holed up somewhere with his honey...

"Carly, how are you? Justin's been asking about Tyler. He hasn't been over to play since you got back from vacation." Lisa Chambers, the town's pre-eminent gossip, was in the check-out line across from hers. Lisa could smell trouble in a marriage from a mile away.

"Are you okay, Carly? You look a little pale. Is everything all right?" *Oh no,* thought Carly. *Lisa knows something.* But how could she? Carly wondered if she was becoming paranoid: she knew she needed to pull herself together, to find some response that would seem normal.

But a sweet, wavering voice saved Carly from having to answer. "Mrs. Brennan, is that you? How is Tyler? Such a sweet boy! And Celia? She must be almost all grown-up by now." Carly turned to find the beaming face of Miss Tonelli, Celia's and Tyler's kindergarten teacher, recently retired but a town legend.

"Oh, they're fine, Miss Tonelli." No one in town could snub Miss Tonelli; even Lisa could understand that.

"Whose class is Celia in this year? And is she still such a good scholar?"

"Oh, Mr....Mr. Martin's homeroom. And yes, she's doing very well, thank you."

Carly looked back to see Lisa pushing her loaded groceries away from the register. Another crisis averted. After sharing pleasantries with Miss Tonelli, Carly concluded her transactions, wheeled her cart to the car, deposited the groceries in the trunk, then slammed it shut with all her strength. Safely in the driver's seat, she spent ten minutes resting her head on the steering wheel, tears streaming, helpless with rage and frustration.

Wednesday

Carly returned home from work to find her back door unlocked. When she stepped into her kitchen she knew, as surely as a fox knows that an intruder has violated her lair, that Steve had been in the house. Nothing visible had changed since she had left hours earlier, but she knew.

She rushed first to the bedroom and flung open Steve's dresser drawers—as she suspected, all his socks and underwear were gone, save for a couple of loose socks whose holes at the heels made them candidates for the trash. How considerate of him to leave that little task for her. The closet was empty of his suits, shirts, pants and shoes.

Her next stop was the bathroom, where she found all his toiletries gone and, infuriatingly, her blow dryer as well. What next? His office desk. Sure enough, all their important papers, stock certificates, bank statements were gone. He had left a stack of current bills piled neatly to the right of the desk blotter. Mr. Efficiency!

Everything else looked untouched until she got to the living room, where she found the door to the liquor cabinet open. Nothing had been taken, but the bottles had been shifted around as though someone had been searching. Of course, the scotch. The poor boy couldn't find his precious scotch, and in his grief had been so preoccupied that he had forgotten to close the cabinet door. How slovenly!

But Steve had left many belongings as well, probably in his haste to get out of the house before she got home from work. Methodically, Carly collected everything of his she could find in their, no *her,* bedroom, from his racquetball equipment to the assortment of small personal items left in his dresser junk drawer, and had just enough time to bag them and drop them into the huge dumpster behind an apartment building several blocks away before the kids came home from school.

Thursday

That evening Liz called from Michigan. "Carly, how are you? How was Hawaii?" Her tone was characteristically breathless.

"Oh, Liz, fine. We had a great time."

"Great news, Carly. I've got a conference to attend in Chicago early next week, and I figured I'd come in Saturday and spend some time with my best friends in the whole world. You busy this weekend?"

Carly listened closely for indications that Liz knew something about her problems, but couldn't come to any conclusions. "Well, stuff with the kids." But then, how would Liz know? She hadn't told a soul. Was she being paranoid again?

"Carly, the three of us haven't had a girls' night out in ages. What say we go out for dinner Saturday night and take it from there? Maybe an all-night talk-it-out like we used to have at school, what was it, five, ten years ago?"

"Actually, Liz, it feels like fifty. But..."

"Let Steve watch the kids for once, and let's the three of us have some fun."

"Well, Steve is traveling again." Carly was surprised at how easily the lie came out. Was she getting better at this? And if she was, was that a good or a bad thing? "But I'm sure Celia would love to spend a weekend with Ashley, and Mom and Dad are always happy to spoil Tyler overnight."

"Then we're on."

"Should I call Beth? Maybe she's doing something else this weekend."

"Oh, I already talked to Beth earlier this week. She's up for it. See you Saturday night. *Ciao.*"

So, Liz had already talked to Beth. Carly sensed a red flag. But what did Beth know, really?

Friday

Despite a whole week of waiting for his call, hoping for and dreading it, and uselessly imagining elaborate scripts of the direction the conversation would take, Carly found herself dumbfounded when she picked up the phone and realized her errant husband was on the other end.

"Carly, I don't know what to say. I'm so sorry for the way things have turned out."

"Sorry? And that's supposed to make things all right? Sorry?"

"I know nothing can make things all right now. I just want you to know that I never wanted to hurt you or the kids."

"Really? Well, you're doing a pretty damn fine job of it anyway."

"No matter what, you'll always be special to me. I'd step in front of a train to save your life or the lives of our kids—even now—you know that, don't you?"

"Well, that's not exactly what's called for here. We don't need a martyr. What we need is a husband and father." Carly waited a full ten seconds for Steve to respond. Had she touched a nerve? Was he reconsidering—maybe realizing that they needed to try a lot harder to save their marriage and family? If that were true...

"I can't be that right now. I just can't. I don't know how things will be in the future, I just can't be with all of you right now." The slump in Carly's shoulders mirrored her feeling of defeat, soon followed by anger. What was he asking her to do—just sit around waiting for him to decide what *he* wanted? She suggested counseling, and was shocked when he told her he'd been seeing a counselor for over six months. *Who, really, is this man?* she wondered. *What else don't I know about him?*

"Dr. Irving has been helping me a lot," offered Steve.

"Is he telling you to cut the crap and go back to your wife and family?"

"Well, no. Actually, Carly, he's the one who says I need to get out of my current situation—to find myself. He says my problems come from *denying* my own needs. That I've been doing that all my life. He says I've been denying my Inner Child for too long."

"Your Inner Child? What the hell are you talking about?" Carly had read something about this latest psychological garbage in a magazine. Even then, it had sounded like just another excuse for adults to behave badly. And leave it to Steve to find a counselor—maybe the only one in town—who would give him an excuse for his behavior. "How about your own children?" she shouted into the receiver. "Don't they need something too? Like a father?"

"I'll always be their father. But I just can't continue the way I've been going."

"Steve, haven't you ever heard of a mid-life crisis? Don't you think that's what this is all about? A lot of men your age..."

"I'm not a lot of men. I'm me. Don't try to put my feelings into some neat little category of yours."

"What about my feelings? How am I supposed to deal with this, to tell the kids?" What was Steve really trying to tell her? She hated to say the word, to even think the word, but she had to know what she was up against. "Steve, do you...do you want a divorce?"

"It's a little early for that, don't you think? I don't know what I want right now. Can you give me some time? You know, some couples have open marriages—they stay married, but see other people. Maybe that's what we need to do for a little..."

Carly slammed the phone onto its base so hard her fingers tingled.

Saturday

It didn't take long for Carly to realize that her instincts had been correct. Saturday evening was an ambush—or *intervention* might be a kinder word, more indicative of Liz and Beth's motivation.

The women returned from dinner and had no more settled into the comfortable chairs of Carly's family room before Liz began. "Okay, come clean. What's going on?"

"Liz, I have no idea..."

"It's Steve, isn't it?" suggested Beth. "Something's wrong between the two of you."

"What could possibly..."

"Look at who you're talking to," Liz interrupted sharply. "Beth and I share a little history of relationships gone sour. We can see the signs. And we know *you*."

"We just want to help," cajoled Beth. "We can tell something is terribly wrong."

Carly's innate sense of dignity fought disclosure, and her stubborn optimism still held on to the hope that, in some way, her problems with Steve would be resolved. But Liz's obvious concern and the compassion she saw in Beth's eyes made her realize she had already harbored too many secrets for too long. It was time to let go. "All right." Her body wilted with the words. "Steve moved out. He's having an affair."

Beth hurried to embrace her. "There, there, go on and cry."

"That's all I've been doing, and it doesn't do any damn good," Carly sobbed.

"It will help now, Carly," said Beth. "You've said it out loud. It's real now—out in the open."

"That bastard!" Liz's velvety tones had risen at least an octave. "I always knew you were too good for him. Even from the beginning."

"Liz..." cautioned Beth, then turned to Carly. "How long has he been gone?"

"Since Hawaii—he came back one day and then later to get some of his things—but he did that when I wasn't home."

"And you've been keeping this all to yourself? Why didn't you tell us?"

"I don't know—maybe I was just hoping it would all go away. That maybe he'd come back, and..." Carly was stunned by the look of incredulity on Liz's face. A sudden realization made her incredulous as well. "You...you don't seem surprised. Neither of you. Did you... did *you* know?" Carly felt enmeshed in one of the world's oldest clichés—the wife is always the last to know.

"Well, not directly. It's not like we saw him with anyone or anything like that. But all his absences...the way he treats you when he's around," answered Liz, who, obviously seeing the confusion in Carly's eyes, decided to elaborate. "Like yesterday's newspaper. Like excess baggage. That bastard! That piece of shit! That asshole!" Liz was on a roll.

"I never thought...I would...I would have..."

"What?" asked Liz. "What would you have done? Or more to the point, what *have* you done since you found out?"

"Done? It's only been a week..." Frustration caused Carly's voice to waver almost to the breaking point.

"Yes—a week! You need to get busy, girl. For starters, you need to at least start thinking about what *you* want in this situation."

"What I want? I want Steve back. I want things to be the way they were." Carly hated the petulant whine she heard in her own voice.

"Of course," answered Beth, "but that's not going to happen. Even if you and Steve patched things up, things would never be the way they were. You can't *make* Steve do anything—you never could. You can't turn him into the perfect father or perfect husband or perfect lover or whatever else you want him to be. The only thing you can really change is you. You need to start *acting* rather than just *reacting*."

Start acting? Carly thought. How could she start acting when she didn't know what to do? She was tired, dispirited, completely disjointed in her thoughts and actions. And now her friends wanted her to start acting like someone else? She was having a hard enough time just surviving every day. But Beth asked the one question, the only question, that could make her see the wisdom in their advice.

"Do the kids know?"

"Might Steve fight you for custody of the kids?" Liz followed up.

"Custody?" The very word filled Carly with terror. "This is all so...I haven't begun to even think about...You don't think he would..." Carly's tears began to flow anew.

"I'm sorry," Beth answered, taking both of Carly's hands in her own. "But this can get incredibly dirty. You have to think about your kids right now. That comes first. You need to think of what you're going to say to them. You need to talk to them soon—tomorrow. C'mon, we're here for you. We'll get you through this. Let us help you."

"Damn," said Liz. "You look like you've been through a meat grinder. You've got a ton of stuff to do, but tomorrow is another day. What can we do for you right now?"

"Could you both stay here tonight?" Carly suggested, a small note of hope entering her voice.

"Of course!"

"Let's just talk tonight, like we used to on Morgan Street," suggested Beth.

"About Steve?"

"Or not. We could talk about Morgan Street or Princess Di or whatever," answered Beth. "Whatever you want," agreed Liz. "Did Steve take *everything* out of his liquor cabinet?"

Chapter Eight

February 1983

Intermezzo

The Eagles, "Lyin' Eyes"

Talking to the kids the next day was not nearly as difficult as Carly had expected—could they have suspected something as well? Tyler had cried, though his sobs didn't seem as impassioned as Carly had expected they might be.

"We won't have a daddy no more?" he whimpered.

"Honey, Daddy will always be your daddy. It's just that Daddy and Mommy are having some problems right now." She reached out for Tyler, pulled him to her, held him close.

"But what's gonna happen?" he asked, snuggling into her arms just like he used to years earlier. The warmth of his body pressed closely to hers brought back memories of those years when mothering had been so much easier, so instinctive.

"I really don't know right now. I just want you to know Daddy's not here because..."

"Because you're getting a divorce?" interjected Celia.

"Sweetie, I really don't know that yet. It's just too early to tell."

"Will we have to move?" asked Celia. Carly was amazed at her daughter's composure—Celia expressed almost no emotion whatsoever. That couldn't be a good sign.

"I don't know that yet," Carly answered honestly.

"I don't want no divorce...I don't want to move. I want Daddy..." cried Tyler.

"It's really no big thing, Tyler," responded Celia. "Half the kids in my class have parents who got divorced. Quit being a baby."

"Celia, your brother's not being a baby. He's worried. I don't blame him." Carly held him even tighter, ignoring Celia's glare. "I'm worried too. But this will all work out. I know it will. Daddy will keep on being your dad...things will just be a little different."

"Not so different, Mom," Celia responded sourly. "It's not like he's ever around anyway."

Once the kids were off to school Liz, finally admitting her "conference" was just a ploy, appeared with Beth, both ready for battle. They had instructed Carly to collect whatever papers she could find: old phone bills, credit card statements, check registers, bank statements. They sat down at her kitchen table, coffee mugs brimming, Beth taking notes on a yellow legal pad.

"Have you changed your locks yet?" Beth asked.

"Changed my locks? Why would I do that?" Carly was beginning to realize she had a lot to learn.

"How did you feel when you came home and found that Steve had taken all his stuff?" Beth asked.

"Well, it was *his* stuff."

"Yes, but how did *you* feel?"

Carly considered the question, taking several sips of coffee before answering. "Kind of creepy. Almost violated. Not so much that he took his stuff, but that he did it behind my back."

"He's been doing a lot of shit behind your back. Changing the locks establishes this place as *your* turf—that's going to be important in the future," offered Liz.

"But it's still his house—*our* house."

"With any luck, not for long," grinned Liz, ignoring the pained expression that appeared on Carly's face. "Now how about credit? Have you checked your credit cards? Tried to use them?"

"No, but Steve would never..."

"Oh, Carly," cried Beth, "this is war. You can't make any assumptions about what he'd do—you have to *know*, and fast. You have no idea what he's capable of. Do you have any credit cards in your own name?"

"No. They're all in both our names, I think, or maybe just in Steve's.... There's never been any need to..." Liz's and Beth's sighs were clearly audible, and their shared look told Carly she still wasn't getting it. Had she always been this naïve?

"Then go get your purse. Get your cards out," demanded Liz.

After two hours of interminable voice mail hell, Carly was able to speak to enough actual human beings to learn all her bank, gas and department store credit cards had been cancelled. Another call determined only the minimum balance was left in the savings account she shared with Steve, although several hundred dollars remained in her checking account. Carly collapsed onto a sofa, completely deflated, and felt her world start spinning around her.

"Is that it? Have you checked all the credit cards?" asked Liz.

"Well, his American Express gold card, but he's the only one that uses that, mostly for any unexpected travel expenses, stuff like that."

"Is your name on that account?" continued Liz.

"I really wouldn't know...wait, the bill came yesterday." She started shuffling through the stack of bills Steve had left with her. "Wait. Here it is. He always takes care of this one himself."

"Oh, leaving that could be costly for him," said Liz, robbing both hands together with a smile on her face.

"I don't think I should open it," Carly sighed.

"I'm beginning to think this is hopeless," sighed Beth.

"Oh, for Christ's sake," moaned Liz. "This shouldn't be any great moral dilemma for you." Liz shook her head in frustration. "Just get your teakettle and some clear glue. Not the Elmer's stuff the kids use in school. You can see that when it dries. Steve doesn't even need to know you're reading his mail."

Following Liz's instructions, Carly steamed opened the envelope carefully. Any remaining guilt she had turned to fury when she discovered charges for jewelry purchases, dinners at fine downtown restaurants, and even a short jaunt to a Caribbean couples resort. Carly was surprised to see that the card was actually issued to both Steven and Caroline Brennan and before long, at Liz's insistence, it too was cancelled.

"That ought to bring him around. I guess you'll be hearing from him very soon," snorted Liz.

Before the afternoon was over, Carly had ordered copies of incoming and outgoing phone calls from the previous six months. But the day's work wasn't done. Liz and Beth had questions about Meredith diSalvo, the woman Carly suspected in the affair.

"Do you know her?" asked Beth.

"Yes. Not well, but I met her at Steve's last office Christmas party."

"Do you think he's moved in with her?"

"Actually, Beth, I think she's married. That probably wouldn't sit too well with her husband. But then, who knows these days?" Carly managed a feeble laugh.

"Hey, Carly, you're getting your sense of humor back," smiled Liz. "That's a great sign. But if that's the case, he probably has another place by now. Do you have any idea where it might be?"

"Another place?"

"An apartment, maybe even a condo," suggested Beth. "Let's see what we can find. You said he forgot to take his old check registers? Terrible oversight on his part. That ought to be a gold mine." Beth beamed with anticipation. It took her only a few minutes to find what she sought, $1250.00 checks made out on the first of every month to Townsend Corporation, going back to May 1 of the previous year.

"Let's see if Townsend Corporation is in the phone book," suggested Liz brightly. In minutes she found that the company held a number of rental apartments and condominiums in Chicago and the northwest suburbs. In looking through the listings, one immediately caught Carly's eye—the one located on Lake Shore Drive. Steve often talked about living on the Drive—had even suggested they move there after Celia was born—but Carly convinced him that a suburban lifestyle was better for raising kids.

"Bet you anything that's Steve's place," offered Beth.

"A place on Lake Shore Drive...since May!" Carly was amazed. Could she have been *that* blind? Everything was happening too fast. Just days earlier, she believed herself to be a happily married woman. Not perfectly happy, but certainly happy enough. Suddenly exhausted and feeling a small hammer starting to pound against her temples, she begged off any further detective work for the day and turned down Beth's offer to spend the night at her place. "I don't want the kids to start to wonder what's going on," she explained, promising she'd be ready to dig deeper in the morning.

Carly was ready when Beth and Liz appeared, bright and early, at her door. "You sleep any better?" asked Beth, entering Carly's kitchen. Liz headed straight for the cabinet where Carly kept her coffee cups. "You look chipper this morning."

"Last night—yes. But I got an early phone call this morning."

"Not from?"

"Steve."

"Really? How is the old philanderer?" asked Liz, pouring cups for Beth and herself.

"Furious—some restaurant last night declined his American Express card."

"Well, imagine that," Liz laughed.

"Yep, that usually brings them around," added Beth.

"We only talked for a minute or so—actually, he yelled. I couldn't get a word in edgewise, so I hung up."

"Way to go. You're learning!" beamed Liz.

"Do you know where he called from?" asked Beth.

"Yes—I checked the area code on caller ID. He's in San Antonio."

"Really!" Liz's voiced dripped venom. "Maybe he's got another chickie on the side."

"Maybe, but it's probably business. He does have clients there. He flies to San Antonio pretty often."

"Hmmm," noted Liz, thumb and forefinger rubbing her chin. "This opens some interesting possibilities."

"What have you got in that devious mind of yours?" asked Beth.

"You girls up for a field trip?"

"A field trip?" Carly was mystified, but one look at Beth's face made her wonder if they'd planned something the night before. They seemed to be sharing the unmistakable look of co-conspirators.

"Let's check out that condo on Lake Shore Drive!"

"No! I couldn't!"

"Aren't you curious? Don't you want to see if he has a place there?" asked Beth. "What have you got to lose?"

Carly hesitated. This was all too much, too soon. But she *was* curious. And it would be good to get out of the house for a few hours. What harm could there be in just *looking* at the place?

As Beth made the wide curve off the expressway onto the ramp leading to Lake Shore Drive, Carly gasped at the frigid, pristine beauty before her. Lake Michigan sparkled on this early February day. On the horizon, a clear blue sky met silvery ice gleaming in the late morning sunshine, separated only by a narrow, far-off band of open water where gentle waves stirred. The van sailed along the Drive, lake and deserted beach to the right, Grant Park to the left, everything solemn and majestic in its coat of fresh-fallen snow.

"This is all so beautiful. I haven't been down here in years. Why don't we come downtown more often?" Carly wondered.

"You'll remember why when we try to find a parking space," Liz grumbled.

The building they sought was one of many Old Grand Dames that graced the area north of Lincoln Park. Its distinguished façade of red brick and stone rose eight stories, short by comparison with many more-recently built structures, but tall enough to give residents of the upper floors outstanding views of the lake. They managed to find street-side parking after only five or six turns around the block and stood before the building for a few minutes.

"We don't even know if Steve has a place here. The listing in the phone book was for S. Brennan. Brennan is a common name," Carly said, sounding as though she was losing her nerve.

"Ah, but you're forgetting the checks he made out to Townsend Corporation. That's the smoking gun. And this is our chance to find out. All you have to do is walk up to the desk and ask."

"Do you think they'll tell us anything?" Carly didn't think it would be as easy as Beth suggested.

"Carly, you're still Mrs. Steven Brennan," commented Liz. "You've got your identification. You don't look like some bum or hooker that came off the street."

"What do hookers look like these days?"

"You're just trying to change the subject. Let's just go in and go up to the desk. Let's see what happens. What have you got to lose?" That question again. Carly wondered what, indeed, she still had to lose. Hadn't she lost a lot already? Could walking into this building make things any worse?

They walked through the door into a lobby paneled in mahogany and decorated with comfortable chairs and sofas upholstered in forest green velvet and maroon leather. The room whispered *"Money. Privacy. Privilege."* Carly approached the information desk where an elderly man shuffled through some papers while a younger man slumped idly in a chair.

"Excuse me. Could you tell me the number of Steve Brennan's apartment?" Carly asked firmly, consciously steeling her voice against the wavering she felt deep in her throat.

"And you would be?" asked the older man.

Pulling out her driver's license, she answered "Mrs. Brennan. Mrs. Steven Brennan."

"Ah, of course," he answered, recovering quickly from what appeared like confusion. "Mr. Brennan said you had lost your key and would be stopping by for a new one. Here." He reached into a drawer for an envelope which he handed to Carly. "We changed the locks at your husband's request after he reported your key missing."

"Oh, thank you," Carly was able to stammer as she and Beth turned away from the desk. As she walked away, she could almost make out a few words the older desk clerk had whispered to the younger man, causing them both to laugh. Had he really said, "*Another* Mrs. Brennan"?

Before Carly could consider the implications of that statement any further, Beth asked, "What's that written on the envelope?"

"Eight fourteen."

"That's got to be his apartment number," suggested Liz. "Talk about luck. Maybe his girlfriend is careless with keys."

"Or maybe he's juggling two girlfriends," suggested Beth.

"Carly, it's your call. Do you want to see his place?" asked Liz.

"Go into his apartment? Are you crazy?" What Liz was suggesting was definitely going too far.

But Liz persisted. "Look. This fell right into our laps. The elevators are over here to our right. What do you say?"

Carly looked to Beth for support. Surely Beth would put an end to this crazy idea. But she was taken aback by Beth's response. "This is an opportunity, maybe the only one you'll get. I'd take it."

Carly wasn't surprised that Liz had suggested something so bizarre, but Beth? Beth was always so level-headed. Still, Beth seemed very sure. "I don't know. Is it even legal?"

"You're still Mrs. Steven Brennan. The key was left for Mrs. Steven Brennan. I think you ought to use it," Liz insisted.

"What was that business about changing locks?"

"Who knows? Maybe he needs to change locks every time he gets a new live-in. But you're looking a gift horse in the mouth here."

"What if Steve showed up and found us here?"

"Steve called from San Antonio this morning, remember? Unless he was able to take a rocket ship home..." Liz sounded frustrated.

"But what if she's there?"

"Haven't you ever heard of serendipity, Carly?" Beth's show of frustration was far more discrete. "Or maybe it's karma. Do we take the elevators or not? It's your call."

"C'mon, you chicken!" taunted Liz. "I'll go in first—if she's there I'll pretend I'm a cleaning lady, or something like that. You'll hate yourself tomorrow if we don't do this."

Carly looked once more around the lobby, then at a particularly attractive impressionist print on the wall directly in front of her. This was the moment when she could discover the answers to many of the questions that kept her tossing in bed every night. But did she want to know the answers? "Let's do it," she finally whispered, hardly believing she'd actually spoken those words.

Moments later Carly's hands shook as she tore the envelope open and removed the freshly cut key to Apartment 814. Once she opened the door, the first thing that struck her was the magnificent view of the lake before her—a picture window took up practically the whole eastern wall of the living room. The room was exquisitely decorated in pale yellow and navy blue, with floral patterns predominating.

"Wow!" breathed Beth. "I figured it would be a studio, but look, there's a bedroom."

This has got to cost a lot more than $1250 a month."

"They must be sharing the rent," suggested Liz. The implications of this were not lost on Carly. Steve wasn't involved in a short-term fling. It was much more than that.

The floral motif continued in the bedroom where Laura Ashley prints predominated. The whole apartment was so...feminine. Definitely not what Steve would have chosen on his own.

But Carly had little time to wonder. Beth was already sliding open a mirrored door, disclosing the contents of one of two closets in the room. Carly spied two men's suits, one the pinstripe that Steve had told her the cleaners lost and another she did not recognize. *Ah,* thought Carly, *It really is his place!* She also saw a few shirts, none of which looked familiar, and several ties she remembered buying. Steve had always admired her taste in ties, she thought bitterly.

Liz slid open the other mirrored door, where she found a number of women's pencil-skirted business suits and silk blouses—all expensive, all designer, all in impeccable taste. "Size 4," she shouted, looking at a label. "Meredith diSalvo has good taste, at least in clothing."

Carly dropped onto the bed, her face in her hands, her shoulders shaking convulsively.

"Carly, I...I'm sorry. The last thing I wanted to do was to start you crying again," Liz apologized. When Carly looked up, Liz saw tears in her eyes, but they were not from crying. Carly was laughing so hard that she soon began choking.

"I've been such a fool! It's so pathetic it's actually funny."

"Then this'll make you laugh, too," added Beth, waving a magazine she had picked up from the nightstand. "Here's a copy of *Cosmo*." Even from the bed Carly could see the title of the feature article, "25 Ways to Spark His Desire." "And the cover story is dog-eared. Maybe Stevie-baby is getting a bit tired of Meredith."

"That would serve her right. And to think I liked her at that party. She seemed so sweet. We talked for almost an hour. Do you think she was seeing Steve even then?"

"Carly, he's had this place since May. And, oh, look at this." Beth picked up a framed photo that graced the nightstand. It pictured Steve, looking relaxed and happy in the swim trunks Carly had so admired during their Hawaiian trip, embracing Meredith, clad in a tiny bikini that showcased her trim figure. The photo had been taken on a beach, graceful palm trees swaying in the ocean breezes behind them.

"Damn, look at them! I just want to kill him! And her! What kind of people are they? I can't believe she talked to me about my kids—I showed her pictures. She seemed so interested. And all that time the bitch was sleeping with my husband!"

"Finally!" said Liz. "Anger! Keep it coming."

"Carly, do you have a nail clipper in your purse?"

Carly, looking in her purse with a frown, replied "I don't know, Beth. Do you really need to manicure your nails right now?"

But Liz was already brandishing a Swiss Army knife she'd rummaged for in her purse. "Will this do?"

"Perfect! Carly, open the clipper part. It's going to be your instrument of revenge—not a lot of revenge, but all you can reasonably have right now." Beth was already taking armfuls of Meredith diSalvo's clothing and piling it on the bed. She took a slim, well-tailored skirt and turned it inside out. "Watch what I do. Here, at the seam. Clip out just three stitches every two inches or so. Be careful not to cut the cloth." She handed the skirt and clippers to Carly.

"Beth, what...?"

"She won't notice when she puts the clothes on in the morning. But after she's sat down a few times, well, every day at work she'll wonder what the hell is happening to her wonderful designer outfits—they're all falling apart! We'll do just the skirts and pants, right at the stress points."

"Lookee what I found on Steve's desk, ladies!" Liz held an expensive-looking leather box decorated with a gold monogram. "Steve's Rolex!"

"What are you going to do..."

Liz, in her enthusiasm, cut Beth off. "Let me have that knife when Carly's done with it. It has a tiny screwdriver—just the size for loosening these little screws. And when the watch falls off his wrist and hits the floor—well, Rolexes are a lot more fragile than they look."

"You are diabolical, Liz!"

"Just my scientific mind at work."

Carly joined in their laughter, but surprised herself when she admitted she wanted to do much more—rip stuff apart, break a mirror. But Beth had good advice. "No, you need to be a bit more circumspect than that. You don't know what's ahead—what could be brought up against you in court."

"Court? I don't care about court."

"Not now, but you will later."

"But I feel so...so angry, so helpless. I want to get back at him—or maybe to just crawl up into a ball and die."

"I know. This has been a shock for you. But for now, this will help. It's a pretty harmless bit of revenge, when you think of it. Here," Beth said, pointing to the seam. "Three stitches every two inches or so. With the very tip of the nail clippers." Beth folded Carly's hands around the cloth and guided her just as mothers must have taught daughters needlework for centuries. "Just do it."

Carly did as she was told.

Chapter Nine

March 1983

Intermezzo

Tom Petty and the Heartbreakers, "Wildflowers"

Hell hath no fury like Carly Brennan scorned. Carly ate, breathed, slept fury. Every night she slept only after hours of thrashing about, fury burning her eyes, and she tasted its bitter ashes as she wakened just an hour or two later. She felt her whole life with Steve, from that damned party on Morgan Street when they had first met, through their relocations, the births of their children, was all a travesty. A sick joke. She grew suspicious of every kind word he had said. She hated him, but perhaps hated herself even more for playing his fool.

She no longer jumped in fear when the phone rang. She pounced on it eagerly, hoping to hear Steve's voice. And when he did finally call on Monday night, sounding much more reasonable than he had his previous call, this time she did the screaming. "You bastard! Who the hell do you think you..." But he hung up on her again, though this time, Carly hoped, from his own sense of self-preservation.

Thank heavens for Caller ID. Carly was able to determine that he was in Missouri, in a hotel in St. Louis, before she called him back. He answered the first time she called and quickly tried to talk through her stream of invective. When he hung up she called again; this time he waited eight rings before picking up. He didn't pick up at all the rest of the evening and into the night. She hoped he was in the room, jumping every time the phone rang, or that her calls had forced him to abandon his lair.

Carly eagerly anticipated her appointment with Ronald J. Kaszmarek, Esq., the attorney who had handled Beth's divorce, and was impressed when she entered his office suite. The mahogany paneling and lush cream-colored carpeting suggested financial success—a good sign, she thought, for an attorney. She spent a few minutes perusing the numerous framed diplomas and awards that adorned one full wall of his office before his receptionist, looking professional in her tailored gray suit, ushered her into his inner sanctum.

There she found an elderly, distinguished-looking man, whose reddish hair, mustache, and formal demeanor reminded her of the funeral director who had handled her grandmother's service. Kazmarek was sitting behind a desk that, had it been a dining room table, could have seated eight. She patiently sat through the formalities of becoming acquainted with both the man and many of the intricacies of Illinois divorce law. The visit was becoming painfully tedious for her when Kaszmarek suddenly said, "Mrs. Brennan, we can proceed with a divorce, if that's what you wish to do, in any number of ways. For example, we can work towards an equitable settlement and try to get it over with as quickly and painlessly as possible. Or," he paused, scrutinizing her expression, "we can take the S.O.B. for whatever he's worth."

"The second one," she blurted out. *Well,* she thought, *Kazmarek is more of a bulldog than he looks!* This thought pleased her.

"Are you sure?" he asked, peering at her as if he were assessing her determination and grit.

"Yes. Take him for all he's worth. Screw the bastard." *Now,* she thought, *I sound just like Liz.* But she rationalized that the situation called for a bit more bluster than her conversation usually carried.

"Mrs. Brennan, surely you need a bit more time to consider this," Kazmarek said smoothly. "You're obviously very angry right now. Are you sure you'll be up for this fight?"

"Damn sure." Carly wondered whether she was venting too strongly at this man, but as Mr. Kaszmarek reached into a file drawer for some papers, seemingly nonplussed by her words, she realized that he probably had encountered similar reactions, and even worse, every working day of his life.

"Very well then. The State of Illinois, in its wisdom, mandates a six-month separation before divorce papers can be filed."

"Six months? You have *got* to be kidding."

"Well, no, Mrs. Brennan," Kazmarek answered, obviously anticipating her reaction. "You and Mr. Brennan have only been separated for approximately three weeks, is that correct?"

"Yes, but six months! I have to wait six months? That's impossible!"

"Yes, it is very difficult. But many couples reconsider getting divorced during this time, so waiting saves the couple and court system a great deal of money and effort. I can begin to prepare the papers, of course, or we can hold off until the six-month period is over."

"No. Prepare the papers. Right away. Trust me, Mr. Kaszmarek, this effort will not be wasted."

Kaszmarek opened his desk drawer, taking out a leather-covered notebook and a fountain pen. Carly reflected that she hadn't seen one of those in many years—but at least it wasn't a feathered quill! All right, so the man was old-fashioned. But he exuded an air of knowledge and confidence. And Beth had done very well in her divorce, remaining in her home with full custody of her children. Carly decided it was in her best interest to trust him.

"Very well then, Mrs. Brennan. Illinois offers several ways to file for divorce. There's No Fault, which stipulates that the divorce is not directly the fault of either of the parties."

"Oh, I think I can point to some pretty serious fault on his part."

"You can file for the divorce based on his adultery, but you may wish to consider that carefully, as it does make his actions a matter of public record. And please excuse me for asking this, but his attorney will certainly do so. Have you, during the course of your marriage, also engaged in any sexual activity outside of your marriage?"

"Of course not!" The thought that anyone would suggest such a thing disgusted Carly. She had to force herself to remember the situation: that Mr. Kaszmarek was only doing his job.

"Please don't be offended, Mrs. Brennan, but when a marriage begins to fall apart, it's not unusual for both parties to seek companionship outside the marriage."

"Do I have to make this No Fault decision right now?" Carly asked, fingering to shreds the tissue she had been holding.

"No, not at all." Kaszmarek seemed to sense that his new client was beginning to fade. "We can schedule another appointment after you've collected the documents I will need. There is also the matter of the retainer."

"Oh," Carly stammered, "the retainer. Can you send a bill to the house?" She had no idea how she would pay the bill when it came. She hadn't even considered the retainer.

"Of course," he said smoothly, rising to indicate their time was up. "I'll begin your paperwork just as soon as I receive your check."

Carly's anger found new cause when she got home and listened to the message Steve had left on her machine:

Carly, I know you're very angry right now, but you have to settle down enough for us to make some decisions. I'll be back from my business trip this weekend and whether you want to see me or not I do want to see the kids. How about Sunday morning? I'd like to take them out for breakfast and spend some time with them during the afternoon. Call my number at the office and leave a message, okay?

Carly grabbed the phone and dialed—not Steve, but her new knight, *Sir* Ronald Kaszmarek. His reasoned tones only fed her flame.

"Mrs. Brennan, I'm sorry but Mr. Brennan does have the right to see his children. In fact, for the next six months he could move back into your home, if he so desired."

"What? What damn good is the law in this state anyway?" Carly asked, vaguely realizing that she'd adopted a new and cathartic habit of swearing when she spoke to her attorney.

"You don't believe Mr. Brennan poses any danger to your children, do you? From abuse? Or...he wouldn't kidnap them, do you think?"

"Hardly likely. He acts most of the time like he has no children. And no, he wouldn't abuse them. Neglect maybe, but certainly not abuse."

"Neglect?" Kaszmarek suddenly sounded more hopeful. "Would the children be endangered if they were with him?"

Carly thought for a moment, but realized she could not truthfully answer his question in a way that would feed his hope. "No, I wouldn't say that. I just mean that he's...I don't know...kind of distant with them, not that he'd let them run wild in the streets without supervision, or anything like that."

"Oh. Well, then my advice to you, Mrs. Brennan, is to accept this as graciously as you possibly can. I give you this advice for many reasons—legal ones, of course, but also, and I speak as a person who has seen this type of situation many times, in the long run it's usually best for children if they can maintain a relationship with both parents following a divorce.”

“What if they don’t want to see him?”

“Then you might inform him of that. But Mrs. Brennan, your children may feel much differently about your husband than you do right now.”

Carly decided to broach the subject about a visit with their father during dinner. She had lately insisted, despite Celia and Tyler’s resistance, that they eat in the dining room every evening. She always felt uncomfortable with the way mealtime evolved in the Brennan household—first an occasional meal in front of the TV to accommodate a special program or game, this leading step by step to virtually all meals being eaten in front of the tube. Another of Steve’s damaging innovations! This was not the way a proper family shared dinner.

She made tacos, which was probably the only dinner both of her children agreed was a favorite. Dessert was slightly more challenging: Celia loved pecan brownies, while Tyler favored a disgusting concoction of cherry jello cubes swimming in Cool Whip. Carly decided to make both. But as dinner progressed, she had reason to wonder if Kaszmarek was psychic.

“Hooray!” shouted Tyler when she, as casually as possible, mentioned that their dad wanted to see them that weekend. Even Celia’s customary pout seemed to relax a bit. “Is Daddy coming home?” asked Tyler with more animation than Carly had seen in weeks.

“Honestly, dorkhead,” answered Celia, “don’t you know anything? This is a weekend visitation. We live with Mom during the week and see Daddy during the weekends.”

“We’re not quite there yet,” corrected Carly. “That’s something a court decides after a divorce has been granted.” Carly immediately regretted having said the D-word. She quickly asked if anything interesting had happened at school, daring to hope that her children would allow her to change the topic.

“But you are getting a divorce, aren’t you?” Celia’s glare made Carly realize she had been foolish in thinking she could extricate herself from this conversation so easily.

“I don’t know yet. Maybe.”

“Yeah, right. Whatever. May I be excused from the table?” Celia asked with feigned civility. Adherence to the formal table manners imposed by her own parents was another policy Carly had lately instituted.

"Without dessert? I made pecan brownies," tempted Carly, torn between her mounting anger at the insolent tone in her daughter's voice and her desire to placate Celia at any cost.

"No, thank you, Mom. I'm on a diet."

"Honey, you're only twelve years old. And you're thin enough as it is." To Carly, Celia looked stick-thin in her jeans and tee shirt. It seemed girls were worrying about their weight much too early these days.

"All the other girls are on diets—even girls in second and third grade. And I am *not* thin. Is eating brownies something *else* I *have* to do now?"

"No, of course not. And, yes, you may be excused from the table. And I can do without your rotten attitude right now, young lady."

"My attitude? You're the one who's been treating us like three-year-olds since Dad left. It's like a concentration camp here lately."

"What's a construnation camp?" asked Tyler.

"A prison, Tyler. It's like we're in a prison."

"That is quite enough, Celia," Carly retorted, trying to regain control of the situation.

"Quit being so mean to Mommy," whimpered Tyler.

"It's okay, Tyler. Celia is just upset." Carly wondered how this conversation had become so volatile. "She doesn't mean what she's saying."

"I do too mean what I'm saying. And at least I'm being honest. Not like some people sitting right at this table. Right, Tyler?"

"Now what?" asked Carly, turning first to Celia staring triumphantly at her brother, and then to Tyler who was pushing cheese crumbs and lettuce shards around his plate with his finger.

"The note, Tyler?" Celia snickered.

"You promised. You promised you wouldn't tell."

"Wouldn't tell what?" asked Carly.

"It was Jimmy's fault. He pushed me off the swing."

"Miss Perot gave Tyler a note for you, and he's been hiding it. He got into a fight at school. She wants to see you."

"Tyler! Fighting?" How could this be? Tyler was always so gentle, so loving. The little boy who took care of hurt sparrows, who cried over dead butterflies. The look of pure hatred Tyler shot toward his sister alarmed her.

"You promised!" he shouted.

"Don't be such a dork. Mom would have found out. Miss Perot knows our phone number. You are such an idiot."

Tyler darted up from the table, shaking a fist at his sister. "I'm not an idiot! You're a rotten snitch. You told."

"Like I wasn't going to tell Mom? It's your own fault for being stupid enough to tell me."

"Stop it, both of you," Carly shouted, running to intercept her son before he made his way around the table. She grabbed him, still shaking his fist at his sister, and held him tight. "Tyler," she said, looking directly into his eyes, "get that note right now and bring it to me, and then go upstairs. Celia, you too. And both of you, stay in your rooms until tomorrow morning. I'm very disappointed with both of you."

"It was Jimmy's fault. He started it," pouted Tyler.

"Enough! And I'd better not hear another peep from either of you tonight. No arguing upstairs. Do you hear me?"

"Loud and clear, Mom," snarled Celia.

Carly feared the glimpse of the future she saw as she watched her children's backs retreating toward the stairs: Celia's ramrod straight with insolence, Tyler's slumped, his head down, angel wings trembling with sorrow and fury. Of course her children were upset, but Carly couldn't tell whether this was a natural response to the changes of the past couple of weeks or a foreshadowing of serious problems ahead. Tyler, her sweet baby boy, fighting. And Celia's petulance was taking on a new, nasty turn.

She willed herself out of her seat and began clearing the table, hoping the headache that had teased her all day would not explode into a blinding, debilitating monster. Placing the milk and salsa on the refrigerator shelf, she noticed a bottle of good white wine, her favorite Bernkastler, half hidden behind a head of lettuce and some cucumbers. She had bought it for some special occasion, but could not remember now what that occasion was. *Screw it,* she thought, pulling the bottle out and rummaging through her junk drawer for the corkscrew.

The week dragged on interminably, with every task a struggle. Despite this, Sunday morning seemed to lunge at her without warning—a clear, cold day, blinding sunshine reflecting diamonds off the snow. Since Celia and Tyler would not be with her, Carly had decided to skip church and head to the health club, determined to leave well before Steve's arrival, not yet ready to see him face-to-face. The health club was a new diversion for her. She tried it out a few times when Steve had first signed up for a family membership three years earlier, but quickly quit, justifying this decision by telling herself that chasing after the kids was certainly enough exercise for her. Besides, she didn't need to see all those female hardbodies taunting her—surely women weren't even supposed to look that muscular. But when Beth suggested she start working out a bit to relieve stress, she was willing to return.

She found that the mindlessness of repeated activity at the health club gave her some solace. She would force herself onto the machines and the walking track despite the assorted aches and pains she knew she'd feel the next morning. And the health club had one other advantage: she noticed that after an hour or two there, she slept better at night. Not much better, but having the last anxious glance at the alarm clock occur at 1:00 a.m. rather than at 3:00 a.m. was at least marginal improvement.

To forestall another argument, she avoided asking her children about their visit with their father once they came home. But the remainder of the day hung like a dense, stifling fog on all of them. This whole situation—Steve, the divorce, their reluctant march into the unknown—reminded her of that saying about an elephant in the room that everyone saw but no one would talk about. But bringing up the visit might only lead to angry words and hurt feelings, which was surely worse. Better to try to keep a lid on things.

Her children gave her no arguments when bedtime came, trooping upstairs without being asked, obviously eager to escape the cloying atmosphere of their family room. Carly thought she might be able to get to sleep early herself, but as she entered the kitchen to turn off the lights and check that the stove and all appliances were safely off, she spied an envelope on the kitchen table. One of the kids must have left it there.

As she opened it she gasped to find an anniversary card, beautifully adorned with pictures of roses, the words *To My Beloved Wife* jabbing her heart with each letter. For the first time that day, she remembered it was their anniversary. Years ago they had stood in that hideous Vegas wedding chapel and vowed to love each other forever.

She dropped the card as if it were a writhing snake, but then had to read it, through the blur of bitter tears:

Dear Carly,

This is probably inappropriate, to send this card now. But I've had it for a while, and it really does, believe it or not, say what I feel about you. I'm sorry, so sorry, about everything. I know you're very angry. I understand some of the things you've been doing—I made a mistake in cancelling your credit cards, but my counselor said I should for my own protection. I know now that was a stupid thing to do. This is all just such new territory for me.

I know you can't understand what's going on right now—but believe me, I don't understand either. I never meant to hurt you. I don't know how things will turn out, but I do know that I love you as much right now as I did on this day 17 years ago, as hard as that may be for you to believe.

Damn the man. He'd already torn her heart in two. Was he now trying to shred it into little pieces?

The next day tested the endurance of both her co-workers and the customers of *Sound Decisions*. Roger finally set her to work restocking some shelves with new inventory, perhaps sensing that human contact with Carly was dangerous for all concerned. This was highly unusual for Carly, who enjoyed her work at the record store. She liked the customers and the atmosphere, which was laid back and casual, with music a constant accompaniment. Most often the store was filled with the sounds of the newer groups with funny names like the Stone Temple Pilots, Soundgarden and the funniest of all— Smashing Pumpkins. But wasn't that the way with rock music—after all, her generation had listened to Iron Butterfly and Blue Oyster Cult.

Some days Roger's taste reverted to classic rock—the Stones and Zeppelin. Funny how those songs took her back to previous times— happier times that were now blurred by persistent melancholy. Hearing the Stones reminded her of a concert she and Steve had attended. They really couldn't afford the scalped tickets and drove all the way to Indianapolis in a December snowstorm to see the show—but Steve knew she had always loved that band. He'd frequently done sweet things like that. What had happened?

When Roger came back from lunch, he found her emptying a box of new CD's. One look at his face told Carly she was in trouble. "Jeez, Carly, what have you been doing? What are all the classic rock anthologies doing with the longhair music? Bachman Turner Overdrive just above Beethoven? And the new Spanish stuff—what's Gloria Estefan doing with the Spanish language CD's? What is going on with you? Stocking shelves has got to be the easiest job in the place."

"Roger, I'm sorry. I..." Carly had to stop to bite hard on her lower lip. *Damn,* she thought, *will I never be able to speak to anyone about this without crying?*

"It's okay." Roger's tone changed abruptly. "We can refile the CDs. It's not that big a deal. I didn't mean to sound so harsh."

"It's not anything you said." Carly could no longer hold back tears.

Roger looked around, obviously embarrassed by the turn this conversation was taking. "Do you want to talk about it my office?" he finally asked.

Carly trooped after Roger into his cluttered office, really just a remodeled stock room in the back of the store. He cleared some inventory forms from the cheap plastic chair he used for employee interviews and seated her in his best gentlemanly fashion. Maybe she was getting fired—big deal—what was yet another failure? She was becoming used to them. Roger closed the door behind them, obviously concerned about privacy, and asked again, "What's up, Carly?"

"I'm sorry. I know I've been distracted. Family problems."

"I didn't know. The kids? Somebody sick?"

"No, it's...it's Steve, my husband. I think we're getting a divorce." Carly was disappointed to realize that saying that word wasn't becoming any easier.

"So sorry to hear that. I know how hard that is. My wife and I divorced after only two years of marriage—and it was really rough even without kids and a house and everything. I can only imagine what you're going through."

"It's just...*everything's* so hard right now. I don't know what to do."

"I know. When Stella left me I could hardly get out of bed in the morning. There just didn't seem to be any point in doing anything any more."

"She left you? God, it must be some kind of epidemic. Steve left me." She was encouraged by Roger's sympathetic, understanding look. "He left me for another woman." Carly immediately regretted having shared so much information with Roger. It was not like her to display her feelings so carelessly. What must he be thinking of her?

Roger hesitantly placed his hand lightly on Carly's arm. "I can't imagine any man doing that, Carly. He must be the biggest fool in the world."

Carly looked at Roger as if for the first time. He suddenly seemed more attractive than he had before—not her type, of course. Slim, almost slight. Very dark hair, already starting to thin at the temples, but really sensitive blue eyes under the kind of thick lashes Carly always believed were wasted on a man.

And his mustache—he probably grew it to make himself look older—but it did suit him. Gave him kind of a Clark Gable insouciance. Should she pull her arm away from his hand, which felt uncomfortably warm and moist? Would he be offended?

"I should go back to work. You're not paying me to bawl away here in your office." Carly reached in the pocket of her jeans for a tissue—she found that lately she needed almost a constant supply of them.

"Don't worry about that. It's a slow day anyway. Stay in here for as long as you need." He got up and turned toward the door. Then he paused, obviously reconsidered, and came over to her chair. Squatting so he could look directly into her eyes, he awkwardly placed his hand on her knee. "Carly, whatever I can do to help." She was touched by his obvious uneasiness. "Anything. If you need some time off, or just someone to talk to, or..."

Carly looked deeply into those sensitive blue eyes. How long had it been since Steve had looked at her so caringly? Steve...could she not stop thinking of him for even a minute? Steve—who probably betrayed her, over and over again, with a number of women.

She realized she'd stumbled upon a crossroads. For just a moment she hesitated, then decided the road she would take. "Just knowing you're here for me, Roger, that you understand. I can't tell you how good that makes me feel." Dabbing at her eyes with the tissue, she attempted a weak smile.

"I do, Carly. I do understand."

Later, Carly couldn't remember at what point Roger's embrace had begun to feel less awkward and more comforting. How good it had been to lean into his warm, hard body, to breathe in the smell of him—some type of men's scent, obviously a very popular one, as she had smelled it on many of the young male patrons of Sound Decisions, overlaid by the faint pungency of cigarettes. Yes, smoking was certainly becoming politically incorrect these days, but the smell of cigarettes on a man always strangely attracted her. It reminded her of high school.

Roger's first kiss was a revelation—tickly at first because of the mustache and just a bit tentative, but then...

Roger, it seemed, had talents she had never suspected.

Chapter Ten

March 1983

Intermezzo

The Doors, "Break on Through"

Liz and Beth blew into Carly's foyer, stomping snow off their boots, chatting excitedly about the blizzard outside, removing hats and coats, shivering with cold. "Geez, we hardly made it," offered Beth. "It's awful out there!" Liz had come in for the weekend and the friends had planned a lavish dinner out. But a fierce March blizzard had made them decide that a get-together at Carly's with pizza delivery was adventurous enough.

"Come in, warm up," invited Carly. "Let me take your coats. Can I get you some wine?"

"Sounds great," answered Beth, "have you got any of that German white left? The one from last week?"

"No, but I can open another bottle. Liz, some of that merlot from last time for you?" Liz nodded her approval.

"This room looks wonderful," exclaimed Beth, entering Carly's living room, the most formal but least used room in the house. "Are these new?" she asked, lifting an accent pillow in a subdued floral print.

"Yes. I've been pretty busy. This room needed painting, and once I did that I realized how shabby and old-fashioned everything else looked. Mostly it was a matter of just moving things around and adding a few new touches. I've also re-papered the kitchen and two of the bathrooms." Carly was amazed at her new-found energy. Could it possibly be the result of her relationship with Roger? What they had wasn't really meaningful—she doubted it would lead to anything. Still, there was something invigorating about attracting the attention of a younger man.

"Wow, you *have* been busy!"

"And you look great," added Liz. "What have you been doing? You've lost weight."

"A few pounds. I guess a combination of not being hungry and going to the health club every day—it's starting to pay off. I'm actually beginning to enjoy exercising—never thought *that* would happen." Carly could barely contain the giggle that wanted to escape from her body: her friends would *love* to know about the new form of exercise she was engaging in.

"Your eyes still look tired, though," added Beth. "Are you getting enough sleep? Those dark circles—you never had those before."

"Actually, Beth, I think they look good on her. Make her look a bit more—mysterious? Romantic? In kind of a Charlotte Bronte sort of way."

Carly laughed. "Nothing all that romantic about tossing and turning every night. But I am sleeping better than I did last month. I'm calling the pizza guy—sausage and pepperoni still good?"

"I ought to go with all veggie, but let's live it up. Hope the pizza guy can make it through the storm," Beth said.

"Better that he's driving in this crap than us!" Liz countered.

The pizza man took a very long time getting there, giving the friends plenty of time to catch up on each other's lives. Beth was enjoying the suburban mom's respite—neither soccer nor Little League had begun—and Liz was busy catching up with preliminary research from her last conference. Carly had been so busy with the minutiae of divorce proceedings—establishing credit, visiting her attorney, catching up with household bills and obligations, that she saw little of Beth the last couple of weeks.

Other activities had kept her busy as well, but she wasn't entirely certain that she was ready to divulge this information, even to her best friends, just yet. She did, however, share with them her frustration with dealing with overdue bills, a first-time experience for her.

"Why didn't you call me?" questioned Liz, settling more deeply into the sofa as she sipped her wine. "I'm always good for a loan."

"Or me. I could have helped out."

"No, I think the financial agreement my attorney is writing will work out. At least I'll be able to keep the wolf from the door until I can actually file for divorce."

"You're definitely going ahead with it?" asked Liz.

"I really don't see any other choice. I've lost all faith in him."

"Have you talked to him at all?"

"Just a few words on the phone, mostly when he wants to see the kids. One good thing about this, I guess he finally remembers he's a father." Carly's resistance to Steve's time with Celia and Tyler had turned to resignation, and then, because of new developments in her life, had become quite useful. She fought to hide a sudden smile that might have seemed strange to her friends who, after all, didn't *have* to know everything about her life. Still, another part of her was eager to tell them about Roger.

"You should talk to him, though, if only to settle financial and custody matters. Whatever you and Steve can settle between the two of you is something a lawyer can't charge you for," counseled Beth. "It would work out better financially for both of you."

"I know you're right. But every time I hear his voice on the phone my skin crawls. I can't believe what a bastard he turned out to be. Or what a fool I was."

"Now don't go blaming yourself," Beth suggested.

"From now on, just remember those three rules about men. Rule 1: All men are pigs. Rule 2: Some men are less piggish than others. Rule 3: Never forget Rule 1."

"Honesty, Liz," laughed Carly, "that's a bit harsh, even for you."

"Okay, not all men. I'm sure there are some decent ones out there—it's just I never find them!"

"Speaking of Antonio..." Carly teased.

"Or not," Liz responded drily.

"I guess my biggest problem with men is that I can never understand them. I mean, sometimes they just seem to be an entirely different species," said Beth.

"Mars and Venus, Beth?" queried Carly.

"Well, yes, almost. Not so much when you're going out with them. But once you're married, everything changes. Like Marty—he's an intelligent guy. That's why I married him."

"Right." Carly, remembering what a hunk Marty had been as a young man, shared a clandestine smile with Liz.

"But after we were married he'd spend weekends watching stock car races. Cars, going around and around in circles. For hours. What was that all about?"

"Men! They only watch those for the damned crashes," offered Liz.

"Without men, there'd certainly be no NASCAR," Beth affirmed.

"Or boxing," offered Carly. "Or ice fishing."

"Or monster trucks," added Liz, "or pork rinds."

"Or oral sex," suggested Beth, eliciting laughter from Liz and a choking fit from Carly, who had just taken a sip of wine.

"Now wait a sec," countered Liz once her laughter subsided, "what's the big deal? Men and women have always been different. Isn't that the whole point?"

"Sure," said Beth. "But the whole male-female dynamic has changed completely in the last, oh, maybe twenty years? Why are relationships so difficult now? Have people changed so much in one generation? All our parents are still together, and I don't imagine life was any easier for them."

"Women accepted a lot more then. My dad fooled around a lot when he was younger...maybe still does, for all I know."

"Really, Liz? And your mom just accepted it?" Carly was aghast.

"Hardly. They fought like cats and dogs about it, but they always got over it."

"Infidelity has been around forever. Our generation didn't exactly invent it," reminded Beth.

"I guess our generation just perfected it—made it the norm," Carly scornfully concluded. "But the biggest problem is the kids. When we were young we just naturally expected our parents would always be together. Our kids don't have that kind of security. I sometimes wonder how they'll handle relationships when they're older."

"Speaking of relationships," segued Liz, glancing, perhaps for affirmation, toward Beth. "There's something to getting back on the horse once you've been thrown. I know it's early, but have you thought at all about dating?"

"Well, I...I don't..."

"Slow down, Liz. It's kind of early. Carly and Steve have been separated for only what, about ten weeks? I wasn't ready to start seeing anyone until about six months after Marty left. Maybe in a couple of months Carly will be more ready."

"But that's just my point. The longer she waits the harder it's going to become to get back out into the couples' world. And Carly, there are some great singles bars around here—a lot of people complain they're just meat markets, but you know, sometimes you just gotta have meat. Or there are other ways—personals in the paper, Internet chat rooms, as long as you're careful about those. I've known women who had a lot of luck that way."

"I don't...it's just..." stammered Carly. She felt she had allowed this conversation to continue for too long, that her reluctance to confide in them was closing in on actual dishonesty. She didn't want to share this information quite yet, but felt disloyal, as if she were wrongfully withholding the intimacy Beth and Liz deserved from her. Finally she blurted out, "I'm already seeing someone."

"What?"

Carly's confession left both her friends wide-eyed, their wine glasses suspended mid-drink.

"Who?" Beth finally asked.

"Roger, my boss. I don't know...it just kind of happened one day at work when I was really down."

"Roger?" queried Beth. "He can't be any older than 25!"

"He's 28, actually almost 29," Carly responded, sounding just a bit defensive.

"Way to go, girl!" exclaimed Liz, lifting her drink in frank admiration. "Do tell."

"Well, there's not a lot to tell. It started the day I told him Steve and I were getting a divorce. I never really thought of him sexually before, but he was just so sweet and understanding. We see each other when we can—usually at his place."

"Does this feel like something that's going to develop into a serious relationship?" queried Beth.

"No, and that's what's so amazing to me. I don't see any future with Roger—and I doubt that he sees any with me. We have nothing to talk about. Well, except for music, which we're both interested in. But honestly, our whole relationship is mostly about sex. Somehow that's just fine for now. I can't believe I feel this way." Carly first sipped, then gulped down her remaining wine. There, she'd said it. She shared with her friends her confusion about the very new feelings she was experiencing. As she looked at them, she couldn't discern shock on either of their faces.

"Carly, it's normal. You're in the semi-obligatory-roll-in-the-hay-with-a-much-younger-man phase. Very common, especially when a woman gets dumped by her husband for a younger woman. Just enjoy it while it lasts. Let's toast Carly and the new love of her life," suggested Liz, raising her glass. "To Carly's new horizons."

"To Carly's new horizons," echoed Beth.

Carly basked in the acceptance her friends bestowed on her. Why did she hesitate in telling them about Roger? She had to know they would understand, would support her in any decisions she made. As the evening progressed, their conversation turned to many things—just like in the old days on Morgan Street. Old reminiscences, good wine, good conversation—Carly hadn't enjoyed an evening so much in more years than she could remember.

Beth shared some interesting news: her brother Jason was coming in for the weekend. She invited Carly to join them for dinner on Saturday night. Carly accepted with pleasure. "I haven't seen Jason in a while."

"Remember when he tried to teach you how to play guitar?" Beth asked.

"A real flop. I don't know why he even kept trying."

"I can guess, Carly. I always thought he was hot for you when we were in college. And I thought I detected a bit of a spark from you, too, whenever he was around," Liz recalled.

"Of course, that was only when Steve wasn't around," added Beth. "When he was in a room our Carly couldn't see another thing in the world."

"So, what is that good-looking brother of yours up to these days, anyway? Still in the music business?" asked Liz.

"Yep. Managing a new group—some kind of alternative music. He's actually doing very well for himself. He's got a place in LA right on the beach—*mucho dinero*."

"And to think how upset your parents were when he wanted to go into music," added Carly. "I thought they were going to disown him."

"It came pretty close to that."

"I was always surprised that he never married," commented Carly.

"He's had some pretty serious relationships through the years, but nothing ever really clicked. Of course, when I think of some of the women he hung around with, that's probably a blessing."

"It's still surprising that someone didn't reel him in, considering what a fine looking guy your brother was," Liz added.

"He still is," answered Beth.

Beth called late Saturday afternoon. Marc had a fever and she couldn't leave him, but Jason hoped Carly would still be willing to keep their dinner date. Carly's first inclination was to decline, but she remembered how much fun Jason was. She had no other plans for this evening—Roger was working at the record shop—so she agreed.

She discovered that Beth's assessment of her brother wasn't colored by sisterly subjectivity: the years had only intensified the qualities that were so attractive in the younger man. While still slim, he had filled out somewhat, and while this caused him to lose the boyish appeal he had once had, it gave him a certain ruggedness which was far more appealing. His hair was still dark and full and curly, framing his narrow face like a halo. And his eyes were as captivating as ever...a woman could drown in the depths of those indigo eyes... dark, deep, expressive.

He took her to an Italian restaurant which, though not far from her home, she had never noticed before, a small place, out of the way, but extraordinarily comfortable in its old-world charm. Good red and white checkered cotton tablecloths, starched linen napkins and fresh flowers graced every table. And the food was likewise exceptional: the restaurant featured northern Italian cuisine, with a wide assortment of fish entrees and the lighter sauces for which northern Italy was known.

Jason's connections to the music world fascinated her; he had met, worked with, and developed friendships with people she only knew through their music. But his many references to musicians and singers didn't sound like name-dropping, a bad habit Carly had always loathed. Jason clearly wasn't trying to impress her. These were simply the people he worked with, and it was apparent that he was passionate about his work.

He asked her about hers. "Well," she responded, "I'm kind of in the music business too—at a very different level. I work in a record store—actually a pretty big one—Sound Decisions. Have you ever heard of it?"

"Sure," he answered, "it's one of those new chains. The stores are almost as big as warehouses. Do you like your work?"

"You know, actually I do. Sound Decisions has a really diverse group of customers—we carry every kind of music you can imagine.

And I like the diversity. Sometimes the suburbs can be kind of white bread, if you know what I mean." Jason's quick laugh reminded her of how poorly he had fit into suburban life himself. He'd always rebelled against conformity.

"I like being able to help my customers when they forget the name of a particular artist or a song," she continued. "I've got one of those memories that latches on to things like that, especially for music." Carly wondered if she was rambling. Was she nervous being with Jason? But then, why would she be? He was just an old friend—the brother of her best friend.

"I remember that about you—how you always seemed to know a little bit about everything."

"I guess I was pretty obnoxious in college."

"Not at all. You never came off as a know-it-all. In fact you always seemed kind of shy. But that kind of skill—that great memory for detail—could be very important in your work."

"Well, I suppose."

"Especially if you want to make a career with Sound Decisions. They're a good company, well-established. Opening up franchises right and left, especially in the West."

"Right now I don't really know what I want to do. I'm kind of undecided about things, what with my divorce coming up and everything."

"I've known a lot of women, and guys too, actually, who seemed to just sprout wings after they divorced."

"Funny, I usually just feel like burrowing in the ground."

"Well sure. You've hit a really rough patch of road. But you've always seemed like the kind of person who would make lemonade whenever all they had was lemons."

Carly was surprised. Was this really the way people saw her? Or was Jason just being kind? Not knowing how to respond, she turned her attention back to her primavera.

"But back to Sound Decisions," Jason continued. "Do you see any opportunities there? How about management? With your knack for detail and your people skills you could be a natural. Music is a huge business today, and it draws people with all kinds of skills."

"I don't think our manager is thinking of leaving."

"You never know. And remember, Sound Decisions is a franchise. You could manage another store. They're popping up all over LA right now."

"California? I don't think so, what with the kids and all."

"It's not like California is on another planet."

"Some folks would disagree with you on that. But I just can't see myself as a manager." Carly was shocked that Jason saw her that way. What was he thinking?

"Fair enough. Then how about concentrating on your creativity?"

"Creativity? In music? Don't you remember how awful I was on the guitar?"

"Well, yes." They both laughed. "But there are all kinds of other creative things you can do in the music business without performing. Writing lyrics. Stage design. Marketing. The list is endless. You always struck me as a creative person, but you're also level-headed. There are plenty of jobs for people with those skills—they don't often come together in one person, at least in the music industry."

Carly looked bemused, but knew Jason was right. The music industry was full of creative people with no common sense and businessmen who didn't understand creativity. That seemed to be one of the biggest causes of all the tragedy that attached itself to the musician's lifestyle. But what was Jason really trying to tell her? He looked sincere. But she honestly did not see herself as the person he was describing.

"Well, I *am* good with numbers," she finally admitted.

"And with a lot of other things, too. Think about your strengths, about what you love to do. And then think about a way you can make money doing it."

Carly's response was interrupted by the waiter, who expertly slipped dishes of *tiramisu* before them. For a couple of minutes both were engrossed in tasting the bitter-sweet delight. "You make it sound so simple," Carly finally sighed.

"It's not simple—I don't mean to say that it is. I know with your situation it would be very hard. It's just that I've always sensed, Carly, that there was so much you wanted to do, but you've never realized how capable and talented you really are."

As the evening progressed, Jason and Carly fell easily into a communication pattern that felt natural to both of them, as though they had seen each other frequently through the many years of their acquaintance. Carly started to feel more comfortable with him, but at the same time more energized than she had felt in years. After what seemed like only a very short time, perhaps an hour at most, Carly noticed that she and Jason were alone in the restaurant.

"Where is everyone?"

"Probably home, and we'd better be heading out, too. It's nearly closing time."

"What time is it?"

"Almost 1:00."

"You have *got* to be kidding." Carly couldn't remember the last time she had been out this late.

He dropped her off at her front door and bent down to receive the friendly kiss she planted on his cheek. "Let's do this again some time, Carly. I'll call you the next time I come back to Chicago for business, probably in a month or so," he offered.

"Do that," she answered. Carly watched him saunter out to his car. As she turned the key in her lock, she caught herself humming a simple tune and considered the possibility that Jason's laid-back amiability was catching. Or was it more than that? Liz was right. She'd been attracted to him from the first time she met him—that same evening when she'd met Steve. Things might have turned out differently if Steve had missed that party.

She realized that somehow, quite unexpectedly, she had begun to see herself as a woman blessed, with two beautiful children, a loving family, dear friends, a nice home, a job she enjoyed and a boyfriend she had a lot of fun with. Even in the dark of the night, a time that had become filled with doubts, fears and hopelessness, her world suddenly seemed clear, bright, and full of possibility. And now a good friend was about to re-enter her life. She had never had an actual male friend before.

And if Jason were to become more than a good friend—well, time would tell. The thought that two very attractive men could possibly be interested in her was intoxicating. Liz had often talked about the power of pheromones—that men, like moths, could sense availability from a mile away. Well, if she was destined to be a moth, she was ready for it. She just hoped she wasn't headed toward any particularly dangerous flames.

Chapter Eleven

April 1983

Intermezzo

Janis Joplin, "Me and Bobby McGee"

On a dreary, overcast April morning Carly, toying with the leftover crumbs from her English muffin, wondered why the despondency of the previous months had again mantled her like a gray gauze shroud. To say her life was a roller coaster ride seemed a cliché, but one that was all too appropriate. On this day, her life felt like...

Limbo.

How had the nuns described it when she was in grade school? A place of silence, a place of waiting. Limbo was for those who had no opportunity to embrace the word of God before they died, including infants who had died before they had been baptized. Carly and her school friends, who naively accepted more mysterious concepts about faith and proper behavior from their habited teachers, had found limbo incredibly unfair—why should babies, surely the most innocent of God's creatures, be denied the joy of His presence?

Carly tried to remember if limbo had been abolished with Vatican II. But even if the Catholic Church did abolish limbo, the concept remained.

Limbo.

She knew she was there right now.

Her blinding, raging fury toward Steve had passed, thank God. That had threatened to burn her to ash. But it had been replaced by a vague, inexpressible hollowness deep within her. Her visits with Mr. Kaszmarek were much more productive these days in terms of getting things accomplished, but less cathartic. The maelstrom of divorce had modulated into the tedium of divorce arrangements: decisions about the disposition of particular jointly-owned investments, the establishment of a timetable for holiday visitation, lists denoting the future ownership of various household items.

And it was becoming clear that the vacuum caused by Steve's absence from her life was not going to be filled by Roger. He was a nice enough young man, to be sure, but their lovemaking had lost its allure very early. The fact that they had nothing to talk about before or after sex increasingly bothered Carly, and she began to believe that, while a meaningless affair might put zest into the life of some women, it only depressed her. Roger seemed willing enough to continue with the affair, but meeting him even once a week had become a chore. And seeing him at work didn't help; his little insinuations, his surreptitious winks and smiles at her, which had seemed so winning albeit somewhat childish when they had first begun to be conspirators in their affair, had lately become annoying.

And what about Jason? Carly had sensed something during their dinner "date," but was what she had sensed a romantic interest, or just an old friendship that had been brought into being by their connections with Beth? It was hard to tell with Jason.

Carly knew her family and friends would continue to support her through her divorce and beyond, but even the most loyal fan becomes tired of hearing the same old song played over and over. She realized that her lamentations about Steve—his betrayal, her resulting problems, her sense of loss and vulnerability—would inevitably become less fascinating to her listeners; actually, her whining had already become boring even to her. And people had to get on with their own lives.

The children—well, that was a tricky call. Things seemed fine on the surface. There had been no further notes from Tyler's teacher, and Celia seemed no more difficult to reach than she was for the last year or so. But their house was so quiet these days. Sometimes Carly actually missed the bickering and minor outbreaks of hostility that had kept things jumping. Her children seemed to be in limbo as well.

She awakened every day feeling suspended in some type of highly viscous liquid—arms, legs and torso valiantly resisting the dull heaviness that held her. But eventually she gave up, earlier and earlier every day, and sank into torpor. How did Tom Petty describe it: "Something about it being worse than anything." That was certainly true. But the next line of the song did not seem to apply to her current situation of turning up one card every day. Carly didn't feel she was turning up any new cards. She had no way of knowing that very soon she'd have the whole deck exploding in her face.

Carly rushed up the basement stairs to answer the phone. Winter had lost its stranglehold on northern Illinois, allowing its weary residents to believe that spring might actually come. Carly, bitten by the spring cleaning bug, was already washing her third load of curtains. Both Celia and Tyler were at friends' houses and she didn't want the answering machine to pick up: she hoped this was the long-awaited call from the carpet cleaning service and that she'd be able to set up an appointment for early next week. They were probably swamped with calls. The first warm spring day was almost an instinctive signal to women like Carly that it was time to loosen the winter grime and get their homes in order.

But the voice on the other end didn't belong to the man from Karpet Kleen. It was a Mr. Connors, who identified himself as the manager of the local convenience store. Carly had popped into that establishment hundreds of times to pick up bread or milk or to purchase slurpees for the kids on hot summer days, but she wasn't what you'd call a regular customer, and didn't know a Mr. Connors. What could he possibly want?

"Could you come over to the store, Mrs. Brennan?" he asked gently.

"Why?"

"Mrs. Brennan, we have your son Tyler here."

"Oh my God, has something happened? Is Tyler all right?"

"Yes, ma'am. He's fine. But I do need you to come over here right now." Mr. Connors' tone convinced Carly that any argument or request for further clarification would be futile.

Grabbing her purse, she rushed out of the house, mindless of her disheveled hair, her old work clothes, the slippers on her feet. When she arrived at the store, she was ushered into a small office in back where a harried-looking middle-aged man, obviously Mr. Connors, sat behind a scattering of paperwork on his desk. Tyler was sitting in a chair in the corner, sniffling, completely deflated, but obviously unhurt. She wanted to rush to her son, but Mr. Connors stood up and offered his hand. Reluctantly shaking it, she asked, "What is this all about?"

"Tyler, why don't you tell your mom why I called her," suggested Connors, not unkindly.

"I can't," he stammered, dissolving into tears.

Connors, turning back to Carly, offered the explanation. "Mrs. Brennan, one of our clerks saw your son shoplifting."

"What? Tyler, shoplifting! That can't be true."

"I'm afraid it is, Mrs. Brennan. He took this pack of cigarettes off a display on the counter and walked out the front door." Mr. Connors held up the incriminating pack of Marlboros.

"Cigarettes? That's ridiculous. Why would a nine-year-old want cigarettes? There must be some mistake." But as she looked at Tyler, who looked away from her, his face buried in his hands, his body convulsed with tears, Carly knew this was no mistake.

"You'd be surprised how young some kids start smoking. And some kids steal them for older friends, or just because they think it's cool."

"Steal? Oh my Lord, have you called the police?"

"Excuse me for just one moment, Mrs. Brennan." Carly panicked as he picked up the phone on his desk. Was he calling the police now? But Mr. Connors pressed only one button. "Julie," he whispered into the receiver, "could you come in here?" In a moment a pretty young woman, whose uniform identified her as a store employee, stuck her head in the door. "Could you take young Mr. Brennan here into the other office for a couple of minutes? I need to talk privately with his mother." Tyler eyed his mother with the startled eyes of a deer caught in headlights, but nevertheless docilely followed Julie out the door.

"Mrs. Brennan, I haven't called the police. I have no intention of calling the police. As you probably know, shoplifting is a very serious problem for stores like ours, but your son is very young and obviously very contrite."

"Oh thank you. Thank you."

"And the 'crime,' if we can call it that, was very unusual. According to Julie, Tyler took the cigarettes right in front of her and walked straight out the door, almost as though he wanted to be caught."

"But, I don't understand..."

"Mrs. Brennan, sometimes children behave very strangely, in an attention-seeking manner, when there's some disturbance in the home?" he questioned, helpfully offering an explanation.

Carly stalled at divulging personal information to this stranger who she still perceived as a threat to her son, but his compassionate look and her own anxiety forced the words out. "Tyler's dad and I are in the process of getting a divorce."

"I thought it was something like that. Obviously, he's a good boy and you're a good parent. I've already told Tyler he's not allowed in the store for a year. I'm sure you'll find a good way to deal with this at home as well." Connors rose, signaling to Carly that the horrible interview was at an end. "Good luck, Mrs. Brennan."

The ride home was very quiet, for Carly had no idea how to react to Tyler's actions and Tyler wasn't ready to volunteer any explanation. She alternated between feeling sorry for him, her darling baby boy, cowering in the passenger seat of the car, too ashamed to even look at her, and firmly deciding that his infraction was too serious to just let pass. He'd certainly made a mistake, but what if this was only the beginning? What if this was a precursor to serious problems ahead? Maybe counseling was the answer. This had to be a difficult time for both of her children; perhaps she should arrange something for both Tyler and Celia.

When they entered the house, Carly banished Tyler to his room, too exhausted to even consider any other action. Within minutes she heard the front door open: Celia was home. Things had been strained between Celia and Tyler for quite a while, Carly knew, but they once had a good relationship, with Celia watching out for her baby brother. Carly thought her daughter might be able to provide some insight into what Tyler was thinking. She shared the morning's experience with Celia, completely and straightforwardly, finishing with the suggestion that both children might benefit from speaking to a counselor.

"Wait a second, Mom," cautioned Celia, "not me. There's nothing wrong with *me*."

"Honey, I'm not saying that anything's wrong with you, or even with your brother. It's just that we've all been under a lot of pressure lately. Maybe talking to someone about it wouldn't be the worst idea in the world."

"Great. Dad has his shrink. Tyler and I will have ours. You getting one too, Mom? It seems to be the thing to do these days. The Brennan family discovers therapy. How cool."

"Well, I hadn't considered that. Actually, I think I'm coping pretty well considering all the stress I've been under."

"Right, Mom. You've been coping real well. It's just that since Dad left the only way you know how to *cope* with things is to invent new rules. I'll bet Tyler's screwing up will just lead to some new rules for both of us."

"Celia, this family has always had rules."

"Yeah, but not like now. For all I know you'll make us go back to an 8:00 bedtime. Maybe you'll figure out that we should go to church *every* day of the week instead of just Sundays. Maybe we should watch *The Brady Bunch* like fifteen times a day so we'd all learn how to act—except no dad, of course. "

"Celia!"

"Well, Mom, that seems to be your answer to everything these days. More rules, more 'time out,' for Christ's sake, like we're both five years old. You sent Tyler up to his room, right? That's how you're 'handling' this?"

"Celia," answered Carly, just barely restraining the urge, new to her, to slap her daughter's smirking face. "You seem to have forgotten who the mother is here. You seem to have the mistaken notion that you're the one in charge."

"Maybe you won't be in charge of us pretty soon."

"What is *that* supposed to mean?"

"Dad asked us to move in with him."

Carly gazed at her daughter open-mouthed. For some time she could think of no response to Celia's bombshell. Finally, "That's preposterous," she said. "Your father doesn't even have a suitable place for you to live in."

"He said he'd get a place, somewhere out here so we wouldn't have to change schools. He said he's going to ask the judge for custody."

"But Celia," Carly fought back the scream building in the back of her throat, "you and your brother wouldn't really want to leave your home, would you? To live with your dad?"

"Tyler doesn't—well, anyway, he's not so sure either way. He told Dad he didn't want you to have to live alone. But Mom, since Dad moved out you treat us like we're little kids."

Carly fought back her first response, to tell Celia to stop acting like a little kid if she didn't want to be treated like one. Deciding that would sound too much like her own mother and remembering how much she hated comments like that, she determined to put the focus back on Steve, where it belonged. "But your dad's not used to being around you all the time. He probably wouldn't really watch you at all." The look on Celia's face told Carly that was precisely what her daughter hoped for. "You'd really want to break up our family like that?" Carly wished the moment she had uttered that question that she could take those words and stuff them back down her throat.

"Right. *I'm* breaking up the family. Not *you*."

"Celia, I didn't mean..."

"Dad's been talking to us. It's not *all* his fault, no matter what you say. And I don't blame him for not wanting to live with you any more. I don't want to either." Celia shouted the final sentence over her shoulder as she ran back to the foyer and out the front door.

Carly followed her daughter but stopped at the door and reluctantly let her go, realizing she had no alternative. There was really nothing she could say to soothe Celia. After all, she herself was becoming tired of living with the person she was beginning to become.

Monday morning it took every ounce of strength Carly possessed to drag herself out of bed. That viscous liquid she was suspended in had hardened to amber, and she felt as trapped as those poor prehistoric dragonflies she had seen embedded in the yellow stuff at the Field Museum. She barely managed to get her children off to school and herself to work.

She'd not yet decided how to punish Tyler, or whether punishment was even a good idea in this case. Funny how she'd never had these kinds of qualms before; she'd always felt she had a pretty good handle on how to deal with her children's difficulties. But this was different. She used to believe that, in most cases, what was right and what was wrong were pretty apparent. Now she found herself questioning not only her children's actions, but her own.

She dragged herself through a long, boring Monday. Just before it was time for her to leave work, Roger beckoned her into his office with a leering wink and asked her to close the door. "I picked up something for us for tomorrow," he smiled, handing her a plastic bag with the name of a popular video rental place imprinted on the front. She and Roger had a regular "date" at his apartment on Tuesday mornings, when Carly had the day off and he worked the afternoon-to-evening shift.

"Debbie Does Dallas?" she asked after peeking into the bag. "Porn?"

"Well, baby, I know it's really old stuff. But it's a classic, one of my favorites. You ever seen it? I thought it might give us some good ideas—like kind of a fantasy."

"Roger, I don't know." Carly, suddenly feeling incredibly queasy, realized it was time, actually past time, to lay this situation to rest. *Debbie Does Dallas* indeed! As if she wanted to spend her free time watching pornography! Roger seemed to respond to the look of apprehension on her face.

"Or not. We don't have to watch it. It's just that, well, sometimes I think you're a little...well, shy isn't really the word. Just maybe not real inspired. Not that I'm complaining, but...you know, everyone could use new ideas once in a while. What do you say?"

Carly sighed. Her degradation at having ever even considered an affair with Roger, whose erstwhile charms were dissipating with each word he uttered, was almost supplanted by her own astonishment and embarrassment at learning that Roger had not been entirely pleased with her either. While she had not wanted to discuss their relationship right then, he at least gave her an opening. "It's not the movie. It's a lot of things. I have so much going on at home right now. My kids seem to be self-destructing before my eyes, and with everything I have to do for the divorce, I just..."

"You won't be coming over tomorrow morning?"

"I won't be coming over at all any more, Roger. This has been great, you've been sweet to me, but I think it's time for us to just go back to the way things were."

"The way things were?"

"Before we started seeing each other." There, it was out. One complication out of her life. Carly was surprised at the relief she felt.

"You think it's that easy?" The vehemence in Roger's tone surprised her. "You think you can just play with my feelings that way?"

"Well, no," Carly stammered, beginning to back toward the door. She didn't like the angry look in Roger's eyes, the tension she sensed in his whole body. The man was practically shaking in anger. She was seeing a side of Roger she'd never even imagined existed. "I didn't think either of us saw our relationship as something permanent."

"No, but you think it's all right for you to just end it like that? 'Good-bye, Roger. It's been fun, Roger. I'm tired of you now, Roger. Just trot along now like a good boy.'"

"I...this is probably not a good time to talk any more about it. I can see you're upset. I have to go home. I'll see you Wednesday, okay?"

"I don't think so." Carly looked at him quizzically. "Unless you're coming in here as a customer, Carly, there's no reason for me to see you here."

"But, Roger, I..." It took a moment for Roger's meaning to sink in. "You're firing me? Is that what you mean? I don't think you can just fire me like that." She wondered if he could actually do it. Weren't there laws against that kind of thing?

But Roger seemed to read her mind. "Oh, I can find plenty of cause. How many days have you missed the last couple of months? How many times did you come in late? You could claim sexual harassment, like all the other broads are doing these days. But somehow, Carly, I don't think you want to do that right now, what with your divorce coming up and everything."

"I can't believe you're saying this." Suddenly his normally languid countenance appeared malevolent to Carly. She'd certainly been a bad judge of character. How did she not see this in him before?

"And you're just part-time anyway. We hire and fire part-time workers all the time. So if you want to make a stink about our affair, tell the big boys in corporate, go right ahead, bitch. But you better think first. After all, you're the married one, not me. Good-bye, Carly. It's been a blast."

Carly had never appreciated her job nearly as much when she had it as she did once it was gone. The money was almost inconsequential and the work itself not particularly challenging, but it gave her time away from home and the distraction of interaction with co-workers and customers every day. Several days later, once the shock had lessened, she listlessly began perusing the Help Wanted section of the newspaper every morning and began revising her resume, but nothing looked worthwhile. Most jobs seemed to require a college degree—her absence of which was yet another addition to her long list of a lifetime of poor decisions.

For a while she considered going back to waitress work; she had the chance of making more money doing that than she would have in any kind of retail sales. Mom and Dad could always use another waitress. And she'd at least be better than that Carlotta, who Dad had hired a couple of years earlier—between Carlotta's carelessness with orders and curtness to customers, Carly couldn't imagine why he had kept her on for so long.

But then she remembered what being a waitress was like—the rude customers, the aching back and feet. She felt she was probably getting too old for that kind of work; the younger, cuter waitresses made the best tips. And it would be embarrassing to go back to her parents for a waitressing job—not that they would criticize her. But she already felt she was taking too many steps backward in her life. This would be another.

Her first few days at home were devoted to her old standby during times of turmoil: frenetic housework. Windows sparkled, floors shone, even the jumble of her closets was beginning to take on some definition. But after three days this activity lost any small charm it had. Carly alternated frenzied restlessness with complete stagnation.

Finally, she forced herself to talk to Tyler about the convenience store. After much stalling and wheedling, many muffled tears and a few sullen stares, his words gushed out with a wash of tears: "It's all my fault."

"Yes, honey, of course you're at fault. You were the one who took the cigarettes, but..."

"No, not that. It's my fault that Daddy went away."

"What? Why would you say such a thing?"

"Because it's true. If I woulda' been a better boy, Daddy woulda' liked me more and he would still be here." Tyler attempted to hold back his tears with balled-up fists, but was unsuccessful.

"Oh, Tyler, baby, is that what you think?" Carly tried to enfold her son into her arms but he resisted. How, *how* could she convince her boy, her baby, that his guilt was completely unfounded—it was common among children whose parents divorced. How could she wipe those tears of anguish and despair from his beautiful face, and bring back that smile that had won her heart the very moment she first beheld him?

"I know it, Mom. I know it's true. It's my fault."

"Oh no, sweetie, your daddy's problems are with himself and with me, not with you kids. You didn't do anything wrong." But after many minutes of trying to convince Tyler of his innocence, Carly realized nothing she could say to her son was going to help him absolve himself of his unearned and damaging guilt. Any thought of punishment left her mind: her boy was already punishing himself severely. And the fact that she did not know how to begin to help him was punishment for her, as well.

If Tyler's unearned guilt had caused a feeling of helplessness in his mother, Celia's reaction to their family's problems produced a dull, thudding ache. Celia said nothing further to Carly about living with her father, but the relationship with her mother, that had earlier been strained by the invisible wall of adolescence, was now fortified with a moat topped with scattered mounds of broken glass, and then mounted with a cannon. Celia had become a phantom child, there only physically, as minimally as possible: mentally and emotionally, not at all.

Carly hoped that once the divorce was over, things would settle into some acceptable pattern. But when would that be? Another two and a half months before the papers could actually be filed, then the wait for a court appearance, and if Steve decided to drag things out this could go on for years. Granted, Steve seemed to be cooperating with Kaszmarek in working out a settlement, but the attorney had warned her that in the intensity of an actual court situation anything could happen. Many couples had scrapped well-wrought agreements and engaged in all-out war once they actually got to the courtroom.

Carly determined to simply take one day at a time, one step at a time, to get herself through the next few months. She would find a job good enough that it could actually allow her to pay the bills on time, would find some way to help her children through their hurt and rage, would somehow put together a good life for all of them. It would just take time.

April turned to May, and the promise of spring began to solidify into fact. Carly had spent a productive Monday putting the finishing touches on her resume and garnering some promising interview appointments for several jobs advertised in Sunday's *Tribune* classifieds. It had been a long time since she'd job-hunted, and Sound Decisions' dress code, or lack of one, did not require professional attire. A quick look in her closet revealed skirts and tops that were not only out of style, but also too large—one of the few benefits of the altered status of her life. Time for a shopping spree—well, not a very big one. No Carson's or Marshall Fields for her. But she hoped to find something suitable at one of the big discount stores.

Beth, always ready for a shopping date, picked her up at noon. Carly was happy to share good news with her friend—her upcoming interviews—and Beth seemed just as happy to hear that good news. Carly wondered how her friends had put up with her so graciously—

she hadn't been a particularly pleasant companion the past few months.

They chatted amiably as they perused the racks at the local K-mart—Carly was delighted when Beth pulled her away from the size 14's toward the 10's. Beth had always had a good eye for clothing sizes. Carly was even more delighted a few minutes later in the dressing room to find that everything Beth had found fit! She knew she'd lost weight, but this much? A bright, sunny day had turned even sunnier.

"I'd go for the red jacket over the navy print shift," Beth suggested.

"Red?" Carly had become accustomed to wearing mostly dark clothing that did a better job of hiding unwanted bulges.

"It's your color, Carly. You'll really stand out at those interviews."

Carefully folding the outfit over her arm, she joined Beth in searching out some suitable accessories. She had shoes that would work, but needed hose and a new navy blue purse. Feeling flush, she picked out a few things at the jewelry counter: a long strand of red glass beads with matching earrings. The bottle of Charlie she picked up in the fragrances department was a complete splurge: she had plenty of cologne at home. But this young, fresh fragrance was just what she needed to build her confidence.

At the check-out counter, Carly and Beth busily chatted about possible lunch destinations when the cashier broke in: "Sorry, ma'am, but your credit card was declined."

"That's impossible!" Carly's voice shook. "The card's new—only a few months old." Carly had applied for credit in her own name soon after she learned Steve had cancelled their joint cards. "Can you run it through again?"

"Of course, ma'am," the cashier complied. The moments Carly waited seemed interminable.

"Sorry, declined again."

"That's okay. I'm sure it's just some misunderstanding." Beth was already reaching in her purse for her wallet. "Let me get this. You can pay me back once it's cleared up."

But Carly, leaving the clothing on the counter, was already rushing for the door. All Beth could do was follow her to the parking lot, where she found her friend prostrate against the car, shaking with tears.

"It's okay. It happens."

"Never to me. Never before."

"Carly..." But Carly wanted nothing more than to go home. She refused Beth's offer to come in—they could talk—Beth didn't want to leave her like this. But Carly was adamant. Once inside she climbed up the stairs to her bedroom, crawled into her unmade bed, covered her head, and cried until she fell asleep.

Hours later she staggered downstairs to the kitchen. Crumbs on the table and unrinsed glasses in the sink told her that Celia and Tyler had come home from school. She called up the stairs to them, but receiving no answer, assumed they went to visit friends: this had become a fairly common after-school occurrence lately. She looked for a note, but found none. That was pretty common as well.

As she walked into the foyer to pick up what mail had fallen through the slot, she could hear the phone ringing. Deciding to let the answering machine take it, a decision she'd been making quite often in the last few weeks, she flipped through the mail, finding only bills and an ominous-looking letter from her bank. She heard only part of the message:

"...Commonwealth Edison. It is important you call today. Please call our accounts receivable office at 1-800-487-3000. This is not a solicitation. Once again, our number is..."

The letter from the bank contained bad, but at least explanatory, news. A check she had deposited—one of Steve's child support payments—had bounced. Therefore, so had several of the checks she had written during the past week, including the one to her credit card company. Glancing at the phone, she saw she had other messages. Thinking she might as well get all the bad news at the same time, she pressed the blinking button for earlier messages.

"Mrs. Brennan, this is Mrs. McNamara again. Could you please tell Tyler one more time to stop tramping through my garden on his way home from school. He's absolutely destroying my impatiens. I hope I don't have to call again."

"Mom, I forgot to leave a note. I'm having dinner at Sherrie's house. Tyler said he was going to Tony's. See you later."

"Carly, Jason. Just calling to say I'll be in Illinois on Saturday. You up for dinner again? Maybe something different? Have you ever had Thai food? Hope to hear from you soon."

Carly couldn't imagine what was worse: spending this evening alone or with her children. She decided to let things lie—at least the kids had the possibility of having some fun this evening. She couldn't deny them that: she certainly wasn't going to be good company herself.

That thought brought her right back to the embarrassment of the afternoon. She'd have to talk to Steve—why did his check bounce? Did he lose his job? Was this some kind of revenge—she wouldn't put that past him. There was so much she needed to do, so many things to worry about.

And Jason's call. How do deal with that? Her last dinner with Jason was one of the bright spots of the last few dismal months. Still, would she be up to it by Saturday? Did she really need any further complication in her life?

Well, dinner alone again. She opened the fridge door, peering for something to eat. Nothing looked appealing. Well, not exactly nothing. That half-empty box of white zinfandel was pretty alluring. Not bothering with a wine glass, she grabbed a clean tumbler from the sink and filled it to the brim.

Chapter Twelve

April 1983

Intermezzo

Creedence Clearwater Revival, "Bad Moon Rising"

Carly filled two wine glasses, venturing one more glance into the living room, where Jason sat on her loveseat casually flipping through the pages of one of her magazines. He looked completely relaxed, whereas her heart was racing. She searched her cabinets for half a bag of pretzels she knew was there, somewhere.

He'd taken her to the promised Thai restaurant, which had recently opened in a nearby suburb. Thai food was new to her, and the atmosphere of the restaurant couldn't have been more exotic. Dark red walls, black chairs surrounding a gold-toned marble table top, a statue of a slim Hindu goddess in Namaste pose before a grotto painted with a huge lotus blossom. Of course, he was the one who had explained the goddess, the pose, and the lotus blossom; in some ways, this friend of many years seemed as exotic as the restaurant.

She was grateful she had accepted Jason's dinner invitation; it seemed to be exactly what she needed after the awful week she'd just experienced. Getting ready for her "date" had been fun; she tried a new, successful hairstyle and had gone back to the department store to pick up the outfit and the cologne Beth had helped her select, this time making sure to bring cash. She'd even pulled out her old stash of make-up and had fun experimenting. It had all seemed a bit silly; after all, Jason was just the brother of her best friend. Perhaps that's why nothing had happened between them so many years ago—she certainly felt an attraction. But that would have complicated things, and then, of course, Steve had come along. That changed everything.

But still, Jason was so sweet at the restaurant, patiently listening to an edited summary of her sea of problems and gently offering her not advice, but support. And he had so many interesting things to talk about: his new job managing an alternative rock band, the interesting people he had met, life in LA. It felt good to step away from her own dreary existence, if only for a short while.

Being with him made her feel more hopeful, more confident that she could deal with the challenges she faced. Of course, he had some pretty strange ideas. That she should develop her love of music beyond pure enjoyment at listening to some of her favorite classic rock groups. That she could take her experience at Sound Decisions and develop it into a career. That she should consider moving out of Illinois—maybe even to California. That she was a competent, intelligent, interesting person with a great future ahead of her. She didn't quite believe she was the person he thought she was, but it was nice to know he saw her in such a positive light.

She wondered if it were possible that Jason's interest in her went beyond friendship. Liz did not believe in the existence of male-female friendship, asserting that whenever a man showed any interest in a woman, or even spoke to a woman, he was interested in taking her to bed. But that was Liz. She'd always been suspicious of the concept of "true love."

Finding the elusive pretzels, she poured them into a bowl and, placing the glasses, the bowl and the wine bottle on a tray, made her way to the living room. She felt just a little light-headed. She'd already had quite a bit of wine at the restaurant.

"So, what did I eat again?" she asked, carefully placing the tray on the coffee table.

"Pad Thai," he responded, his slow smile warming her heart. "Did you like it?"

"Loved it," she said, glancing at the sofa and at an armchair. But drawn to sit closer to him, she found herself joining him on the loveseat. He made room for her, casually placing his arm on the backrest behind her. "And the restaurant was so beautiful," she added.

"Yeah, that's kind of a traditional look for a Thai restaurant. They're very popular in California right now," he said, reaching over her to grab a handful of pretzels.

Damn, he smelled good! She didn't know what scent he wore, but it was working on her. Hardly believing what she was doing, she placed a hand lightly on his arm. Pausing, he looked up at her.

Was that surprise she saw in his eyes? Had she been missing signals he had been sending—she was so removed from the "dating" scene. Perhaps he had been waiting for her to make the first move. Women were a lot more aggressive than they had been when she was in college.

She decided to take a chance; she had little to lose. She kissed him, hard, on the lips.

His jolt was electrifying, but not in the way she had hoped. "Carly," he said, gently pushing away from her.

Damn, what have I done? she cursed herself. "I'm so sorry. I shouldn't have done that."

"No, Carly, it's just that..."

"I'm just so stupid. Maybe a little too much to drink. I don't know why I would even think for a second that you..."

"It's not..."

"...could even be interested in me." She covered her eyes with her hand, trying to hide the tears she felt beginning to emerge.

"Carly, look at me."

She forced herself to look into his eyes. His look was kind; he probably sympathized with her in her embarrassment. That's the kind of good friend he was. She hoped she hadn't ruined a great friendship at a time when she really needed friends.

"It's not you. You're a beautiful, desirable woman. But not for me."

Of course not, Carly thought. *I'm not in his league. He's handsome in a winsome sort of way—a lot of women are attracted to that. A successful businessman in the music industry. He could probably have any woman...*

"Carly, I'm gay."

Later that evening, Carly wasn't surprised she hadn't suspected as much. After all, Jason didn't fit her perception of a gay man. He was anything but flamboyant. He dressed well, but was no fashion plate. He was certainly good-looking, but was no Greek god. He showed no interest in fashion or modern dance.

But after a talk that lasted well into the night, she realized how stereotypical her conception of gay men had been. Jason assured her that gays came in assorted sizes, shapes and colors, and had as much variety in interests and pursuits as anyone else. Her first question, once she got over the shock, was "How long have you known?"

"Probably since I was about five. Even when I was in kindergarten, I was more interested in the girls than the boys. I liked to talk to them—we seemed to have so much more in common, and I felt a lot more in tune with how they thought."

"But if you were interested in girls..."

"As friends. Think back to kindergarten—how the boys hated the girls. Boys don't start to get interested in girls until the hormones start kicking in."

"But when were you sure?"

"Well, I became pretty sure one day when I was twelve, sitting in my dentist's office, thumbing through a copy of *Sports Illustrated.* I saw a picture of the U.S. Olympic Swim Team, standing in line, dressed only in their Speedos. I couldn't turn the page. Of course, the clincher came when I saw Chad Everett in *The Wild Wild West.* That pretty much resolved any doubts I had."

Carly laughed. "But you dated women in college."

"Sure. I was in no way ready to come out."

"How about now? Do your parents know?"

"God knows I've wanted to tell them. But when I think of all the times I heard Dad's references to "fairies" and "fags" when I was a teenager, I know he wouldn't accept it very well. And Mom has never been able to keep a secret from him. Besides, even though being gay is a lot more accepted now, it's not exactly the kind of announcement that would make them want to throw a party. Where do you think Beth gets her latent judgmental side from? You know how straitlaced she can be sometimes."

"Jason, she's your sister, and she loves you. She'll always love you."

"I know that. And she'll know pretty soon—I'm determined to tell her. Not this trip, but maybe next time."

Carly looked at him skeptically. "It's not like we're living in the 1960s."

"I know. I should tell Beth. But it's just seemed easier somehow not to let people know, especially after I moved to California. I was able to start a whole new life there."

Carly had never known Jason to be a procrastinator, but then, this was a whole new situation. She was beginning to realize how much he had to deal with throughout his life.

"And what about you?" he asked. "Are you angry with me?"

"Angry? Why?"

"For keeping this a secret from you for so long." Carly reflected for just a moment on the damage caused by secrets, but also on their absolute ubiquity—everyone had secrets.

"How could I ever be angry with you? You've always been a great friend to me."

"Well, once you remove sex, men and women can get along."

Carly saw truth in that statement. One of the reasons she'd always considered Jason a friend—her only true male friend—was that their relationship was different. He'd never had an agenda, had never pressured her.

That was her last thought late that night as she slipped into a deep, dreamless sleep.

When she heard the sharp ringing she first reached for her alarm clock, but a quick glance at the time, 3:00 a.m., made her realize the sound was coming from her phone. A phone call in the middle of the night—never a good thing. Her hand shaking, Carly uttered a quick prayer before reaching for the receiver.

"Carly?" She could hear the fear in the male voice, but could not at first identify it. "Carly, you got to come to the hospital. It's Ma."

"Carl, is that you?"

"Yeah, but you gotta come now."

"What happened?"

"They don't know yet. It happened while she was sleeping. The doctor thinks it might be a stroke. She's at Holy Family, on Harlem Avenue. She's in intensive care."

"Oh my God. I'm on my way."

Carly tossed on the first pair of pants and sweater her hands encountered and shoved her feet into a pair of old sneakers while trying to determine her best course of action. Should she wake her children and take them to the hospital? Should she call Beth and ask her to come over to get the kids ready for school? Even though it was 3:00 a.m., she knew Beth would bundle Marc up and come right over to help if she called. Or maybe the kids shouldn't go to school at all.

Suddenly she knew exactly what to do.

She hurried past Tyler's partially opened door and gently opened Celia's tightly shut one. Sitting carefully on the bed, she gently shook her daughter's shoulder until Celia's eyes opened just a slit. "Mom?" Celia questioned, taking in at once the dark room and obviously knowing this wasn't a normal wake-up call.

"I'm sorry, but I have to wake you up right now. It's very early in the morning, but I need you to take care of your brother. Grandma's very sick—she's in the hospital. I need to go there right now."

"Is Grandma going to be okay?"

"I don't know."

"What do you want me to do? Should we go to school?"

"I'll call you from the hospital just as soon as I get some idea about what's going on. We'll decide from there. Get your brother up at his regular time and both of you get dressed, so if I decide you should go to school or come to the hospital, you'll both be ready. And please call Aunt Beth at about 7:00 and tell her what's happening."

"Okay, Mom. I'll take care of everything. You go to the hospital. Don't worry about us."

"Thank you, sweetie," Carly answered, quickly kissing her daughter on the cheek as she got up.

"Mom, I'll pray hard for Grandma."

"We'll both be doing that."

Carly raced up Interstate 88 to the Eisenhower Expressway which, though not stalled by the heavy traffic that would commence in just two hours, was still being traversed by more cars than she would have expected at 3:30 in the morning. By the time she parked haphazardly in the hospital's massive lot, her thoughts had turned into a mantra which, though it did not provide comfort, at least allowed her the presence of mind to function: *God, please let her be all right. God, please let her be all right.*

She dashed past the sleepy night clerk at the reception desk, pausing for just one moment at the statue of the Holy Family that dominated the lobby. *Jesus, Mary and Joseph,* she whispered, remembering a prayer from her childhood, *help our family in this our time of need.* She took the elevator to the intensive care unit, and stepping into its white, antiseptic waiting room, immediately saw her brother slumped in a chair, chin resting on hands folded as if in prayer. "Carl," she cried, "Ma isn't..." No, it couldn't be. Her mother couldn't be dead, without her only daughter getting a chance to say good-bye.

"She's still hanging on. They'll be getting her ready for surgery very soon," answered Carl. "But it don't look good. The doctor says it's an aneurysm in her brain, and they can operate on it, but it's very risky. They gotta do the operation right away."

"Oh God. Can I see her?"

"Yeah, probably, but for just a minute. Dad's in there with her. But you better kinda prepare yourself—they got her—there are tubes everywhere." His voice cracked; Carly saw a side of her brother she had never before seen. Embracing him, she held him close, feeling the heavy sobs he refused to release. "You might not even recognize her," he added, pulling away and wiping at tears that were just beginning to appear.

Carl led his sister to yet another reception desk. Here there was no sleepiness, no laxity. All staff were sharp and alert, insensible to the lateness of the hour. The cool, efficient nurse at the desk stopped them with the warning, "Your mother can have only one visitor at a time, and only for a couple of minutes. I'll send an aide to tell your father that you're here and ask him to come out of her room."

Moments felt like hours as Carly waited for her father, but finally he appeared, looking perhaps twenty years older than when she had last seen him a few days earlier. "Oh, Dad," she cried, reaching up to hug him. But he roughly pushed her arms away.

"Go," he said. "Go see you mama. Go now."

No warning words could have prepared Carly for the horrendous change in her mother. She first saw the tubes and wires Carl had mentioned—IV, catheter, various wires ominously attached to beeping and flashing monitors. Most frightening of all was the mask connected to the respirator humming steadily behind her bed. What Carly could see of that beloved face was deadly ashen, every bit of vivid color drained away. Worst of all was her mother's complete stillness; Carly realized she had never before seen her mother so still and quiet, even while sleeping. Zosia always exuded such vibrance, such energy.

"Oh, Ma," she whispered. Only then did she notice the nurse standing off to the other side of the room, marking monitor readings on a clipboard. "Nurse, can she hear me?"

"We can't really know," answered the woman kindly. "We always act toward our comatose patients as though they could hear us. Say to her what you would say if you knew she could hear you."

Carly had only moments to whisper words of love and encouragement to her mother before the nurse again spoke. "I'm sorry, but you'll have to leave now. Your mother is about to get prepped for surgery." Carly kissed her mother's flaccid, powdery cheek one more time, squeezed her hand gently, and reluctantly left the room. She headed toward the door to the waiting room blinded by tears, praying she had not just spoken the last words she would ever say to her mother, and almost stumbled into Carl's arms when she found him there.

"She looks so bad. I'm so afraid. I don't think...I don't see how she can make it."

"Now stop it, Carly. Don't say that," Carl admonished. "Mom is strong, and she's got more will and determination than anyone I've ever known. If anyone can make it through this surgery she can."

Karol was sitting desolately in a chair across the room, pitifully alone, blankly staring into space. When Carly tried to break away from her brother's hold to comfort him, Carl tried to restrain her with, "No, wait..." but she was already rushing to her father. She sank into the adjacent chair and reached for his hand, but he pulled it away, glaring at her fiercely.

"Dad?" she questioned.

"Go away. Lemme be."

"But we have to help each other through this. I know you're upset." Carly learned through many years that her father's actions were often confusing, but this reaction mystified her.

"Upset? Is you fault mama been so upset. Up every night worried about you. Dat's why she so sick now."

"Dad!" Carl rushed to his sister's defense. "Don't talk to Carly like that. It's not true and it's not fair. This aneurysm—it could have happened at any time to Ma. It's probably something she was born with. The doctor said so."

But their father's rage could not be assuaged. "Damn doctors don't know everytink. Dey don't see how you been worryin' her so much. You run off wit' a man you don' even marry, den finally marry him and now you gettin' a divorce. Is shame and worry dat makin' my Zosia so sick."

"Please, you can't believe..." But one look at his face, contorted with rage, convinced her that he did believe her responsible for her mother's condition.

"Dad, stop it!" Carl was almost shouting. "Carly didn't cause this. Ma didn't have problems with Carly moving away—you did. You were the one who was so upset. You're just looking for someone to blame. And there is no blame. It just happened. These things sometimes just happen." Carl grasped Carly's elbow and led her across the room, depositing her firmly in a chair and filling a small paper cup with chilled water from the nearby cooler. "Here, drink this. Don't listen to Dad. He's just a bitter old man, looking for someone to blame for something he can't control. And he's so worried about Ma, which only makes him worse."

"Oh, Carl, you don't think...it was anything that I...?"

"No, of course not. It was nothing you did or didn't do. There's a chapel at the end of the hall. Why don't you go there and pray for Ma and for all of us. I'll talk to Dad later, when I can get through his bull-headedness and make him see reason."

"But I should talk to him now. Maybe I can make him see..."

"No, not now. He don't see nothin' right now but his own fear. Later. When...when we know more. Go to the chapel. I'll be there with you in a few minutes."

The chapel was cool, still, beautiful in its simplicity, designed to comfort the desolate souls whom circumstance had brought here. A contemporary statue of the Holy Family graced the altar, and Carly directed many of her prayers toward the peaceful marble countenance of the Blessed Mother, whose compassionate and knowing features reminded Carly of her own mother, battling for her life right now in some antiseptic operating room located only God knew where within this behemoth of a building.

Could Dad be right? Am I at fault? Could I have caused this? Carly's modern understanding of causal reaction and her knowledge of medicine, gleaned from any number of magazine articles she had read through the years, told her it could not be so. Illnesses happened, sometimes quite suddenly, and were not usually caused by the actions of others. Her father was wrong—and terribly unfair—to blame her. Her brother was right. He was just a bitter, frightened old man, looking for someone to blame.

But Carly also knew how dangerous stress was: she'd certainly been feeling its physical effects herself for the past few months—the headaches, the sleepless nights. Could her lifestyle have so stressed her mother that it caused something in her brain to snap?

But if it was stress that placed her mother into that terrible state, Carly reasoned that it surely couldn't be *her* fault alone. It was mostly *Steve's* fault. It was Steve who caused the break-up of her marriage, the problems with her children, even...even her affair with Roger. What else could she have been expected to do? She was only human. Roger was just a natural consequence of her loneliness. *But she was still married. Roger was a sin. This was her punishment.*

Oh God, no!

The thought was so powerful that Carly almost screamed it out. *This couldn't be a punishment—not because of Roger.* Carly had long ago banished from her mind the God of her youth—the vengeful God the nuns spoke of, frightful in His retribution. But in that peaceful chapel fear of that God returned, haunting her, edging out her belief in a loving God, a God of compassion, a God of forgiveness and hope. Carly willed her adult consciousness, her adult understanding of life and faith, to banish the useless childish recriminations that threatened to drown her.

Carl stopped in perhaps a half hour later to tell Carly that her mother had been taken down for surgery. Now all they could do was wait. Carl spent the next hours alternating between the chapel and the waiting room, attempting to comfort first his sister, then his father, who though united in their grief and physically separated by only a few dozen feet of glistening white floor tile, were emotionally facing a chasm that seemed to open further with each passing minute. During a time when Carl was with their father, Carly, lost in her fears and prayers, was startled by a sudden embrace.

"Carly, I'm so sorry." Beth held on even more tightly as she slid next to her into the pew.

"Thank God you're here. I was going to call. "Did Celia..."

"Yes, Celia called. The kids are at my house," answered Beth, "with Jason. His flight doesn't leave until tonight. I didn't think they could concentrate on school today. I hope I did the right thing."

"Yes, of course." Carly considered for just one moment how this was pure Beth—she always knew what to do. And Jason. Was it only hours ago that she had been with Jason? It felt like a week had passed since he'd revealed so much about himself—so much that his sister, here comforting her, did not know. Life certainly led a person down some pretty strange avenues. What...what time is it?" she asked.

"About 8:00."

"Oh God, Mom's been in surgery for...almost two hours. What am I going to do? What if she dies? I can't bear that."

"Your mother is strong—a real life force. If anyone can survive, she can. What exactly happened? Was it a stroke?"

"No, an aneurysm. In her brain." Carly could not help but notice the shadow that crossed Beth's eyes. Then Beth knew, too, that the situation was next to hopeless. Few people survived such a physical cataclysm, and those who did were often worse off than those who died. Carly surrendered herself completely to Beth's embrace and wept helplessly the tears she had been trying so hard to control. Beth tightened her embrace as if she were trying to hold a fragmented Carly together.

"The kids can stay with us as long as you need them to. And I called Liz—she's taking the first plane out. When she gets here she can wait with you here or spell me at home. I didn't expect her to come out, but she insisted."

"I don't know what I'd do without the two of you."

"So don't worry about the kids—you've got plenty of other things to worry about right now."

Zosia's surgery lasted almost three hours. Once she was returned to intensive care, family members were permitted to visit her room individually for just a few minutes each. Carly could not have borne more than a few minutes by her mother's side, looking down at her bruised and bloated face beneath a swath of white bandages. The words of encouragement and love she whispered in her mother's ear were more for herself than for her mother; Carly knew this mass of battered flesh could not comprehend anything she said.

The next two days took on a strange pattern of their own for Carly: up early to get the kids off to school, then back to the hospital to wait... and wait...and wait. Home late at night, to kiss her sleeping children after Beth had seen to Celia and Tyler's dinner. Then a long sleepless night filled with self-doubt and fear.

Her mother had not yet wakened, and the doctors could not tell Carly much about her condition, much less give any predictions about the future. Carly grew to love the chapel, her refuge when she needed a quiet place to think away from the bustle of the busy hospital.

It was during one of these quiet periods when she heard the chapel door open, as she had heard it many times that day when some petitioner had come in to kneel quietly in one of the vacant pews.

But Carly knew immediately this visitor was someone she knew: she sensed his presence even before she could see or hear him.

"Carly, I'm so sorry. I came as soon as I heard."

"Steve..." Carly hardly heard herself over the beating of her heart, but what emotion this rapid beating signified she could not determine. She noticed how much older he looked, how he had seemed to age several years in just several weeks' time. Recent events had surely affected him as well. "What are you...why are you here?" she asked.

"Please don't send me away. I just wanted to be here for you and for your mom. She's been almost like another mother to me."

"You have a lot of nerve coming here."

"I know you're angry. But just let me be here with you for a little while. Or tell me what I can do to help." Carly only then noticed the package he had placed on the pew beside her.

"Mom can't have flowers. Not in intensive care."

"I know. I brought them for you. Red roses. Your favorite. And some flowers for Celia too." Carly was drawn unexpectedly to the memory of the day of Celia's birth, in this very hospital. Steve brought red roses for Carly and tiny pink tea roses for his new daughter. It was a time of so much joy, so much hope. Her remembrance was cut short by Steve's question, "Are the kids okay?"

"They're with Beth."

"Good. Then they'll be fine. And your mom. What's her condition? Tell me what happened."

Talking with Steve about this new horror that had entered her life helped to relieve Carly's anguish. She realized this was probably only from longstanding habit; after all, they'd shared many years and two children. But Steve's concern and gentle words, the familiarity of having him close, calmed her and gave her some peace. After listening carefully to her recounting of the details of her mother's illness and hospital treatment, he asked, "Have you eaten anything today?"

Carly had to think. "No, but I couldn't. I don't think I could get anything down."

"You have to eat if only to keep up your strength. Let me take you out of the hospital for a while. We can grab something down the street."

"No, not now." But Carly was beginning to waver, to think she perhaps needed some time out of the hospital, when the chapel door opened again and suddenly she was enveloped in an energetic swirl of silk and musky perfume.

"Carly, I came as soon as I could," cried Liz. Seeming to suddenly notice Steve's presence, Liz shot a spiteful look in his direction. Then, turning away from him, she embraced Carly, determinedly planting herself in the pew on her other side, as far away from Steve as she could get. She continued to ignore Steve's presence altogether. "How is your mom?"

Steve rose and, taking Carly's hand, said gently, "I'll go now. Let me know if you need anything, anything at all. And please, let's get together in the next couple of days, when things settle down and your mom is on her way to recovery. We have to talk."

Steve bent down and hugged Carly clumsily, surely discomfited by the icy daggers from Liz's eyes boring into him. After he left, Liz asked Carly many questions about her mother's illness and treatment, the children, and her father's and brother's reactions. Carly shared with her all the anguish of the past days. Finally, hesitantly, Liz asked about Steve.

"I was surprised to see him myself," Carly answered. "I think he just came over to help. I know he became very fond of my mother over the years."

"Just be careful, Carly. Please. You're very vulnerable right now. Just concentrate on your mother and the kids. And on what *you* need."

"Of course," Carly answered, but her fear and worry had been joined by other emotions—confusion of course, but also, and completely incomprehensibly to her, a small sliver of relief.

Chapter Thirteen

April 1983

The Eagles, "Hotel California"

The next three days were interminable for Carly, who spent most of her time at the hospital monitoring her mother's progress. Although Zosia had not yet regained consciousness, the doctors assured Carly that her mother's coma was drug-induced and was intended to give her battered brain time to heal. They indicated that she was doing exceptionally well under the circumstances.

Carly had spoken just briefly to her father the few times they ran into each other going into or out of her mother's room in the intensive care ward. Both Beth and Liz, however, spent a great deal of time in the hospital with her, switching off between that and caring for Celia, Tyler and Beth's son Marc, and their support helped a great deal. She hadn't told either of them that she had several phone conversations with Steve and reluctantly agreed to have dinner with him that evening.

Steve picked her up at the hospital promptly at 8:00, driving her to their favorite Chinese restaurant in the new red sports car the children had mentioned but Carly had not yet seen. She never had any particular interest in cars, but thought briefly that a good name for that particular model might be the Mid-Life Crisis.

As she nibbled disinterestedly at her *lo mein,* she suspected why Steve had brought her to this restaurant. It was not only the memory of many pleasant evenings spent there. Of all the places in their area, it was the one which provided the most privacy. The booths were separated by mahogany paneling topped by red silk curtains, furthering the sense that each group of diners was the only one present.

Carly sensed Steve had a greater purpose in mind than providing her with sustenance, but he waited until after dinner, as they were served fresh tea and almond cookies, to make his appeal.

"Carly," he began, "I've been a fool. I've made the biggest mistake of my life."

She thought those lines sounded rehearsed. *But dammit, why is he still so attractive to me?* she thought, with concern bordering on despair. His golden good looks were only intensified by small laugh lines forming around his eyes and an occasional silver strand nestled amid the spun gold of his hair. Forcing herself back into this moment, she coldly asked, "What mistake would that be?"

"Leaving you and our kids."

"It's a little too late for apologies."

"Please don't say that. It's never too late, not if two people love each other the way we do." Steve reached for her hand.

"Stop it," Carly responded, pulling her hand away and grabbing a glass of ice water. "You've shown me precious little love the past couple of years."

"I know it's my fault. It's *all* my fault. I know I've been acting crazy. But there's a reason for that. It appears I really am crazy, or kind of crazy, anyway."

"What are you talking about?"

Steve explained that Doctor Irving, his psychiatrist, had diagnosed him with manic depression, a condition that could be the cause of his mood swings. Carly remembered Beth's disparaging name for Doctor Irving—Doctor Feelgood. Leave it to Steve to seek out the doctor most likely to toss him some simple explanation to excuse his unforgivable behavior. And wasn't manic depression the new *disease du jour*?

But then visions of their life together flashed into Carly's mind: that long, crazy ride to Albuquerque, the Christmas skis, his one-day war on chocolate, his unfathomable behavior in Hawaii. Their life together had been laced with the bizarre; early on she had ascribed that to his personality. Later in their marriage she thought his idiosyncrasies might have been caused by his unconventional childhood. Neglect. Abuse. Poverty. They all left marks on children that could haunt them through adulthood.

And truly, Steve's spontaneity, so different from her own deliberate manner of approaching life, was one of the things she had found so attractive in him. Life with Steve had been very stressful at times, but she could never say it was boring. From the moment he walked into that Morgan Street apartment she had been drawn to him with magnetic force: was he what she'd sought to free herself from her own stultifying conventionality?

"Well," she finally answered, "I imagine that's possible. I don't know a lot about it. I guess I would have to describe you as moody, but a psychological disorder?"

"It would explain a lot of things. Like how sometimes I feel like Superman—invulnerable, indomitable. And then other times, I feel incapable of doing anything, as though everything in my life is meaningless."

Carly was surprised by his openness; throughout their marriage she had wished he'd been more forthcoming with her. There was so much about him she did not know, even after many years of marriage. But she refused to offer him an easy way out. "Everyone has their ups and downs," she commented drily, although she had to admit that his mood swings had been well beyond the norm.

"I know that. But my moods don't seem to have anything to do with what's going on in my life. I could be high as a kite when the whole world's blowing up in my face and sick of it all when everything's going along fine."

Carly thought of her own bad moods: they always seemed to be caused by some present negativity in her life. She could always explain them. But she couldn't say that was true for Steve. Still, she wasn't ready to just accept his explanation. "Are you telling me that this is what caused your cheating?" Her eyes bored deeply into his.

"Well, no," he answered. "But you can't know what it's like to feel the way I've felt for most of my life. I know how wrong I've been, but when I'm in my most depressed state I'd do anything to feel better. Even stop being the husband I always wanted to be to you. I understand that now."

Carly was suspicious, but then, there had been Roger. Hadn't she done pretty much the same thing? Not to the same extent, of course, and there may have been a bit of revenge involved. But she had used an affair to help herself through a rough time. She regretted that now, but still, she had allowed it to happen.

And what about Jason? She'd been ready, eager, to fall into bed with him. If not for his astounding revelation, she was sure she'd be with him now—even though she was still a married woman. Was retaliation a valid excuse for ignoring the vow she'd made in that Las Vegas chapel?

"I understand a lot of other things now," Steve continued. "Like my problems with my own family. Doctor Irving says manic depression runs in families, and I'm almost certain my dad had it. That's probably what made my own childhood so terrible."

Suddenly alarmed at the frightening implications of Steve's last two sentences, Carly asked, "Does that mean that Celia or Tyler could have it?"

"There's a definite possibility. And if that's the case, won't they need two parents, a complete family, to help them through? The stress of our break-up—well, you never know what can trigger it."

Carly reflected that Steve was capable of exaggerating this aspect of the disease just to make his point. But Celia's mood swings seemed far beyond what was usual, even for a teen-aged girl. And Tyler's recent shoplifting and other misbehavior—maybe Steve was right to be concerned. "Is there a cure for this?" she asked.

"No, no cure."

"No medication? Nothing that can be done?"

"Well, yeah, there's medication. Lithium. A lot of people take that."

"Does Irving think it would help you?"

"Well, he said yes, but I disagree. In fact, I've stopped seeing him." This surprised Carly. Steve seemed entranced by this doctor, describing him as some kind of guru or magician. "I don't need to see him any more. Now that I know what my problem is I can handle it myself without medication. Hell, Carly, I don't want to be some kind of zombie. I want to be myself. If I was all drugged up I couldn't do my job—wouldn't have the creativity I need, or the judgment."

"But Steve, mental disorders are just like any other disease, aren't they? If you were a diabetic, you couldn't just handle it yourself. You'd have to be taking insulin."

"I know, but this is different. If this is a problem of the mind, I can handle it with my mind."

"I don't think that a person with a psychological disorder..."

"I'm sure I can do this. I've really been a lot better in the last couple of weeks." Carly was skeptical. What if his confidence was just the result of his being in Superman mood?

"But Carly," he continued, taking her hand across the table and holding it firmly, his eyes welling with tears. "I can't do it without you and the kids."

"I don't think I can..."

"We've got too much invested in our lives together to just let it go. We owe it to ourselves and to the kids to try once more to see if we can get back on track. You know it's what they want. It breaks my heart to see them so unhappy."

She knew a lot more about that than he did. She'd been the one dealing with most of their unhappiness, not him. Was he really thinking they could return to the way things were? "It's not like we could go back..."

"That's the best thing" he interrupted. "We don't have to go back. We need to start fresh, maybe even somewhere else. That would be the best thing for all of us. I'm independent enough financially that I can move my company anywhere—I was thinking maybe south, Georgia or South Carolina. There are plenty of opportunities there. Maybe somewhere on the ocean. You'd like that, wouldn't you?"

"I can't just..."

"Don't say no. Please, don't say no. Say you'll think about it. Say there's a chance."

"But there's so much going on. With Mom sick..."

"Of course you have to stay here for a while. I understand. I wouldn't expect you to leave your parents right now when they need you. But later, when...well, when things get resolved, one way or the other. At least tell me you'll think about it."

"I don't think I could ever trust you again. And I can't live with you without trusting you." Carly willed herself to resist the pleading look on his face. But he was her first love, her only love. She wasn't sure that would ever change.

"Honey, I'm not the first man who's ever cheated. You're not the first wife who's ever been cheated on. Other couples work it out. We can too. Please, tell me there's a chance. Even the slightest chance. Give me some hope."

"But I..."

"Please, give me the chance to spend the rest of my life making up to you for the past couple of years. That's all I want. That's all I'll ever want."

Carly felt her inner resources crumbling. It was so much easier to hate him from a distance.

"You're what?" Liz's gypsy eyes flashed. "Tell me again. I don't think I heard you right. You're planning to do *what*?" Her heavily ringed fingers trembled slightly as she lopsidedly placed on its saucer the delicate Mikasa cup, Silk Flowers pattern, with its subdued, impressionistic floral pattern of pinks and greens. For a moment, an almost tangible silence settled upon the three women seated in the dining area of Beth's commodious, tastefully decorated and expensively equipped kitchen. The ceiling fan, whirring silently, could not provide enough draft to lift the heavy tension that had settled on the room. China and silver glittered, catching no one's eye. Slices of almond streusel coffee cake and the crystal bowl of fresh fruit salad Beth had provided for Liz's farewell brunch lingered untouched. Finally Carly, absent-mindedly shredding her paper napkin, responded quietly, "We're just going to be seeing each other. He's not moving back in. We're starting all over, kind of, well, kind of like dating."

"Dating? You and Steve are *dating*?" Beth's incredulous look matched Liz's in quality, if not in intensity.

"Well, not dating exactly. That would be ridiculous. After all, we *are* still married. We'd just be going out together once in a while—to talk—or doing stuff with the kids. It's like we're starting over, trying to give ourselves another chance."

"Another chance?" Liz's eyes radiated incredulity. "This is the man who cheated on you, probably for years."

"I know, Liz," Carly responded. "He's not perfect." She chose to ignore Liz's choking on a sip of coffee and Beth's eyes rolling upward, ever so slightly. "He's made mistakes. He knows that. I have too."

Beth cut in. "We all make mistakes, Carly. We're only human. But what mistakes have you made, compared with his? You can't possibly hold yourself responsible for his behavior."

"No, not for his behavior, but for mine. Why didn't I see what was going on? Why did I ignore so much? Why didn't I know how much trouble he was really in?"

"Trouble...what kind of trouble are you talking about?"

"He's sick."

"Oh my God! Not AIDS!" Liz was aghast.

"No, of course not AIDS."

"Why 'of course not'?" Beth asked. "Anybody who sleeps around and is careless about it could have AIDS. And that person would be jeopardizing everyone he's sleeping with."

"Steve does *not* have AIDS," Carly insisted. "But he has been sick for years." Carly told her friends about Dr. Irving's diagnosis of manic depression.

"Okay. But if he actually has manic depression, does that excuse his cheating on you?" Carly was taken aback by Beth's question, even though she had the same reaction when Steve first told her. But Beth's attitude was really beginning to annoy her. Was Beth interrogating her? It felt like it. She'd expect this kind of thing from Liz, but from Beth? Why were her friends reacting this way?

"No, he didn't say that," she responded icily. "But it was probably a contributing factor, a way for him to act out the frustration the disorder must have caused him. Anyway, now that his problem is out in the open, we can deal with it."

"It just sounds like more of Doctor Feelgood's psychobabble to me." Liz did nothing to hide her disgust.

"It's not psychobabble—we're talking about a very serious condition. I've been looking it up. Millions of Americans are manic depressive, and 15% of them wind up committing suicide. It's not something to be taken lightly."

"You don't think he's suicidal?" asked Beth, concerned. "Have you had any indication he's thinking about killing himself?"

"Not really. But the possibility is always there, and it's frightening."

"Maybe that would be the best solution altoge———-"

"Liz!" Carly and Beth cried in unison.

"Okay, I'm sorry. I was only thinking out loud. But it sounds like more of his manipulation to me," muttered Liz.

Carly smoldered. How could Liz say such a thing? She'd really gone too far this time.

"Maybe you could tell Steve that there are better drugs available today, not to mention psychotherapy and other kinds of behavior modification. The mother of one of Marc's friends is dealing with manic depression—I think she's taking Prozac—and she's also in a therapy group that meets once a week. It's helping her a lot." The soothing tone of Beth's voice was intended, Carly was certain, to gentle the troubled waters their conversation had dived into. But this effort was lost on Liz.

"This is all bullshit," she fairly thundered. "He just doesn't want to give up his highs—his manic stages. He's unwilling to do what it would take to really help himself—or you and the kids, for that matter."

"Steve doesn't think he needs all that. He thinks he can handle it himself—mind over matter, more or less. He's smarter than you think." Carly couldn't believe she was defending Steve. After all, Beth and Liz still weren't saying anything she hadn't thought, and said, herself. But she didn't want to hear it from them. "And he does want to help himself—and me and the kids too," she continued. "They're the most important consideration."

"I can't listen to any more of this," Liz muttered, "I'm going upstairs to throw a couple more things in my suitcase. My flight's leaving in a couple of hours."

Carly was relieved to see Liz leave the room: things had gotten too tense. Beth seemed relieved as well. "Do you really think his coming back would be good for the kids? Don't you think this 'dating' thing will just confuse them?" she continued in the same gentle tones.

"Maybe at first, but if Steve and I could salvage our marriage, it would be wonderful for them." Carly appreciated the opportunity to share her many concerns with Beth alone. Liz had never been a mother; she couldn't possibly understand Carly's concerns about her children. "Tyler's been a basket case since Steve left. I swear I don't know what to do with him. A nine-year-old boy really needs his father. And Celia talks about going to live with Steve."

"Steve's in no position to take the kids—no judge would go for that. The kids may threaten—even Steve might talk about fighting for custody—but it won't come to that, Carly."

Beth's obviously loving concern led Carly toward expressing thoughts she'd been unsuccessfully trying to banish. "There have been times when Steve and I have been great together. And I miss him—I can't help it. I'm just so tired of being lonely. Can't you understand that?"

"I don't know exactly what your marriage was like, or what you're feeling right now. But I do know those last couple of years I spent with Marty were the loneliest in my life. Living in a shell of a marriage is about the worst thing in the world."

Beth's statement, though jolting, had the ring of truth for Carly. She had been terribly lonely the last couple of years. But was she *more* lonely without Steve, or *less?* She'd have to think about it later. "I know what you're talking about, Beth, but Steve is so sorry. I know he is. He says he'll do whatever it takes to make this work. And why should I throw away the last sixteen years of my life? Steve and I had a lot of good times. Don't we owe it to ourselves to give our marriage another chance?"

"Now that sounds like *Steve* talking," grumbled Liz, stepping back into the kitchen, forcefully depositing her overpacked suitcase on the floor. Beth winced at the sound.

"Yes, he did say that. But he's right."

"He says that now," Liz interjected. "But you don't know what's been going on in his life. Maybe his girlfriend—or both of them—or however the hell many he has—threw him over. Maybe that's why he wants to come back. Did you at least ask him about that?"

"Liz, you've always had a suspicious nature. And you've never liked Steve. Not from the very beginning."

"Christ, Carly, it's like we're back to square one. Haven't we had this conversation before? Don't be a fool. Give yourself a chance to see if there's another life for you out there."

Fool? Did Liz just call me a fool? It wasn't just the words; it was the tone that Carly so deeply resented. Who did Liz think she was? "That's easy for you to say. Another life..." she responded, looking at Liz with a raw anger never seen before by either of her friends. "You mean another man. But I'm not like you, Liz. I don't need to fall into bed with every other guy I meet, like some two-bit whore."

Liz's olive complexion turned uncharacteristically ashen. Beth often said somewhat the same thing to her years ago, when they were all in college and sexual liberty almost conferred a badge of honor. But this was different. Carly's words were meant to hurt, and the heavy silence in the room indicated that they had.

"Time for me to go," Liz finally said, reaching for her purse. "I have a plane to catch."

Beth tried to intervene. "Liz, your plane doesn't leave for hours. Carly didn't mean that the way it sounded, did you? Liz, don't leave. Please."

"Never mind. I'll be the one to leave." Carly's forceful push away from the table shook Beth's floral arrangement as though it had been caught in a sudden breeze. "I can see I don't belong here."

"No, both of you. Stay and we can work this out."

"You two work out whatever the hell you want. I should have known better than to expect any understanding or support from either of you. I have to go to the hospital. You may have forgotten that my mother is dying."

"Carly, that's not fair," Beth said in a tone that reflected hurt and undeserved pain. "We haven't forgotten for a moment about

Zosia—you were the one who started talking about Steve as soon as you came in. You've got so much on your mind right now—you're not thinking clearly. We only want to help. Don't leave like this. Liz, tell her to stay."

But it was too late. Carly was already halfway down the hall to the front door, leaving a shaken Liz and a sobbing Beth in her wake.

"She had a good night. Her vitals are all stabilizing. Doctor says she's coming along about as best as a person could after this kind of crisis." Carly had fled to the hospital after leaving Beth's home—this formidable structure seemed more of a refuge to her right now than any other place she could be. She scrutinized the nurse who was speaking to her, one she hadn't yet met in the Intensive Care unit. Unlike most of the ICU nurses, whose extreme youth (as it appeared to Carly) was balanced by their crisp professionalism, this was a nurse of the old school: on the far side of middle age, matronly, sporting a graying bun fastened on top of her head, with liquid brown eyes that expressed compassion and understanding. The only thing missing was a sparkling nurse's cap to perch atop her head.

"I don't know. She looks so pale, so much older. And she hasn't moved yet."

"She can't, dear. Doctor has induced a coma to give her brain a chance to heal. She won't move until he brings her out of it."

"Can she hear me if I speak to her?"

"That's hard to tell. But talk to her—it can't hurt. She's your mom. If nothing else, it'll help *you* to talk to her. I'll leave you two alone." The nurse made a quick but thorough assessment of the information displayed on the myriad machines surrounding Zosia and deftly tapped it into the device she carried attached to her belt. Carly considered for one moment the contradiction of this woman: so old-fashioned in appearance and demeanor, so modern professionally.

Once alone with her mother, Carly studied the strange machines that beeped or thumped, their displays showing various patterns of lines and numbers in green or red. Each machine held a cord or tube attached to Zosia's body in some way, many of them disappearing into the folds of soft white bedding that covered her still form. Carly inspected the oxygen tubes gently balanced on her nostrils and a wire that led to a black clothespin-like contrivance attached to her finger—*this must be for her pulse.* But finally, Carly's eyes rested on her mother's face, her features still, peaceful, and as beautiful as ever.

"Oh, Ma," Carly sighed, gently reaching for the one hand visible outside the bedding, careful to not disturb the monitor. "It's me. It's Carly. I hope you can hear me."

Carly spoke for a few minutes as if her mother were awake and listening, telling her about the children, about the beautiful spring day outside, about how all her friends and relatives were thinking of her, praying for her. Carly began to feel more at ease, as if she were speaking to her mother in the kitchen of the Berwyn home. She even told her about Steve, and about his proposal.

"Ma, I don't know what to do. I don't trust him. I can't ever trust him again. But I don't know how to handle everything that's been going on. I'm afraid. The house—I might lose the house. I already lost my job. I can't make enough money for the mortgage and everything—even with child support, I won't be able to do it. Dammit, I should have listened to you. I should have waited to get married, should have finished college. What was I thinking? I just never expected to be in this position.

"And the kids—how will they feel if they have to move, away from their friends, their school? Will they blame me? Will they even stay with me? It would kill me if they left, if they went with their dad. Beth says that won't happen—but she doesn't see Tyler's tragic little face every day. He misses his father. And I don't know what to do with a boy—how to raise a boy—by myself. It's not going to get easier as he gets older.

"Celia's even worse: she's become a mystery. I can't begin to figure out what's going on with her. One minute she's so grown-up, so helpful, as if she's the adult and I'm the child. The next minute she's surly and impossible to deal with, or what's even worse, quiet, almost morose, not herself at all. How can I help her?

"I just feel...so worthless...like everything I've done since Steve left has turned to shit. I can't do anything right. Yesterday one of the toilet pipes started leaking, and I didn't have the money for a plumber. But I figured—how hard can this be? I found a wrench and started tightening stuff. Ma, I made it worse. There was water all over the floor. You would have laughed—it was like something out of those old *I Love Lucy's* you used to watch over and over. I had to turn off the water line and call the plumber after all, so now the phone bill and electric bill won't get paid—again.

"I just can't do everything by myself. Other women manage this—lots of them, but I can't. How do they do it? And I've made some really big mistakes since Steve left—with men. I obviously don't know what I'm doing when it comes to them. I can't trust myself to make good choices there.

"But if Steve and I got back together—I don't know. I'm not sure I can live with him any more. You and Dad, you must have had problems in your life together, in your marriage. Dad's not the easiest person to live with—I ought to know. How did you manage? How did you do it for all these years?"

She looked lovingly at her mother's face—so beautiful, so peaceful—with what was almost envy, then caught herself. What was she thinking?

During her drive home, Carly began to feel less agitated, if not comforted. Despite her mother's inability to talk, Carly had felt her presence. Her visit to the hospital had helped. As she walked into the foyer she could hear the phone ringing, but decided to let the answering machine take it, a decision she'd been making quite often the last few weeks.

"Carly, are you home? Can you pick up? Please, Carly? It's Beth." Of course Carly knew who it was—that voice had been a big part of her life for seventeen years. *"Please, call me when you get home. We have to work this out. Liz is heart-broken—I hated to see her leave for the airport, she was just so shook up. Carly, we're sorry. We should have listened more and kept our big traps shut. We were just so surprised. Call me as soon as you get in. Or stop over. Come for dinner. Bring the kids, and I'll order a pizza. I want to know how your mom is. Let's talk."*

Carly battled the urge to pick up the phone. Realizing she wasn't ready to talk to Beth just yet and observing intermittent flashes on the machine, she pushed the button to hear the other messages, thinking how this simple task had been transformed from a mundane diversion to a fearful encounter:

"Please call our accounts receivable office at 1-800-487-3000 immediately. This is not a solicitation."

"Carly, it's Liz. I'm calling from O'Hare. My flight's leaving in just a few minutes. I'm so sorry I upset you. You know me—sensitivity is not my strong suit. I just get so mad at Steve for hurting you. But you know what's best for you—I'm behind you all the way, whatever you decide to do. Please don't be mad. Oh shit, they're announcing my flight. I have to go. Call me. Please."

"Mrs. Brennan, please speak to your son. Today I caught him deliberately destroying flowers in my rose bed. When I caught him he called me a...well, I don't want to say the word. We've been neighbors for so long. I'd hate to have to call the authorities on this."

"...Commonwealth Edison. It is important you call today. Our phone number is..."

Pressing the delete button, Carly collapsed into the overstuffed chair next to the phone, thinking about the million things she needed to do, knowing she would do none of them that day.

Chapter Fourteen

July 1983

Billy Joel, "You May Be Right"

"Hello. Hello. Who is this? Look, I wish you'd..."
Once again, Carly was speaking into dead air. This had been her second hang-up call this week, perhaps the tenth she had received in the last two months, usually on nights when she had been out with Steve.

The calls were always the same: always at night, after 10:00, sometimes as late as 1:00 a.m. Carly's Caller ID told her that each call had been made from one of several pay phones in northwest Chicago. The caller never spoke.

Carly had phoned the local police department, who sent over a pleasant enough young man with a blonde crew cut that made him look approximately old enough to be a junior in high school. He interviewed her briefly but told her there was nothing much he could do. The calls couldn't be traced to one phone number, and after all, no threats had been made. It could be kids—perhaps friends of her son or daughter—who were just playing pranks. There had been a lot of that in the neighborhood recently. Or it could be legitimate wrong number calls; nowadays, with the lapse in civility among strangers, people who called the wrong number often hung up rather than apologizing to the person they had disturbed. He suggested Carly keep a journal of the calls—when they occurred, what she had been doing that day—which is how she determined the correlation between "call nights" and "date nights."

"Date nights." Carly laughed. She remembered how much she had anticipated dates as a high school student: the time she spent trying on numerous outfits, various hairstyles, make-up looks from the subdued to the truly dramatic. But it wasn't like that with her nights out with Steve. Of course, it probably shouldn't have been the same; after all, this situation was different. She and Steve were not living together, but they were still married. And they still shared two children. He had kept his apartment on Lake Shore Drive: "Until things get normalized between us," he said. Carly did not challenge his assertion that he'd started renting it after their separation; she had absolutely no intention of telling him about her earlier foray into his lair with Beth and Liz.

But she missed that sense of heightened anticipation date nights once had. Not that there wasn't a great deal of raw emotion the first time she and Steve had "gone out" in June. She was a bundle of jangled nerves, spilling a glass of wine in the restaurant, tripping over her words in the simplest conversation. They planned the evening to give themselves the opportunity to talk things over, but there didn't seem to be much to say. Too many topics were *verboten*; neither she nor Steve wanted to risk a flare-up in a public place. Now their date-night conversations were mostly concerned with filler topics: references to current items of interest in the news, chat about neighbors and mutual acquaintances.

They resumed a sexual relationship their third night "out," when Carly had invited Steve in for a drink after a particularly promising evening at a Thai restaurant. The drink had turned to several, and before she knew it, Carly was overcome with desire for this man who had been central to her life for so long. But the sex was awkward and unfulfilling—curiously flat. Several subsequent attempts proved no more gratifying to Carly.

Their afternoons out with their children, to the zoo, to museums, to the beach, to the forest preserve, to movies, were no better. Of course, the kids were getting older: Tyler had turned ten over the summer, and Celia would be thirteen this month, both beyond the age of desire for parental attention and time. Often they made it very clear that they would much rather be doing something different. Tyler usually wanted to play video games with Marc, and Celia preferred spending the day at the mall with her friends. Steve seemed to resent this, which seemed unreasonable. He'd missed out on so many opportunities to be with his children when they were younger and would have loved to spend time with him. Nevertheless, she and Steve scheduled another family outing for this Sunday afternoon, back to Brookfield Zoo. Perhaps this time things would be better.

At least the financial pressure had let up. Steve was once again a full contributor toward the family expenses—thank God she didn't have to worry about dunning calls any more. And she found another part-time job in the older section of town, at a small shop that sold musical instruments. The job didn't pay much, but Carly enjoyed dealing with the offbeat but friendly clientele, and during slack times her boss never objected when she removed a guitar from the display and tried to strum a few chords.

The brightest part of Carly's life was her mother's partial recovery. To the amazement of both her family and her doctors, Zosia, once brought out of her coma, not only survived but made great gains toward normalcy. She was still mostly bed-ridden, but had been home for over a month. Karol arranged nursing care during the day, and Carl and Carly worked out a schedule to let their father keep up with the restaurant several evenings during the week and to get their mother to her frequent physical therapy sessions.

Once the giddy excitement over her mother's survival passed, Carly became more realistic about her chances for a full recovery. Often Zosia's mind seemed lost in the past, and other days she was resistant to any of Carly's attempts at communication. But Carly was heartened by the occasional day when her mother was both responsive and lucid. Having her back under any terms was a blessing.

Another bright element of Carly's life, to her amazement, came from a completely unexpected source. In May she received a flyer from the local community college and, almost as a lark, had signed up for two summer courses: 20th Century British Literature and Music and Culture. She faced her first evening class with trepidation—had, in fact, almost turned the car around and gone back home—worried she would stick out and not be able to compete with a bunch of fresh-faced kids who were only a few years older than her own children.

But surprisingly, about half the class was composed of older students—*non-trads*, her music professor called them—who were returning to school for a variety of reasons. Two or three of her classmates were even older than she was, and one classmate, Esther, was a lively seventy-something whose contributions to class discussion were always pertinent and useful, and often hilarious. When she and Esther stopped for "coffee and" after class to marvel at what they learned about how music had affected culture over time, Carly thoroughly enjoyed their discussion. The whole college experience was completely different from her ill-fated attempt at eighteen, and Carly often wondered whether this was because college had changed or because she had.

With all this activity in her life—work, school, the kids, Steve— it was no wonder she had little or no time to spend with Beth and Liz. She reopened contact with them just a few weeks after their blow-up—it was impossible to think of dropping friendships of so many years. But the relationship wasn't the same. She now felt uncomfortable discussing Steve with Beth, and she had really never felt comfortable discussing him with Liz. It was probably better just to let her relationships with her best friends seek their own courses for a while.

One thing was certain: Carly's plans for getting to bed early this evening were abandoned. The late-night phone calls disturbed her so much that, if she attempted to go to sleep, she would only spend futile hours tossing and turning. And there was always the chance she would get a second hang-up call—that had happened twice already.

It made more sense to read her assignment for tomorrow's lit class—the last half of Virginia Woolf's *To the Lighthouse*, and to try to catch an hour or so of sleep in the morning after she sent the kids off to school. She'd need that sleep: tomorrow would be another busy day, with a couple of hours at work, two late afternoon classes, a trip to the grocery, and then a shift with her mother in the evening. *Ah, Virginia,* she mused, taking up the novel, *what are you trying to tell me in this strange, strange book?*

Taking up the book where she had left off, she found that Virginia had, indeed, something to say to her: "...it is useless in such confusion to ask the night those questions as to what, and why, and wherefore, which tempt the sleeper from his bed to seek an answer." *So,* thought Carly, *Virginia Woolf was an insomniac too, and also a seeker of answers.* She hoped, based on the biography she had been given by her literature teacher, that she would find more acceptable answers than this tragic author, a suicide, had found.

Oh, look at him! He's doing it again." Tyler pointed at a scruffy, yellowish polar bear executing a passable swan dive into the bear pool. The bear swam out just a few feet, then returned, pulling himself onto the rock ledge with more grace than one would expect from such a lumbering mass of flesh and fur. In just moments, the bear was readying himself for another dive.

"So, we've watched him do this, what, twenty times already? Don't you ever get bored, Peabrain?"

"Celia, don't call your brother names." Carly felt as though she had said those same words two hundred times that day. She thought she might as well make a recording, to save herself aggravation. "Did you know," she tried gamely, "that even though they look cute, polar bears are among the most dangerous animals in the world?"

"Yeah, Mom, I think you told us that the last time we were here. Or maybe it was the time before? Can't we just go to the souvenir shop? I'm melting out here."

Carly, too, felt as though she were melting. Today the temperature hovered in the low 90s and the humidity was stultifying. Brookfield Zoo, with its wide expanses of open spaces, its gorgeous formal gardens and its innovative animal habitats (so much more pleasant for the animals, Carly hoped, than those sad cages of years ago) was usually an oasis for Chicagoans trying to escape the heat. But today, without even a whisper of wind, the park felt more like a swamp. Carly, despite what she knew about the temperament of polar bears, would have liked to jump into the pool with them.

"Time for some souvenirs, Punkin'?" Steve asked, embracing his daughter and pulling her close, either oblivious to or heedless of her peevish resistance. "I bet you want some of those cute stuffed animals for your bed." *Typical,* Carly thought, *he hasn't noticed that she packed away all those stuffed animals years ago. Or maybe he'd just rather not see all the posters of popular rappers that took their place.*

"It's too hot," Celia whined, pushing herself away. "I just want to go somewhere where it's air conditioned."

"No!" Tyler was insistent. "I wanna stay here. I like the bears. I wanna watch the bears." Was it Carly's imagination, or was Tyler regressing? He seemed so childish these days. Yesterday he had surprised her with a full-fledged tantrum, the type he had outgrown when he was three.

"I know. Let's get some ice cream. Where's that cart with the fudge bars?" Steve offered.

"Steve, they've already had ice cream. And hot dogs, and cotton candy, and French fries. Nobody's going to want dinner." Carly wondered if her voice had always sounded so shrill, so nagging.

"Can't we just leave? I told Jennifer I might meet her at the mall later. Please?"

But Celia's pleas were drowned by Tyler's chant, "Fudge bars, fudge bars, fudge bars."

"I'll tell you what," suggested Steve in his most persuasive sales voice. "Here's the plan. Celia and Tyler, you go back toward the lions. That's where we saw the ice cream cart. Then a quick stop to the souvenir shop, then home. How does that sound?"

"I wanna see the porpoise show!" Tyler practically screamed.

"We saw that *last* time. How many times do you want to see a stupid fish jump?" Celia bristled frustration. Carly almost mentioned that a porpoise was a mammal, not a fish, but wisely decided to withhold that information for the moment.

"Just get the ice cream, okay?" Steve handed his daughter a five dollar bill. "Celia, sweetheart, humor your brother a little. He's younger than you." Steve should have known better. Celia had figured out a response to that old parental standby years ago—that Tyler would *always* be younger than her—but today she seemed to decide it wasn't worth the effort to argue. She resignedly turned her back on her parents and started walking toward the lions' den. Tyler followed her, plaintively calling, "Wait up. Wait up."

Steve and Carly started following their children, but at a leisurely pace. "Why do you think they're so cranky?" Steve finally asked.

"I don't know. The weather. The humidity," Carly began. But then she caught herself. She had vowed during this trial reconciliation to be more open with Steve, to tell him exactly what she was thinking. She knew they didn't have a chance together if she continued in her old patterns of dissimulation and retreat. "Actually, I think this whole situation is kind of hard for them. They don't really know what's going on between us. Hell, Steve, *I* don't really know what's going on between us, or what all this is leading to."

"We're just going to have to take things as they come. I don't have a crystal ball either."

"It's like we're married, but we're not. We still don't see a lot of you. You were gone all week again, and I couldn't get in touch with you."

"I was out of town on a business trip. A very lucrative trip, I might mention. If this contract comes through, we'll be able to pay that outrageous bill your attorney sent last week."

"All right," Carly sighed. Steve had mentioned that bill three times this week—did he think she was at fault for having sought legal counsel? He was the one who left their marriage. What other choice did she have? "But the number for the hotel you gave me—you weren't there."

"I told you there was a screw-up with the reservation. I know I should have called, but I was at one meeting after another—it just slipped my mind. I can't be checking in with you all the time and do my job. Christ, you make me feel like I'm on a leash."

"Things are different now."

"Yes, I know. You don't have to tell me that. But things aren't ever going to get better between us until you lighten up a little. I told you I'm sorry. I told you that a hundred times. Are you going to make me pay for my sins every day for the rest of my life?" One look at Carly's flashing eyes must have told Steve that he had gone too far. "Look, I didn't really mean that. But think about it. It took years for our marriage to fall apart. Putting it back together isn't going to happen overnight."

Carly walked quietly for a moment or two. Steve was right: the problems in their marriage weren't going to be resolved quickly. But Carly couldn't help wondering whether there was any real chance they would ever be resolved. It often seemed that they were right back to just before the Hawaii trip; nothing had changed. "Steve," she finally responded. "I got another one of those calls last night. The hang-up calls."

"Not again. Did you call the police?"

"No, I don't think that's doing any good."

"It's probably just some kids fooling around."

"I don't think so. It's been happening for weeks. And I'm almost certain it's the same person. Are you sure you don't know who's making the calls?"

"Honey, I swear. I haven't got a clue. Don't you think I'd tell you if I knew who was doing it? Don't you think I'd stop it? Look—here come the kids. They've got their ice cream. Try to smile, would you? You look like you've just lost your best friend. Maybe that's why they're so cranky lately—you're just not yourself. Hey, I bet I know what it is. Isn't it about that time of the month?"

Carly's withering look was lost on Steve as he grabbed Celia at the waist, swiping a lick at the Fudge Bar she unsuccessfully tried to hold away from him.

"How's Ma been today?" Carly asked hopefully, kissing her father's cheek as she entered the living room. Two months after the doctor had released her mother from the hospital, Karol had called his daughter to ask her to handle some of the paper work, acting as though nothing unpleasant had occurred between them. This was characteristic, and despite the lingering pain at her father's accusations, now slowly morphing into simmering resentment, Carly had resumed her role in the family without ever again mentioning their argument.

"Is good. She been askin' about you all day."

"She eating?"

"Yeah. All dat soup you bring. How's da kids?"

"Good. Not so thrilled about being back to school. They'll be over to see you and Ma this weekend."

"Good. And you husband?"

"He's okay, Dad. Anyway, I guess he is. He's traveling again this week."

"Is good. You doin' de right ting. Is better you not be alone—better for you and you kids. Between a husband and wife—sometimes dey fight. Dat jus' how it is."

Karol had supported Steve's moving back into their home wholeheartedly. Now he acted almost as though the previous nine months never happened. "You mama sleepin' right now. I gotta go to de restaurant. I see you later tonight," he said.

Carly locked the door after he left, then watched him through the front room bay window as he walked toward the restaurant. As she brushed against the gold brocaded draperies, a cloud of dust motes told her it was time to pull out her mother's old Kirby and vacuum this room. Ma would surely be horrified to see her immaculate housekeeping so summarily abandoned. The house plants needed a watering as well.

As she began these chores, she considered that her father wasn't the only one who seemed to be acting as though the previous nine months had not happened. Steve was back, but she was disheartened at the thought that nothing had really been resolved between them.

She wished she had the sense to demand they enter a marital counseling program before allowing him back into their home; now she'd lost any leverage she might have had. He argued that he was far too busy at work to commit to any sort of regularly scheduled meetings and used his frequent business trips and late nights out with clients to verify that. But did those excuses actually verify anything? Knowing how easily he deceived her, she was torn between wanting to believe him and fearing that she'd be a fool to do so.

Once the kids had gone back to school she was able to pick up a few extra hours at work. She liked the diversion, but between that and the hours spent with her mother, continuing with classes at the community college was out of the question. She really missed the stimulation—had joined Esther for one more "coffee and," but it wasn't the same. Esther was all caught up in her latest class—sociology—and this made Carly feel only more left out.

Limbo. Had she entered it again? This time, of her own volition? She'd put her life on hold, but for what? To save her marriage? For the sake of her children? Or was it because she realized she couldn't make it on her own? In many ways, she'd taken the easy way out. Her financial worries were over. She wasn't getting calls from neighbors complaining about Tyler's behavior. She didn't need to worry about dating—she'd certainly had no success with that during the time she and Steve were separated!

She decided to peek in on her mother, who was now lodged in what had been Carly's room when she was a child, the only bedroom on the first floor of the house. It had long ago been converted into a den, but now it resembled a hospital room, with a mechanical bed, a counter full of various medications, and an oxygen tank standing nearby if needed. As she entered, Carly gently straightened the soft flannel sheet that had become tangled around her mother's feet.

"Carly?"

"Oh, Ma. I'm sorry I wakened you." Carly bent to kiss her mother's pale, tissue-soft cheek.

"No. Is time I get up. I been doing nothin' but sleepin' all day." Zosia's smile warmed Carly's heart.

"Can I get you something? Are you hungry?"

"No, just sit. You do too much. How's Celia and Tyler?"

"Good, Ma. Not real thrilled to be back in school. Do you want me to read to you?" Carly picked up the novel she had begun reading to her mother earlier in the week. During her long evening watches, she started reading out loud, more for the companionship of her own voice than for any other reason. One day her mother, who had been fading in and out of full consciousness for several days, pointedly asked what happened to one of the characters in the novel.

From that time Carly had chosen books that appealed to her mother's taste—usually romances with incredibly pure heroines and preposterously rakish, though always handsomely rugged, heroes. This particular one featured a world-weary pirate who was in the process of falling madly in love with the young noblewoman he had kidnapped. "Do you want to find out what's going to happen next between the beautiful Lady Katherine and the pirate Reginald LaPierre?"

"Maybe not tonight. You look so tired."

"No, I'm all right."

"Everything okay at home?"

"Sure, Ma. Everything's okay." How characteristic this was of her mother. Here she'd been feeling sorry for herself for being in limbo, while her mom, who'd been through hell the past few months, had concerns only for her daughter. Zosia was such a great role model; Carly vowed to become more like her.

Carly had been in bed for over an hour when the phone rang. In her exhaustion, she tried to ignore it, to let the machine pick it up, knowing her late night caller wouldn't leave a message. Then she thought of her parents. What if it were her dad? Could something have happened?

Just before the fourth ring, her hand reached out, almost of its own volition. "Hello? Hello? Who is this?" Again she heard nothing but dead silence.

But the caller did not hang up. This was a different response. Carly tried again. "Hello? Who are you? Why do you keep calling me?" she asked softly into the speaker. "What do you want?" Finally, she heard a sigh. "Look, you want to tell me something, don't you? That's why you keep calling. Tell me what it is."

"Your husband..." The voice was young, tentative, breathy. It sounded as if the caller had been crying.

"Yes?"

"Your husband is an asshole."

Carly felt strangely relieved. Finally, this person had connected, had given her a message. She answered steadily, "No one knows that more than I do, whoever you are. But why are *you* saying that?"

"Because he's cheating on me!"

Carly heard the phone click. Strangely, for a few long moments she felt no reaction at all. Then she became surprised by her own laughter. *Pity you hung up, poor soul, whoever you are,* she thought, *before I got a chance to thank you.* What kind of idiot would make such a call—Steve certainly knew how to pick them! But very soon her laughter stopped. *I knew it*, she thought miserably. *I knew this damn reconciliation wasn't going to work.*

"What do you mean, evidence? If anything, it's evidence that what I'm telling you is the truth!" Two hours after the phone call, Steve stood amid assorted boxes, bags and motley pieces of luggage, items spilling out attesting to the speed and fury with which they had been packed. Here a zipper snagged half-closed on a pair of navy blue Jockey shorts; there a travel alarm perched atop a terry cloth bathrobe stuffed into a dark green Field's shopping bag.

"Do you think I'm crazy? Or just stupid?" Carly looked incredulous. She thought she had cornered a rat, only to find that this particular rodent wasn't about to give up the search for a way out.

"I told her it was over weeks before I moved back home. She just isn't taking it well. She'd do anything she could to break us up—that's what these calls are all about."

"The calls that you denied. You swore you didn't know who was calling." Carly punctuated her words with a small kick to an old gray suitcase lying innocently on its side at her feet. "And I believed you, you bastard!"

"I didn't know it was her. I realized she was a little unbalanced..."

"She'd have to be—to have anything to do with you!"

"...but I never imagined she'd call here. I didn't know it was her. I swear!"

"Yeah, that means a lot to me—your oath. I can really trust that."

"I know I'm asking a lot, that you have no reason to believe me. It's just so ironic: now, when I'm trying to make things right, everything's blowing up in my face. You trusted me before when I was lying to you, and now, when I'm telling the truth..."

"Do you even know what truth is?" But Carly was crying now, deep painful sobs that convulsed her body and robbed her of the ability to speak. "I...I don't...I can't..."

Steve took three tentative steps toward her, gently touching her shoulder, but backed off quickly as she instinctively flinched and jerked away from him. "Carly, I'm taking these bags into the guest room. Okay? I can stay there until we work this out. You don't really want to throw me out—not now, do you? Not after all we've been through, all we've meant to each other?" Carly could not respond through her tears.

Faced with no response from her, he continued. "Okay. I'll unpack now. Things will work out, you'll see. It'll be all right." Lifting the box closest to him, he turned away from her and headed toward the hall.

Chapter Fifteen

September 1983

Led Zeppelin, "Kashmir"

"Ah, poor Lady Katherine."

"Oh, I don't know, Ma. I think she's beginning to enjoy her adventure. And Reginald is a lot more interesting than that boring Lord Baldwin she was engaged to."

Carly hoped her voice sounded normal; it had already been a very difficult day. She'd tossed in bed for hours, then managed perhaps only an hour of sleep. Fortunately, Steve was gone before she wakened. She muttered a prayer of thanks upon seeing that—she had no desire to speak to him. Once she got the kids off to school, she fled to her parents' home, seeking refuge in time spent with her mother. She needed respite from the turbulence that was overtaking her mind and the weariness that was overtaking her body.

"But he is bad man."

"Reginald?" Her mother's involvement in these romances, her interest in their characters, was a source of astonishment to her daughter. Carly had never seen her mother read a book—Zosia was always too busy with the restaurant, her family, the church and her home. And of course, the English language presented a barrier. Now she acted as though these entirely predictable stock characters (a phrase Carly had recently picked up in literature class) were real people: acquaintances perhaps, or neighbors. "He's not so bad, Ma. He's a pirate. He's not supposed to be a saint. And he's so handsome."

"Handsome, yes. But bad."

"Well, yeah, but pirating is his business. We have to look at his life in its context." *Whoops,* thought Carly, *something else from literature class.* She'd have to stop doing this—she was visiting her mother, not conducting a lecture.

"Not the pirate job," clarified Zosia, "all the woman."

"Well, Ma," Carly laughed, "he's supposed to be a ladies man. Don't you think he'll change once he and Lady Katherine get together? Become faithful?"

"Change? No. Men. They never change."

"Oh sure, Ma, people change all the time."

"No, not men. Not when they always running after woman. You Papa never change."

The clank of the old air conditioner, hastily brought into the room to provide comfort during this uncharacteristically hot autumn, was the only sound Carly heard as she scrutinized her mother's face. Zosia's countenance seemed composed, even serene, but Carly noticed her right hand picking nervously at the embroidered decoration on the collar of her robe. Her mother seemed more lucid today than she had been over the past week, but she could not be saying what her words seemed to indicate. Carly considered that perhaps in her mother's still often bewildered mind, she was confusing her father with Reginald.

"You mean Reginald? Reginald's running after women."

"Yes, yes, Reginald. And you Papa too. Always running after woman."

Carly felt soldered to her chair, her mind spinning. She was unable to process what her mother was saying.

"Yes. With *Pani* Poniatowski, for many years. And *Pani* Tomczak." These were respectable women of her parents' social group, women who frequented the restaurant and attended St. Casimir's Church. "And young girls—waitresses. You remember Regina?"

"Regina?"

"You was young, grade school."

"The pretty one? The one who had to leave when she got pregnant?" Carly vaguely remembered her mother having used that unfortunate young woman as an object lesson about what happened to girls who engaged in sex before marriage."

"Yes. Regina. Carlotta's mama."

"Carlotta! Carlotta from the restaurant?" Zosia only nodded. Carlotta! That inept, lazy, sloppy waitress that her father refused to fire. Carlotta—Carlotta was her sister? How could this be? Why was she never told?

You Papa...so many woman." One heavy tear glistened on Zosia's tissue-soft cheek.

"But, Ma, you never told me. You never said anything in all these years."

"What is to tell? You tell Celia and Tyler everything go on between you and Steve? Is some things only husband and wife know. Is how things is."

That was true. She didn't discuss her marriage with Celia and Tyler. And there were things she'd never told Steve—and many things he'd never told her. Still...this was different. Her father unfaithful for many years. A half-sister. These revelations were mind-boggling. "What did you do when you found out? What did you say to him?"

"Nothing. What could I do? There was you...and you brother. And the restaurant. What could I do in this country—I hardly speak English then. I have no one here. There is nothing for me to do."

"Oh, Ma." Carly felt weak, light-headed. All those years of believing in the absolute sanctity of her parents' marriage—all a lie. And her mother's role for many years: to play the part of the loving wife to an unfaithful husband.

"But that's from before. I should maybe not even tell you now. It don't matter. You papa is not so bad man. Many men act like that. Many men are much worse. You papa and me get along good now. It don't matter."

But it did matter. Her father—a cheat! A half-sister she didn't know...and really didn't want to know. *Carlotta! He had the nerve to name his bastard daughter after himself! Just like his other children: Carl. Carly. Carlotta. No wonder he couldn't fire her!*

But soon the kinder side of Carly appeared. *I guess Carlotta has her reasons for being so surly. She must know who her father is—and she's got to be angry that he won't call her his own.*

Carly didn't quite know where to cast blame, until...

Her mother! Keeping all this a secret for so long! Hot anger filled Carly's heart, but only for moments. Could she really blame her mother? Zosia traded her happiness for the happiness of her children and devoted her heart and soul to making a secure life for her family in this new country. As an immigrant in a time when women had little recourse, she chose the course of sacrifice, not selfishness.

How could she do any less in her own situation, especially when she'd been incapable of succeeding in any aspect of her life once Steve had left?

She was tired of the late payment phone calls that made her feel incapable of sustaining herself financially. Tired of dealing with the myriad problems of two children whose lives had been turned upside down. The other relationships in her life had been likewise compromised, if not destroyed. Her father was hardly speaking to her, and she feared that Carl, though trying to be supportive, was beginning to lose faith in her capabilities. She wondered whether she'd ever be able to mend fences with Beth and Liz. And her forays into the dating scene had been ludicrously unsuccessful.

She was beginning to believe she was incapable of succeeding on her own. And hadn't she vowed to make her mother's life a model for her own? Other women had found ways to live with unfaithful husbands. She could, too. She whispered, almost to herself, "I'll try much harder with Steve. I'll try to make my marriage work."

"No, no. Not you." Zosia's voice, for the first time in months, resounded with close to its usual strength. "Do not do this."

"But Ma, you yourself..." Carly was stunned at the look of alarm on her mother's face.

"That was me. With you is different. This is different time, different place. You are American woman—smart, strong woman. You make a life for you'self. There is much you can do. Steve is not for you. He will never change. Do not stay with man who lies to you, who cheats on you. I was wrong to do that. You do the right thing, the smart thing. Promise me. Please!"

Carly looked at her mother with wonder, as if she were seeing her for the first time.

"Listen to you mama," Zosia continued with a small smile. "Now, I am getting so tired. Read to me more about this Lady Katherine and her pirate."

Chapter Sixteen

Several Years Later

Dr. Hook and the Medicine Show,
"On the Cover of the Rolling Stone"

An old man, wearing a toga and holding a staff, stands at the edge of a mountainous chasm. He peers at agile young men running a race. Behind these men he can see a background of a cream-colored stream that bisects a golden fountain. *"What is he thinking?"* wonders Carly as she slowly mounts the magnificently curved double staircase of Radio City Music Hall.

A quick skimming of her program informs her that this magnificent Art Deco mural, "The Fountain of Youth," is the work of one Ezra Winter. She wonders if the man in the toga is remembering the days when he was a young man. Had he found a magical fountain of youth? Did he wish he could join those young athletes in their race?

Carly reflects that over the past few years she has, in a sense, entered the stream of her own fountain of youth. She's experienced rebirth of a sort, and it has brought her to this place. *If it hadn't been for Jason...if it hadn't been for Jake...if, in a very strange way, it hadn't been for Steve,* she reflects.

If it hadn't been for Mom...I wouldn't be here now: attending the Grammys.

The day after her mother's revelation, Carly had returned to Mr. Kaszmarek's office to request that he reinstate her divorce proceedings.

"Very well, Mrs. Brennan. I'll start working on that today," he responded smoothly. "And then after the six month waiting period..."

"Six months! I've already served a six month sentence with this man. And then some." The anger in her voice surprised her.

"But Mrs. Brennan..."

"Please. There must be something you can do."

"I'll try, but..."

It had worked. Kaszmarek rewrote the paperwork to reflect a more recent separation. Steve had not objected, but then, she didn't give him the opportunity to do so.

Over time she came to realize that the only way she could extricate herself from Steve's emotional hold was to avoid seeing or even speaking to him. They shared too much history—history that was getting in the way of her path toward a better future. When he tried to call, she did not answer the phone. When he emailed, she deleted without opening. When he finally appeared at her door, she had only two words for him—"Restraining Order"—before slamming it. She left letters from him unopened.

Once their divorce was actually final, she and Steve had worked very hard to develop a relationship that was, if not friendly, at least non-combative. It wasn't easy, but they both realized it would be beneficial for their children to see them together at birthday parties, graduations, and other events. This was why she had found herself sitting in her living room with him once the other guests had left Tyler's grade school graduation party. She'd listened patiently to the insights Steve felt he'd gained from therapy —that his bipolarism, apparently the new name for manic depression—was finally under his control.

"That must make Meredith happy," she'd offered, with only a modicum of bitterness surfacing in her comment.

"Oh. Meredith. That didn't work out."

"Really?" Carly was surprised. She assumed they were still together. She reflected that not knowing very much about Steve's current life was one of the major benefits of living in California.

"She's not a very compassionate person," he explained. "Actually, being with her made me realize the treasure I lost when we separated."

Carly scrutinized the hang-dog look he was giving her. Years earlier, that look would have charmed her into embracing him, encouraging him, comforting him. But not this day.

He seemed to be waiting expectantly for a response. When none was forthcoming, he continued. "When I needed her support the most, she wasn't there for me. And it was just at the time that I found out what my real problem was."

Carly ignored the pause that signaled it was time for her to ask exactly what that problem was. Instead, she began stacking the paper plates and cups that had been left on her coffee table.

"I went back to my old therapist," he continued, "Dr. Irving. Do you remember him?"

Yes, Carly remembered him well: good old Dr. Feelgood. She answered Steve's question with a slight nod.

"Well, he finally found the true diagnosis."

Another pause. Carly remained silent.

"He determined that I have a serious sex addiction."

This time Carly responded, but not, perhaps, in any way that Steve had expected. It was hard to repress her laughter: the hang-dog look on his face, once so compelling, appeared purely manipulative to her. Looking at her watch she smiled and asked him what time he needed to check into the motel. "I think you'd better head out before you lose your reservation," she advised while gathering the plates and cups she'd been stacking. She headed toward the kitchen, not leaving it until she heard the slamming of the front door.

A sex addiction. That was rich. Feelgood had found another popular diagnosis to keep Steve paying his exorbitant fees. And was his newfound "sex addiction" the reason that Meredith hadn't "worked out"? It would serve Meredith right if she'd caught him cheating on *her.*

Although Carly accepted the fact that this diagnosis might be genuine for some people, perhaps even for Steve, she knew any treatment would be unsuccessful for him. Steve was never going to do anything to change; his ego would forever trick him into believing he was indomitable.

Radiant reds, oranges and golds adorn every surface of the immense foyer. Massive elongated cylindrical chandeliers provide a soft glow that emanates throughout the room. Carly stands among a crowd of people, all lavishly dressed, some recognizable from the covers of entertainment magazines. She can hardly wait to reach the Great Stage, literally and figuratively. It had been a long, steep climb in every way.

If it weren't for her mom...Carly and her mother had never again referred to their conversation of that fateful afternoon. But that conversation set Carly on a different course, had given her the strength to redirect her life. She began to realize that it was time to let go of any guilt she felt for the failure of her marriage. Liz always said it was useless to feel guilty about another's actions: "A person cheats and lies because he's a cheater and a liar," she insisted."We're not responsible for another's actions." Carly's realization that her mother, a woman of great wisdom and virtue, could not prevent her own husband from cheating, gave her a new perspective on how limited the likelihood was that she'd ever be able to change Steve's behavior.

Of course, her father had urged her to remain married. "For better or worse," he had thundered when she'd first told him. "You make you bed, you lay in it!" It was all she could do to resist yelling back—to berate him for his own lack of faithfulness to her mother. He, who had the audacity to further demean his wife by hiring his own bastard child, the worthless Carlotta, to work in the family restaurant. Who was he to give anyone advice? The only thing that restrained Carly from voicing her anger was the realization that doing so would break a promise she'd made to her mother.

But even her father, faced with his daughter's determination, came around in his own way. "So, you gonna be okay wit money?" he had finally asked, days later when she had come to do an errand for her mother. "You wanna work at de restaurant?" Carly did not want that, but she did request his assistance in helping her get through two years at the local community college: a loan to cover some expenses, as well as help with child care. Her parents were happy to keep an eye on Celia and Tyler while she attended classes, and spending more time with the grandchildren seemed to hasten her mother's slow recovery.

Things became more difficult when she decided to enroll in a new program at a small college in northern Michigan. Woodbridge College had been among the first to establish a bachelor's degree in Music Industry Management, which the college advertised as a blend of art and commerce. The program coordinator assured her that her accounting background, limited though it was, was a benefit, as was being a woman in a male-dominated business. Not only would she be a novelty, but she'd be able to offer a unique spin to an industry that was beginning to attract more females, not only as performers, but also as managers and staffers.

She spent weekdays at the university and long weekends at home, once again with the help of her parents who stayed with the children when she was in Michigan. By taking course overloads and attending classes during the summer, she received her bachelor's degree in only two years. She'd hated leaving Celia and Tyler every week but consoled herself with the realization that what she was doing, letting them see her as a person with goals and the ability to achieve those goals, was good for them.

The day Carly attended her college graduation affirmed this belief. The sight of her parents and children beaming at her and cheering when she received her degree convinced her that she had made the right decision. Celia needed a model of a woman who could take charge of her own life. Tyler needed some distance from the model Steve had provided of a disengaged parent whose outside interests always trumped the needs of his children. She was determined to give them both what they needed.

A tuxedoed usher takes her ticket and leads Carly toward the front of the auditorium. And she worried about being over-dressed! Looking around at the variety of ensembles, she feels very comfortable with what she's wearing. Her gold lamé sheath suits her, and the diamond-encrusted choker and ankle bracelet, lent to her by a generous client, add plenty of dazzle. She worries about the four-inch heels on her strappy sandals—tripping on her way up the stairs to the stage, should that be required, is a fear she knows other women in the audience must be sharing.

Moving to California was, perhaps, the most difficult challenge of all. Steve had objected, threatening legal action to keep their kids in Illinois. But in the end, he was too preoccupied pleasing his new girlfriend Rosemary, who certainly had no desire to help raise another woman's teen-agers, to follow through with his threat.

The last day she spent in Illinois with Liz and Beth was emblematic of the relationship they'd shared. Why had she ever doubted their love? Why had she wasted time being angry with them, when their words and actions really expressed only their concern for her? The day she finally steeled herself to call first Beth, then Liz, turned out to be one of the happiest of her life. They both welcomed her joyfully back into their lives. No recriminations. No "I told you so's."

Then, as always, they were there for her. "Where do we pack this?" Beth asked, holding up a quilted, down-filled jacket.

"I don't know," Carly answered. "Liz, you've been to southern California in the winter. Will it ever get cold enough for...?"

"Hell no. Just toss in some bikinis and some short shorts and you'll be fine. Stick it in the Goodwill box, Beth." Carly scanned her bedroom, her bed a jumble of clothing, shoes, and linens, the floor a mass of packing boxes of every imaginable size. She despaired of getting everything sorted away, and she had only a few more days in which to do it.

"Did you bury St. Joseph yet?" Liz asked. Carly shrugged. "You know, Carly, your house isn't going to sell until you do."

"Is this another one of those Catholic things? Or is it a Polish thing? Or both?" Beth asked.

"Definitely Catholic," responded Carly, "but more Italian, I think. Or maybe it's just Chicago craziness. I don't know who else does it."

"I never thought you were so superstitious, Liz," Beth accused.

"It's not superstition," Liz insisted. "Besides, it works all the time. If you want to sell your house, you need to bury a statue of St. Joseph upside down in your back yard. The house will sell within six weeks. I can give you the names of ten people I know who did it, and it worked every time." Beth's eyes rolled toward the ceiling. "You shouldn't be so skeptical, Beth. You can't argue with success."

"Carly, you don't believe in all this mumbo jumbo, do you?" Carly was intently scrutinizing a small, gold beaded evening bag and obviously was not about to answer her question, so Beth shot an exasperated look at Liz. "I swear, Liz, for a girl who hasn't set foot inside a church in twenty years, you sure have retained some strange ideas." She looked once again to Carly for support, but Carly was now studying a pale blue cotton sweater before finally dropping it into a box labeled "California."

"Carly, does your mother believe in this silly St. Joseph business?" Beth persisted.

"She said she didn't *really* believe in it."

"There!" laughed a triumphant Beth. "Even Carly's mom's doesn't believe in it, and she has a house full of religious statues!"

"Well...she also said that it couldn't hurt," added Carly.

"So there," retorted Liz. "Do you want me to pick up a St. Joseph from the religious supplies store before I head home, Carly?"

"You don't have to. He's already buried," Carly admitted to howls of laughter from Beth and a smug look of satisfaction from Liz. "And it wasn't easy getting through all the ice and snow and the rock solid ground. Not to mention buying the statue. What an embarrassment! When I asked the saleslady for a statue of St. Joseph, she wanted to know if it was for burying or for my shrine."

"You mean they have separate statues?" Beth's head tipped to one side, her eyebrows arching with incredulity. "What a hoot!"

"Don't listen to Beth, Carly—you did the right thing. Just wait and see. Your house will sell before you leave, and then who will be laughing last?"

"I hope you're right." Carly held up a tattered Hard Rock Café/Chicago tee shirt for only a moment before her friends unanimously decided "Garbage!" But they agreed immediately that, faded though it was, Carly's 1981 Rolling Stones *Tattoo You* tour shirt was a keeper, if only for sentimental reasons.

"I still can't believe you're actually selling your house and moving so far from home," Beth said. Carly could hear the pain in her best friend's voice; she felt much the same way. The thought of moving so far from Beth and Liz was heartbreaking.

Firmly biting her lower lip, Carly raised a spaghetti-strapped, blue checked sundress, peering at it intently. She was not ready to share in words, even with Beth and Liz, her own deep sense of loss at having to give up the home in which she had raised her children, a home that held so many happy memories. *Oh well,* she thought, *this home holds a lot of sad memories as well. The kids and I will just have to make new happy memories wherever we are.* Then, dropping the dress onto the California pile, she responded by giving Beth a hug that said everything she could not verbalize. Beth's returning hug, which became a tight circle of love and support once Liz joined in, told her that her friends understood.

"What about this leather jacket? California or Goodwill?" Carly asked, breaking away from their three-way embrace as she quickly brushed at her eyes.

"California," Liz answered. She, too, wiped away a tear. "You'll fit in with your rock and roll friends. That music: the last relic of your childhood." Liz, in keeping with the drama that always defined her, had become an avid fan of Italian opera some fifteen years earlier.

"All those rock and roll songs about sex, drugs and...well, rock and roll," Beth added, shaking her head in mild disapproval. Her music preference over the years had turned to easy listening.

"And social change, and relationships, and love, and just about everything you can think of," retorted Carly. "Admit it—it speaks to you, too—or it used to, before you two decided to get all grown-up and sophisticated."

"The important thing is that it keeps speaking to you. You do want to be a success in your new career," answered Beth.

Carly retreated to the closet to fill a box with shoes, spending a considerable amount of time speculating about what she should take. When she returned to the bedroom she beheld a reflection from many years earlier: Liz sitting on the bed peering into an open book, Beth reclining stomach-down on the bed, knees bent, legs lifting gently up and down, chin on one hand, the other hand slowly turning a page. Carly thought they looked like a picture out of a 1960s-era teen magazine, or was that just nostalgia kicking in?

"Great helpers you turned out to be," she chided. "With your help and fifty cents I could buy a cup of coffee."

"You need to update your cliché collection. Fifty cents? Have you been to Starbucks lately?" asked Liz. "Here. Quit bitchin' and take a look at some of these. I'll bet you haven't seen these pictures in almost twenty years. Can you believe our hair?" asked Liz.

Liz and Beth had unearthed an old photo album, one that contained pictures Liz had taken during a celebratory shopping trip to downtown Chicago just days after Beth's college graduation. Carly pointed to a shot taken by a friendly passerby. The three of them stood before the entrance to the Sears Tower—big hair, make-up to the hilt—mugging for the camera *a la* Farrah Fawcett. "God, what gorgeous dolls," she exclaimed. "We look like we're sitting on top of the world."

"Well, we were," responded Beth.

"And still are," laughed Liz. "Gorgeous, anyway."

"You know, I hardly know who that girl is." Carly pointed at her image square in the middle of the photo. "When I was in college I just thought that by now I'd be settled, know exactly what I wanted out of life. I figured I'd have all the answers. Sometimes I'm not even sure I have all the questions."

"This is coming from our all-time Trivial Pursuits champ? Then I guess there's no hope for the rest of us mere mortals," Liz sighed.

"I'm not talking about the simple questions and the simple answers, Liz."

"We know what you mean, Carly," Beth responded. "But I wouldn't feel too bad about it. Everything that's happened to you in the last couple of years...that would throw anyone for a loop."

"But that's the thing. I *don't* feel bad about it. I kind of feel that's the way things are supposed to be right now, at least for me. For the first time in my life I don't need to know all the answers." This insight, if that's what it was, had been one Carly had considered often in the past few months, sometimes with delight, sometimes with what bordered on panic. She missed the sense of surety she'd had in life; at the same time, she relished her new sense of freedom.

One other insight infused Carly with an even greater sense of freedom, although this was one she would never share with her friends. She was no longer that lost soul who had spent a drunken night singing "It's Over" with Roy Orbison. Instead, her current theme song was the Eagles' "Peaceful Easy Feeling." She lived that feeling, knowing that her feet were now firmly standing on the ground.

What had gotten her there was her new conviction that no adult owed anything to any other adult. Of course, she still believed parents owed their children a great deal: after all, they had brought these young, dependent humans into the world. But her greatest sense of relief and freedom had come the day she had overcome her anger at Steve, which was based on the belief that he had "owed" her fidelity. After all, she had reasoned, she had been a good wife, had done everything she could do to keep their marriage together.

But Steve, like herself, was an adult, who was free to make his own decisions. And so was she. Despite her desire to blame Steve entirely for their divorce, her actions during their marriage, their first separation, their attempted reconciliation, and their divorce, were her actions, her decisions. Steve was not to blame for them. And after all, everything she did was based on what she had wanted for herself.

She feared that others would see her thoughts as being bitter and cynical—but that was not the case at all. Overcoming her belief that Steve had owed her had freed her from the anger that had been destroying her: and not only her anger with Steve, but also her anger with her father and her best friends. It also gave her great joy in realizing that everything she would do for her friends and her family would be done out of love—not out of any sense of accommodation or accountability. Surely that was a positive thing in every aspect.

"Didn't you say something about ordering a pizza?" Liz's plea took Carly away from her reverie. Well, she supposed she owed Liz and Beth lunch—she had promised them that.

"That's your reward—once we're finished. Now what do you think about these jeans? Too faded, or is faded in these days?"

In the end, her house had sold three weeks after St. Joseph's burial. Carly realized Liz would never let them forget that. And Carly would never quit being grateful she had been able to salvage her friendship with Beth and Liz; frequent visits to Illinois and an open invitation to visit her in California at any time would keep the friendship strong.

Once Carly has been seated in her plush red seat, she realizes she's the first of her party to arrive. This gives her the opportunity to take in the grandeur of the Great Stage, which looks like the most spectacular sunset the world has ever known. Rays of orange punctuate golden panels that define its half-bowl construction, causing a brilliant, nearly pulsing, glow.

The hall begins to fill. Carly is caught up in the sound of excited chatter. Craning her neck she peers up to the third balcony, where Tyler, Celia and David are, or soon will be. Jason had been instrumental in getting them tickets—no easy task. But he knew how important it was to Carly to have her children present on this exceptional night.

Although it had been her biggest concern. moving her children to California proved to be less stressful than she'd feared. At their worst moments Celia begged to move in with her friend Ashley, and Tyler threatened to run away. But once they realized the inevitability of the move—or, as Tyler liked to quote from his favorite TV program— "Resistance is futile"—her children weren't entirely opposed to the idea. California did have an aura that appealed to both Celia who, only one year away from college, dreamed of a career in the movies, and Tyler, who as a beginning high school student, dreamed of surfing.

Carly hated to break the news of their move to her mother, who was still grieving the loss of her husband. Karol had passed away quite suddenly from a heart attack just two weeks after Carly's graduation from Woodbridge. Carly grieved too: she had come to see him as a man who, though flawed, had many good qualities. Chief among those were his devotion to his grandchildren and his generosity toward her once he had accepted her decision to divorce Steve.

She was relieved when her brother Carl had invited their mother to live with him and Danuta, a lovely Polish immigrant who got a job as a waitress at the restaurant, and who turned out to be the woman who would finally win his heart. They had a traditional Polish wedding followed by a reception that would have done Warsaw proud. Now Zosia was kept busy helping them raise their three children.

Carly could hardly believe she was soon to become a grandmother herself—this upcoming change in her life had come about much sooner than she would have expected. Celia lasted less than a year in college, deciding that a life with David was what she truly wanted. Carly tried to dissuade her, but then, she lacked leverage: hadn't she done the same thing?

Celia's pregnancy had soon followed. Most of the time Carly was successful at reminding herself that her daughter was an adult who needed to live her own life and make her own decisions, even if Carly herself believed Celia was making the wrong ones. Still, David seemed to be a nice enough young man. And Carly rejoiced in how excited they both were at becoming parents; that was a good sign.

And Tyler. Carly often wondered if it was that trip to Hawaii that had instilled in her son his love of the water and all it contained. In California, he spent too much of his high school years, she believed, surfing and snorkeling. She feared he'd become a beach bum. But there was little chance of that, now that he was entering a graduate program in marine biology at Stanford.

As show time draws near, Carly cranes her neck to search for Jason and Jake, but cannot find them in the crowd being shown to their seats. She can't stop marveling at the grandeur surrounding her. The hall's walls and ceiling, its carpeting and seats, are all the same vibrant red, the ceiling punctuated by long, slim panels of yellow lighting that furthers the illusion that she is in the center of a stunning sunset. Carly is quite certain she's never been in a more magnificent room.

But she's becoming worried. Jason is known for showing up late, but tonight? He's responsible for bringing Jake, the young man who might very well be the star of the evening's show. Still, without Jason, she would never be here. She owed him so much. But he owed her as well. Their partnership was equal in every way; neither would have found this magnitude of success without the other.

"Will you just think about it, Carly?"

"I can't! I can't just up and leave. Think of my kids! And Mom. She needs me here."

"Carly, I'm not asking you to move to the moon. There are planes, you know—California is only a couple of hours away. Besides, if you don't do anything with your education, what was the purpose of the last couple of years? I'm sure your mom would agree with me."

Jason had a point. She was happy with her job at Sound Decisions, was thrilled and grateful when the manager who replaced Roger had hired her as assistant manager right after graduation. Within a year, she was manager. The salary was decent—enough to pay the bills and have a little left over at the end of the month.

But Jason was right. There was much more opportunity in California, at the center of the music business. And managing a small music store wasn't exactly the career of her dreams, especially now that electronic downloading was threatening to start cutting deeply into music stores' profits. It was entirely possible that within a few years businesses like Sound Decisions would disappear.

But California was risky; Jason wasn't exactly what one would call a success story either, despite the façade he'd presented for so many years. He'd experienced tumultuous ups and downs through his whole time in the Southwest. Once he abandoned performing professionally, he had some success co-managing a band called Dino and da Boyz with Kevin, his partner in both business and life. They put away enough for a down payment on a lush mini-mansion in Beverly Hills, and their pool parties were becoming legendary.

They discovered very soon, however, that even a generous income couldn't support a cocaine habit. And Kevin's creative accounting methods, which Jason learned about only when two IRS agents paid them a visit, spelled the end to both their professional and personal partnerships.

What followed for Jason was a series of short-term stints with various bands. He finally found what, he hoped, might be a more stable position as the sound technician and background guitarist for a country band that played bars in Tucson and some of its surrounding towns. Country was not really his passion, but he faced greater problems with the group, chiefly their tendency to get embroiled in a bar fight every third gig or so.

One night as he knelt over the body of the band's drummer, listening to police sirens coming nearer, he realized he had enough. Once he was sure that Brad was not dead but just unconscious, he jumped into his beat-up Jeep and headed back toward California, determined to find some kind of work in the music business that didn't involve bar fights and the ever-present chance of having to spend a night in a local jail. It was on a holiday visit to his sister that he first got the idea of a business collaboration with Carly.

"Here's the deal," he'd begun. Carly thought he looked much more earnest than she had ever seen him look before. "There's a warehouse in El Segundo that would be a perfect place to start a backline company."

"El Segundo? Backline company?"

"El Segundo—small town south of LA—you'd love it. Backline company—a place that rents out equipment to bands."

"What kind of equipment?"

"Amplifiers. Microphones. Backup instruments. We'd also sell some of the smaller stuff—guitar strings, drum heads."

"But why would bands want to rent stuff? Don't they have their own?" Carly was mystified. She could sense the excitement in Jason's voice, but could not comprehend the need for such a business.

"This is for traveling bands—some of the smaller bands, but big ones too. A lot of them travel by plane these days—some of the smaller ones can't afford band buses, and the bigger bands don't have the time to waste traveling by bus. Sometimes they've got back-to-back gigs across the country, especially if they're really hot. So they rent. That's where we come in."

Carly was skeptical.

"There's also smaller business—local bands who can't afford a lot of equipment. That could be how we start—renting equipment for weddings, graduations, stuff like that. And eventually, maybe even a small recording studio. I'd like to get into managing, even if it's only in a small way."

"How *we* start? Wait a minute. I haven't committed to anything. Besides, is there any money in this business?"

"Yeah, if we do it right. I'd provide the technical background—you'd be the one who kept the business aspect going strong. And we could rent a warehouse for a steal."

What was Jason thinking? Did he really expect her to drop everything—her whole life—and just rush off to California to join him in what seemed a very risky venture? But his excitement was contagious enough to earn from her a promise to visit El Segundo for just a weekend after the first of the year.

That visit changed everything. When she embarked on the plane at O'Hare it was eight degrees and all of northern Illinois was digging itself out of a hundred-year blizzard; when she disembarked at El Segundo airport, she found herself surrounded by palm trees, tropical flowers, and a temperature of seventy-two degrees. Jason was at the airport to meet her: he insisted on taking her immediately to the warehouse.

"What do you think? Is it big enough?"

Carly thought it was cavernous. She couldn't imagine ever filling such a room with musical equipment. "And this would be your office," he added, showing her into a small room equipped with only a desk, a chair, and one ancient file cabinet. Everything had an industrial feel to it. This wasn't quite what she'd expected: no Hollywood glamor here. Still, she hadn't really known what to expect.

"I know it doesn't look like much, but it's wired for all the electronics we'd need and has all that great shelving in the back. And the loading dock is perfect." Most of this didn't make much sense to Carly, but Jason's enthusiasm was beginning to elicit small bursts of excitement in her.

He spent the rest of the day showing her the town's high school, parks and rental possibilities. She was intrigued by the town's name, "El Segundo," until she found out it was Spanish for "The Second" and referred to the town's history of being home to the second oil refinery built on the west coast. Still, there were plenty of interesting residential areas and Jason assured her the town was home to a lot of music businesses.

Jason showed his own business acumen by waiting to take her to the beach until the early evening, just as the sun was setting on the horizon, its rays a band of gold beneath a slate-colored sky. The sand was soft under her feet and warm waves lapped gently against her ankles. Jason didn't mention that the building they could see in the distance was a refinery. Still, she was to later learn that El Segundo Beach, despite its disadvantages, had advantages as well. It may have been the refinery that kept the crowds away, making the shoreline almost private on most days. The sand was pristine, and the waves were just the right height for Tyler's earliest attempts on a boogie board.

Carly took the plunge, agonizing over but eventually deciding to invest some of the income from the equity of her home in the business. It was a mild success from the very beginning. Jason's winning personality and his long experience in all aspects of the music industry made it easy for him to talk to customers and clients, be they performers, technicians, salesmen, managers, or promoters.

Carly found she loved her work and the opportunity of being her own boss. She learned something new every day, particularly on those days when she accompanied Jason setting up equipment for performances. Not only did she find she had more mechanical talent than she'd ever imagined, she got to meet the most interesting people—people she would never have encountered in suburban Chicago. Musicians, of course, but also the myriad music professionals and groupies that accompanied most bands, like the bass guitarist from India who sounded like Jimi Hendrix while looking like Gandhi, or Lulabelle, a tiny sprite of a girl from Alabama who'd spent most of her adulthood following at least six of the bands she and Jason had worked with.

Carly shouldn't have been surprised. Music had always spoken to her. And it had supported her through what she saw as the most transformational period of her life. Music had helped her accomplish something she'd believed was attainable: supporting herself and her family doing something she loved.

It's getting close to show time. Stretching her neck almost to the point of injury, she finally spots Jason and Jake entering the hall. Her first instinct is to stand up and wave, but then she remembers that the ushers know exactly where to seat everyone. Jason looks very handsome in his indigo blue tux—the first time she's ever seen him so formally dressed. And Jake, as always, is a heartbreaker. He'd followed the Grammys' "more casual" guidelines in choosing to wear a black velvet sports coat trimmed at the collar and lapels with black leather. Carly knows he'll be a knock-out if he lands on that stage this evening.

It had been a small job—a wedding reception for about 150 guests. Early in their business, engagements consisted primarily of providing sound equipment for local bands performing at celebrations like weddings, bar and bat mitzvahs, and birthday parties. Carly was surprised at the lavishness of some of the birthday parties: one party for a fourteen-year girl had involved over a hundred guests. And swans.

But then, Carly mused, it was, after all, California; everything needed to be larger than life. These engagements didn't pay much, but they did help keep the lights on and the rent paid.

She was about to finish installing a Fender amp when the band arrived, so she didn't notice Jake until their first sound check. But when he took the stage, she did a double-take. He looked almost exactly like the poster of Jim Morrison that had graced the living room wall at the Morgan Street apartment that she, Beth and Liz had shared. Slim, almost to the point of frailty. Dark curls framing the face of an angel. Deep brown eyes a woman could get lost in. She smiled. He was probably awful—he wouldn't be the first performer who tried to make it solely on his good looks.

From the first few chords he strummed on his acoustic guitar, she could tell he had talent. And his voice: not at all like Morrison's, but exceptional just the same—perhaps having more of a resemblance to a young James Taylor's. Before long she heard Jason, who'd been discussing finances with the father of the bride, pulling out a chair to sit next to her.

"Who is that guy?" he asked.

"Jake. Jake Something. Here." Carly reached into her briefcase for some paperwork. "'Jake Winters. Singing and playing tonight with the Mad Hatters.' The band's so-so, but the kid's really something." Jason listened carefully, nodding along with the beat of the music. "Definitely in the alternative rock tradition. He's got the magnetism of Kurt Cobain. And he can rap too."

"And the looks," Carly mentioned quietly.

Jason laughed. "Yeah, he's the whole package. I wonder if he has a manager."

"Let's see what the audience thinks."

That evening, the wedding guests had been mesmerized. The younger guests danced through every song, and even the grandmas and elderly uncles tapped their toes and nodded with the music. During one of the band's breaks, Jason broke through the throng of young women who were asking for Jake's autograph to invite him to join Carly and himself for a drink after they broke up the set.

"I don't drink. I'm only nineteen," Jake responded. Jason resisted laughing—this young man was like none of the musicians he'd ever known. But Jake agreed to meet them at a local bar across the street from the reception hall. Carly and Jason learned that he was a recent graduate of El Segundo High who had no interest in attending college. He also had no close ties to the Mad Hatters—had met them only two weeks earlier. And he did not have a manager.

Carly worried a bit about Jake's eagerness to sign a contract with them. He was so young. He was untried. He could turn out to be trouble. But she and Jason found managing him a joy: he was hardworking, intelligent, and responsible. They had no problem arranging gigs for him at weddings and parties, then later in bars and casinos. His reputation grew with every engagement.

Their big break came when his first single, which they recorded at the warehouse, became one of the first YouTube miracles; it was Jake who had suggested they post it on this new music site that neither Jason nor Carly had heard of. From there, his rise to the top was, as the media like to say, astronomical.

Both Carly and Jason worried they'd have to fend off other, more established managers whose expensive lawyers could find ways to break Jake's contract with them. And although they knew he must have offers, he never mentioned them. They also feared he'd begin to get into the same bad habits that led to Morrison's and Cobain's early deaths. But other than an occasional beer once he turned 21, Jake showed no interest in alcohol or drugs. His music was everything to him.

When Jake received notification of his nomination for Best New Artist, he went immediately to the warehouse to tell Carly and Jason. After a series of hoots and hugs, his first concern was for the ceremony. "If I win," he had said, puppy dog eyes pleading, "will you two go up on the stage with me?"

"Of course! We'd be honored!"

"I won't win, though," he'd continued. "I'm up against some real talented people."

Humility. Loyalty. Responsibility. Talent. More Talent. Even More Talent. Carly knew this young man had it all. She could not imagine what Jason and she had ever done to deserve Jake Winters.

Carly has only time enough to brush kisses on both Jason's and Jake's cheeks as they squeeze into their seats, Jason to her right, Jake seated on the aisle, the traditional nominee seating, to her left. The program is about to begin, but it will be well over an hour before the name of the Best New Artist is called. She's so excited that she doubts she'll be able to pay much attention to the show, which gives her plenty of time to count her blessings. Family doing well. Career surprisingly successful. Good health. No relationship, although she'd dated quite a bit in California and the man she's currently seeing shows some real possibility. But she's in no particular hurry to settle down.

Her focus drifts from the show onstage to ruminations about the past to plans for the future. The better performances catch her attention, but she pays about as much attention to the series of nominations and speeches here, at Radio City Music Hall, as she would have paid if she were watching the program on her television at home. She is surprised, therefore, when the nominees for Best New Artist are about to be announced. Jason grabs her hand, squeezing it so tightly she feels her borrowed rings digging into her fingers. Jake does the same, but she can feel his hand tremble.

As Jake's name is announced as a nominee, all three of them look directly ahead, radiating a confidence they do not actually feel, but knowing that a camera is directed at their faces and that millions of people are watching. As the other nominees' names are announced, Carly looks at Jason, whose confident smile, which she knows is forced, makes him look like he is the one who might be soon receiving an award, and then to Jake, whose face seems to suggest that he is facing not an honor, but imminent execution. She favors him with her best encouraging grin, the kind she had beamed on her children when she had sent them off on their first days at school. This seems to relieve some of his tension.

"And the winner of the Best New Artist award is..."

Carly wants this win. She has dreamed of it since Jake announced the miracle of his nomination. She prays he'll be taking home that little gold statue of an old-fashioned record player. It would be a wonderful recognition of his great talent. It would forever assure Jason of his worth in this world. It would be a testament to her mother and her friends, who had always supported her, even when she felt defeated. It would give her kids awesome status among their friends. And a Grammy, particularly such a prestigious one, would definitely boost the anticipated profits of their company.

And of course, she wants this for herself. It would be fun to be up on that stage, wallowing in the admiration of millions, especially if she was able to execute all those steps without falling flat on her face. It would be an affirmation of the good choices she's made and the hard work she's done, both in the business, and in finally beginning to understand who she is and what she is capable of achieving.

She wants this win. But deep within herself, she knows she does not truly need it.

After all, she knows she is already a winner.

Discussion Guide

1. The title *Coming to Be* comes from Plato's *Theatetus*, a dialogue that focuses on change: *"Nothing ever is, but everything is coming to be. "* In what ways did Carly "come to be" during the novel?

2. How was Carly influenced by her Polish family? How were they helpful or not helpful to her?

3. How were Carly's children, Tyler and Celia, affected by the changes in their family situation. Did their reactions seem typical for children who experience their parents' divorce?

4. Did you identify with any of the characters? Which one(s) and why?

5. Names were very important in *Coming to Be*. How was Carly's name integral to the story's development?

6. The names Beth and Liz are both nicknames for the name Elizabeth. Based on the discussion the roommates had, do their nicknames describe their personalities?

7. Each chapter in *Coming to Be is* introduced by the title of a classic rock song that was meant to set the tone of the coming chapter. Did you see any connections between the title of the song and the chapter (the Roy Orbison chapter doesn't count!) How did the song titles foreshadow the final chapters of the novel?

8. In what ways did Liz and Beth help toward Carly's development? How helpful was Jason?

9. Have you had any situation in your life in which friends or family members helped you grow in ways you would never have imagined? Did reading *Coming to Be* inspire you in any way?

10. Do you believe Carly's short affair with Roger was justified? Were Carly's and her friends' actions in Steve's apartment on Lake Shore Drive justified?

11. Did anything make you laugh in *Coming to Be*? What and why?

12. Did anything make you angry? What and why?

13. How would *Coming to Be* be different if the story had been written from Steve's perspective?

14. The novel takes place in a number of areas: Chicago, suburban Chicago, Albuquerque, Atlantic Coast, California, New York. In what ways did the different areas affect the characters' actions?

15. How did Zosia's revelation change the course of Carly's life?

16. Manic depression is a mental illness which is currently called bipolarism. Have you had any experience (with yourself or others you know) with bipolarism and the effects it has on not only the sufferer, but also on his or her family and friends? How is Steve's bipolarism central to the story?

About the Author

Rebecca Thaddeus earned a doctorate in Composition and Rhetoric from the University of Illinois at Chicago. Thirty-eight years of teaching English and a great interest in history led her to the conviction that she could write historical fiction. Her first novel, *One Amber Bead*, was set during World War II, while *My Mother's Daughter* is set in early 19th Century Mississippi. Rebecca lives on a century-old farm in northern Michigan where she hosts a writers group and writing workshops.

You can find Rebecca Thaddeus on Facebook, or visit her blog at oneamberblog.blogspot.com. You can purchase her books in bookstores and on Amazon. For wholesale orders, contact Plain View Press: http://plainviewpress.com.

Acknowledgements

I am deeply thankful to all the following:

Nancy Nielsen and Carol Hannah who, with Nancy Kaszyca, lived this book with me.

Pam Knight, whose creativity and professionalism has shepherded me through the creation of three published novels.

Barbara Brice, who provided me with Professor Fishman's accounting language.

Thad Stolarek, whose technical computer support is indispensable, and Tirzah Price, who smooths my way through Word and PDF tasks.

The Mahollands, Rebecca, Mike, Isaac, Ada, and Emilia, and Chris Ebey, for their love and support.

My writers' groups, whose help and encouragement were instrumental in making Coming to Be come to be: Elaine McCullough, Kelly Thompson, Carole Jones, Julia Reges, Olive Mullet, Dan Mullet, Phillip Sterling, and Nancy Scott.

The members of my book club, whose support for my writing has been greatly appreciated for more than twenty-five years: Maryanne Heidemann, Barbara Ross, Jeanette Fleury, Susan Fogarty, Peggy Peterson, Michele Christner, Alice Bandstra, and Cheryl Courtney.

Dane Johnson, who gave me great insight in developing the character of Steve.

Dan Cronk, who provided me with useful information about various areas of the music business.

Mary Murnik and Dave Frank, who gave me insight into the minds of chemists.

Frank Werner, owner of On Stage Services, Inc. in Grand Rapids, MI, who introduced me to the backline music industry.